SECRET OF THE DARK HOUSE

Linda Gaine

authorHOUSE

AuthorHouse™ UK Ltd.
500 Avebury Boulevard
Central Milton Keynes, MK9 2BE
www.authorhouse.co.uk
Phone: 08001974150

©2010 Linda Gaine. All rights reserved.

No part of this book may be reproduced, stored in a retrieval system, or transmitted by any means without the written permission of the author.

First published by AuthorHouse 6/9/2010

ISBN: 978-1-4520-2674-9 (sc)

This book is printed on acid-free paper.

CHAPTER ONE

He walked quickly, arms swinging beside him, taking long heavy strides in army boots strong enough to cope with mountainous terrain. Hailstones streamed down like thick nail heads, clinging to his unshaven face to resemble tiny minuscules of ice. He was beginning to feel as if he had been stuck in a capsule and set adrift in space only to be trapped in time after being incarcerated for so long. But now he was free, he had escaped that capsule; and now he was going home.

It was dark, almost pitch dark, and there were no houses around these parts for miles. It was like the land that time forgot, a remote and desolate place. But it wasn't desolate to him because this is where he grew up. He smiled to himself, a brand new start! That's what he needed, and not long now just one more gate to open and he would see the welcoming glow of the candle light sparkling in the living room window, Mother always kept three candles on the windowsill it gave the place a warm welcoming touch.

He saw the lights on in the lower ground floor, a soft shade of amber with a comforting surrounding; But no candle! Anger stirred inside him, this was not as he remembered! What in hell was going on? Where was everybody? His hand came up and touched the rucksack on his back it seemed to weigh no more than a bag of feathers; it contained a hunting knife, rope, and chisel, a machete slotted into the side pocket, neatly in place. He smiled, his lips widening into a deadly grimace that made his otherwise handsome features grotesquely contorted, someone is having a laugh with him, making out they were someone else, then the door would open and mother would be there laughing at him, her arms outstretched ready to close around him in a loving hug, "Good to see you son." She would say while smothering him in kisses. The surrounding countryside was strangely silent; no birds sang in the trees, they had already nested for the night. The sky shifted by thunderous clouds, passing like shapes in the night.

He reached behind him and pulled out the hunting knife. He stood for silent seconds staring at the big arched door, and then he knocked and rang the bell

A man answered, about to say, "Can I help you?" but the words never passed his lips. He shoved the knife into his belly, twisted and turned. The man looked shocked, he uttered a small inaudible gasp, then blood seeped from his lips, and between the rigid hands that held the knife tightly, he looked up into the killers eyes that were wide and staring, cold unfeeling, bland and soulless.

The body slumped to the floor, blood spilled over the doorstep, onto the rug, building up like a rain soaked puddle. He stepped over the body and silently walked towards the living room. He could hear a television; he looked towards the sound where flashes of light from the dimmed room cast shadows of the changing scenes. It was a programme that he used to watch in the hospital. Sounds of laughter echoed around him, exploding off the walls.

"Who's there darling?" A female voice called, not worried by the shuffling feet that headed toward her.

She looked up, her heart thundered, she gasped at the sight of the blood stained knife. He smiled again, that death grimace, an unpleasant ghastly sight. He reached behind him again and pulled out the machete. He walked towards her, she just stood still, and her hand gripped the arm of the chair, startled wide eyes glared at him, as terror froze her to the spot.

"You're not my mother!" he snarled, the machete cleaved the air and the woman fell. It was a bloodbath, but it didn't matter, he could have all the time in the world cleaning it up afterwards.

Mounting the stairs slowly, yet with feet that thudded on each step, he made his way along the landing, the death grimace wider, to expose healthy white teeth, Hollywood style.

He opened the door to the pink bedroom, a little girl slept soundly in her bed, next to the window a small baby was curled up in her cot; reaching behind him again he pulled out a spike. His iron hard eyes blinked once.

Amanda waited at the bus shelter shivering in the chill evening air. The wind howled past churning up old tin cans and bits of litter. Giant puddles mirrored images of light from the fat sleet drops that still drummed down heavily from a charcoal sky.

Hunching her shoulders she bowed her head from the cold, tucking herself into her coat. This was the worse time of the evening, standing around until her feet were almost numb waiting for the bus to arrive. A chubby round-faced man passed, glancing towards her with a hesitant smile and a slight nod of his head, his eyes red and watery from the cold. Amanda returned the gesture with a soft smile and a blink of her own watery eyes. He hurried on, and she glanced to see if the bus was coming, stamping her feet to bring life back into her frozen toes. It wasn't far from where her grandmother used to live, she could see the big mountain from where she stood, towering above the little house. She had often wondered how long it would take to climb to the top, but she never did get round to climbing that mountain, because a mountaineer she wasn't cut out to be. In the mornings she would stand outside craning her neck to see the mist shedding from its peak on a crisp cold day. She could smell the pungent aroma of damp slate from the old quarries and rooftops, along with the rampant smell of crisp burning coal.

She gazed around at the empty streets. It was certainly quiet for a Friday evening, as if the countryside had taken a deep breath and decided to hold it until the storm had passed. On the opposite side of the street, a woman passed holding tightly to her umbrella that had turned inside out, it looked as if it was about to depart and fly off, and no matter how desperately she struggled to hold on to it, it would only be a matter of seconds before it was snatched from her hands and hurled into the night sky.

Wrapping her coat around her she decided it would be quicker to walk than to stick around at the bus shelter waiting for hypothermia to set in. Amanda strained her eyes shielding them through the mist to see if there was any sign of a bus coming up the hill, if not then she would start the miserable journey home on foot.

The sleet poured down, steadily at first and then in torrents. Walking in the sleet and the cold was a really nasty thought, even though it wasn't far, maybe a mile or so; it would take her at least three quarters of an hour to walk it but it was far enough in the dark on your own, in the freezing cold.

It wasn't really so bad living in North Wales, in the summer it was such a beautiful place, it was quiet and still with just the trill of the birds singing in the trees, the soft gentle breeze that floated from the valley carrying the wonderful scent of wild flowers to scatter in the air, and the view from the mountains was breathtaking. Her parents had purchased the house and moved when she left school so moving hadn't caused too much havoc with her exams. She had passed all her 'O' and 'A' levels winning her a place at Bangor University. She wanted to do law and so far she found that she had realised her vocation in life, it was going to be Forensic medicine or Law, and maybe both if she was clever enough! At first she found it strange after living in London all her life. City life was worlds apart from the calm countryside. It was a suspiciously quiet abode and sometimes reminded her of a ghost town. It should never have felt strange at all really; every single school holiday had been spent visiting her grandparents from the time she had been able to walk.

But sometimes even living in a place that is slightly familiar is never the same as visiting each year. After only a few months of moving, both her grandparents were dead.

Madeline lived next door to Amanda's Grandparents and they had been friends from the age of five, a friendship that would last well into their mature years, and would remain that way until the day they died.

Madeline had boundless energy; she'd move with a brisk bouncy stride, her deep Auburn hair was always tied in a ponytail bobbing along behind her; her eyes were the colour of pale sapphires.

Amanda found herself hunching over from the strength of the wind as it pushed her forcibly from behind. She pursed her lips together tightly as damp and freezing winds ripped through her when she hit a draughty corner.

A cramp in her left side left her gasping; she bent over to catch her breath, her lips slightly apart, and her hands resting on her knees while her heart pounded faster with the effort. She got her breath back and stood up, reaching into her bag to take out a packet of tissues to wipe her runny nose. Her eyes narrowed through the lashing sleet, she thought she could just make out a faint apparition of the house. But surely, it couldn't be the house? She had only just left the bus shelter. It looked like the house and then she realized it was the penetrating shadow of the mountains throwing an illusion; it was tiredness that had got the better of her, she had been straining her eyes as if she had been reading a paperback for a lengthy time, and running and walking for hours instead of minutes.

A subtle movement from behind made her stop. Dark shadows haunted her features as she squinted through the mist. Someone was behind her she was almost certain, but that wouldn't be so unusual at this early part of the evening. Amanda looked behind her, there was no one there, and maybe she imagined it? The noise came suddenly, like someone banging on tin, she jumped; glancing around her again, wishing now she had waited for the bus, maybe it was the sound of a factory horn distorted by the wind? The unwelcome sensation of being grabbed from behind by unseen strong cruel hands spurned her on, and she found herself breaking into a small trot. To her right came another loud bang and now it sounded like someone banging on steel but it was louder this time. Amanda jumped again sucking air through her clenched teeth with shock. There was someone behind her, and then to the side of her, all around her something moved very fast in the blink of an eye. Her trot became a fast walk, a hurried dash to safety. Someone was following she could sense them, almost smell them as if they were walking closely by her side matching each step with her own, imagining she could hear their footsteps softly tapping on the sodden concrete.

She stopped so suddenly, turning her head quickly to the left and then to the right, glancing behind her again but still she couldn't see anyone, and all she could hear in the dull silence was the soughing wind that brushed the trees and the darkness that was her sole companion. She took a deep breath and reasoned with herself, this was just silly! A stupid reaction to nothing! Relax she smiled, it was time to battle her fear because there was no one behind her and if there had been she would have seen them! She shrugged off her irrational behaviour and her hurried dash slowed to a rapid walk. Sleet splashed her face and stung her eyes; she squinted, pulled in a deep breath then sprinted off again. The sleet was thundering down now, bouncing off the puddles like tiny crystals. Her long dark hair was drenched, clinging to her face; she made a sour expression and yanked it away pulling up the collar of her coat as the icy drops of sleet ran down her neck.

The small bridge was straight ahead, it was a lonely quiet place that was never used very much, because it was claimed that in the seventeenth century, human sacrifices were made on the bridge as an offering to Satan; and it didn't take an awful lot to frighten the decent folk in this tiny village. A man had died on the bridge after chopping off his hand in an act of madness and mayhem after joining a Satanic cult, and now people were afraid to walk across the bridge at night in case he came back to haunt them. The bridge resembled a bad Omen a place you must never be after dark.

Amanda had laughed at the stories, of course she knew it was only silly rumours and she wasn't the type to let her imagination run riot. Just a stupid story that's all it was! She didn't believe in Ghosts, or walking dead men either, she believed in fact, not fiction and wasn't about to associate herself with such silly rumours, if she couldn't see it; then it wasn't there! And that was as simple as that! She couldn't remember reading any reports in the papers of a suicide on the bridge or of any satanic cults either! So no one had ever proved it was a true story.

The heels of her shoes tapped noisily on the concrete footpath. She bowed her head from the wind keeping her eyes on the ground that followed the path of the dull amber streetlights. Directly in front of her there was a road that forked in two directions; to her left led to the woods and to her right was a small dirt road that took her almost to her door. The dirt road was more like a tiny alleyway hidden away behind a couple of factory premises and that was going to be her choice. Amanda shoved her hands into her pockets they were beginning to feel numb from the cold, Briefly, she glanced ahead, still squinting from the sleet and carried on walking across the bridge, it wouldn't take long once she had crossed to the other side, and her relief was evident in a long deep sigh. She couldn't wait to get home and out of these wet clothes; only half a mile or so once she got past the alley and she would be able to see the house from there, now she began to smile.

A tall dark figure that the slate grey evening had moulded into the shape of a man pressed his back to the wall in the alley. He looked Bat like in appearance as he shifted in quick fluttery movements. His head jerked to the right as he heard her approach, a lopsided grin that was meant to be one of smug satisfaction crept across his odd features that were cleverly camouflaged behind a latex mask that resembled 'Punch'. He held the machete tightly in his hands, it swung backwards and forwards like a pendulum.

She wasted no time in her rush to get out of the sleet and cold. Walking faster, her heels clicked on the concrete path that echoed the stillness of the shaded countryside, and the only other sound was the noise the sleet made as it thundered to the ground with a dull pattering thud.

He watched and waited, hopping from one foot to the other in eager anticipation of what might come next! He was an animal of super intellect, harbouring a terrible destructive impulse that would be hard for any living creature to match, even in the wildest of animal kingdoms!

Amanda turned her head to the right and even through the darkness she saw something move, it was so swift in its departure that she wasn't exactly sure what it was. Perhaps it was a Fox? How could it be a Fox? It was too big for a Fox. And then she froze; a cold dread settled in the pit of her stomach, her heart lurched in her chest. Out of the alley at the foot of the bridge an exceptionally tall figure emerged just a few feet ahead of her; it wore a long black cloak hung from a misshapen body, an unreal thing with no face except a hood that hung down the front of the garment draping its head, the heavy tread of his army boots sounded like the far distant echo of thunder. Amanda uttered a cry of alarm and stumbled across the rest of the bridge; somehow she had the feeling his hand would snake out and grab her in an unholy embrace as she steered herself to the right to pass him, her heart battered and stuttered against her ribs. She expected it! Waited for it! And for fleeting seconds she did nothing. But it never happened. He seemed to float past like a ghost returning wearily to the graveyard. Once she got to the other side she spun around quickly to see if he was following, but there was no sign of the hooded figure, he had vanished as if he had never been there in the first place. She stood at the end of the bridge her trembling hands gripping the iron railing while she took a couple of deep breaths. Finally her breathing calmed considerably, her fright abated for now. She glanced behind her once more and wondered what the hell it was that had appeared so suddenly and without apology, if someone scared you unintentionally, they would say sorry! But he didn't say anything. For moments she stood there watching, her eyes narrowing down any movement and decided that maybe it was a tramp, or a very old man just making his way to shelter for the night, but a ghost! He certainly wasn't.

By the time she had reached the drive to the three bed-roomed semi detached that she shared with her mother father and brother she was still shaking, she fumbled in her bag for the keys; her fingers curled around the cold steel and she gripped them firmly in her hand. She was happy to be home in one piece, to see the warm welcoming lights that were on in the house. Amanda glanced up at the greyish smoke that filtered from the chimney, it was hardly visible to the naked eye, but she knew it was there fading away like the tails of misshapen tadpoles into the oceanic blackness of night.

She closed the door behind her and shook herself out of her coat, draping it over the shower rail in the downstairs bathroom; she grabbed a towel from the rail and dried her hair until every wet strand lay limply around her shoulders.

"Not a great night to be out without your umbrella is it I bet you're soaked?" Megan said as Amanda walked into the kitchen. "You'd left it here this morning, I knew it would rain."

"I know I remembered it when I got to Uni." She reached over and gave her mother a kiss on her cheek. "Anyway, I just had the fright of my life."

"What do you mean, what happened?" Megan asked.

"I don't know what it was, it was just really scary, as I crossed the bridge a man appeared from nowhere, it was just something about him that spooked me I suppose, he moved so quickly I wasn't expecting someone to appear so suddenly like that, it was like he'd been there for quite some time."

"Don't tell me you've been listening to those silly stories again?" Her mother laughed.

Amanda frowned. "No, of course not, it might have been an old tramp; I don't know what made me so jumpy."

"You're pretty safe around here darling, that's why we moved in the first place."

Megan dried her hands on the tea towel and lifted the lid off the saucepan.

"They aren't true you know just some daft story."

Amanda didn't want to think about the man in the cape so she changed the subject for now.

"I know that, I don't believe in all that rubbish anyway."

She walked over and peered over Megan's shoulder at the beef stew boiling in the pot.

"Mum, did you ever know of anyone who walked about in a hood and cape?"

Megan raised an eyebrow. "No, and apart from Batman, No one I can remember. Why?"

"Oh, that person on the bridge, well, he was wearing a hood and cape."

Megan frowned, and then she looked puzzled. "Ah wait a minute, do you remember when you were a little girl, the man that walked around dressed in a cape and hood?"

"Um, I can vaguely recall someone like that; didn't he go to the town centre a lot?"

"Yes darling that's right, I wonder if it was him you saw?"

"But, wouldn't he be well over eighty now?"

"Yes, you're probably right there, maybe it's not him then, he used to terrify you when you were little, the poor man."

"What was poor about him?"

"He used to wear the hood because he was terribly disfigured."

"Disfigured?" she repeated, her curiosity getting the better of her. "What do you mean, in what way?"

"Because he had his twin growing out of the back of his head, the twin never grew, and apparently that was why he wore the hood."

"How do you mean it grew out of the back of his head? How could he have survived it must have been attached to his brain?" The thought of some kind of deformed baby growing out of someone's head got more monstrous by the minute, and Amanda scrunched up her face in disgust.

"Yes, it was growing out of the back of his head, it was the face only."

"The face of the twin!" she gasped. "How could he survive?"

"Well he did, for many years I remember your grandmother telling me about it he lived in the same village."

"You're teasing me now; no one could survive a thing like that."

Megan looked at her seriously and Amanda knew at once her mother wasn't telling her stories.

"I'm telling you the truth, ask your dad, he knew about it."

"So, how big did the twin grow?"

"It didn't grow as such, it was just the face of the twin, they were Siamese twins I think and one didn't develop, much the same as 'foetus-in-fetu it happens today."

"I never heard of that before, it's macabre, but surely he's dead by now?"

"I think he must be, he was an adult when your father was growing up, it's just that when you said about the man in a hood and cape it reminded me of him."

"It was some other kind of weirdo I expect, never mind Mum it was probably nothing, I think I'll go and get ready before Madeline comes."

Amanda peeled off her clothes, turned the taps on full, then sat on the toilet seat waiting for the bath to fill; she watched the steam rise and curl along the ceiling and walls, to flow in tiny rivulets of condensation down the pink bathroom tiles. She turned on the extractor and sprinkled pink bath salts liberally into the steaming water then lowered her self into the bath, catching her breath as the heat seared her skin turning her into a pinkish lobster colour.

She lay back closing her eyes, but the vision of the hooded man swam into her mind as clearly as if he was standing right in front of her.

The door flew open with such force that she slipped under the water splashing the tiles and drenching the carpet; struggling up, she grabbed the flannel to cover her breasts.

"What the hell are you doing? Why don't you knock first?"

Her brother stood there with an expression of startled surprise on his face.

"I didn't know you were here! Why don't you lock the door?"

"David! We have a shower room downstairs, why can't you use that!"

"Because it's not a shower I want stupid! I want the toilet!"

David ducked for cover as a bottle of shampoo hurtled across the room hitting the doorframe behind him. He slammed the door angrily. Amanda glared at the door for ages with a mixture of anger and acute embarrassment.

David was her half brother, he was her father's son and she often wondered how such a bright intelligent attractive man as her father could spawn such an idiot! Immediately the thought had left her mind, she retracted it, she didn't mean it, David wasn't so bad as brothers go, his mother had died of cancer when he was just four months old, and her mother had brought him up from the age of fifteen months, there was ten years difference between them; and she loved him very much, there was nothing he wouldn't do for her but sometimes he could be a little thoughtless.

She pulled the flannel over her breasts and up towards her face where a tiny sheen of perspiration had trickled slowly towards her brow.

For a long while she lay there in the heat of the water, thinking about the strange figure that appeared so suddenly from nowhere to startle her, she wondered what he was doing there. It was not a place where people usually hang out, so maybe he was a tramp after all searching for somewhere to shelter for the night.

Amanda glanced up at the clock on the wall and was surprised at how late it was. It didn't seem long ago that she had walked into the house freezing cold and soaking wet from the sleet, and now the time was flashing by. If she was planning on going out with Madeline it was time to hurry. She grabbed a towel from the rail and dried herself quickly, then picked up the bottle of shampoo, screwed the top on tightly and put it back on the shelf.

She could hear Madeline's voice as her bare feet hurried down the hall to her bedroom. She had arrived early. "Won't be long Madeline." she yelled.

Outside the night was like one great ocean invaded by one single streetlight that glowed miserably, the rest was spaced out resembling a convoy of spaceships heading down the road to invade the city centre. She hated the dismal glow of the streetlight; it made her feel as if winter was going to last forever.

As she crossed the room to close the curtains she saw movement outside. Squinting through the darkness she saw a black hooded figure scuttling towards the bushes, his head seemed to be so grotesque as if it was too big for his shoulders and appeared to swivel unnaturally at a thirty-degree angle, and seemed to gaze up at her bedroom window, she found herself shuddering at the thought that he could be the misfit with the twin growing out of the back of his head!. Everything about him appeared unnatural. Her breath caught in her throat as his eyes locked onto hers, the face was almost white, and even the paleness of the moons shimmering surface clearly defined what looked to her like the face of a puppet, something that she was familiar with, a subliminal image but couldn't quite place it, but she knew she had seen it before somewhere. She moved away from the window pressing her back to the wall, craning her neck forward so she could see him without him seeing her, but when she looked again he had gone. For one brief second only, she squeezed her eyes shut and then opened them again expecting to see him. Was this just a figment of her imagination? Was she starting to see things that were not there? He looked exactly like the figure on the bridge! The earlier scare was still very fresh in her mind. She closed the curtains tightly so no gap was visible; but the figure was imprinted in her mind there was something unholy about him, he looked like the grim reaper in one of Dennis Wheatley's novel's, or perhaps the vampire in horror films and on T.V.

She ran to her bedroom door "David!" she called. "There's someone outside!"

"Outside Where?" David called back from the foot of the stairs.

"Outside my bedroom window he's standing over by the field."

She heard the door open as her brother went out to look, her hands clasped together in an anxious knot as she paced up and down. It was like forever until she heard the door open once more and David's feet ascending the stairs towards her bedroom.

"There's no one out there love, perhaps it was a cow over in the field or something?"

"There was somebody outside, and it definitely wasn't a cow! He was staring up at the window, and he wore a long black cloak."

"Well they're not there now, they must have gone, but I'll take another look." She watched as he went down the stairs towards the front door. Whoever it was, had long gone.

Amanda sat at her dressing table and gazed into the mirror, her velvet almost black eyes were moist from the heat of her bath, her usually pale unblemished skin had a healthy glow that brought a flush to her cheeks.

Applying her make up carefully, she made sure it was dry before slipping on the black satin dress she had bought a couple of weeks ago. The cool material felt smooth and soft against her skin. She sat down on her bed and slipped on her high heeled black satin shoes, tied her hair into a white bow and then made her way downstairs.

By the time Amanda came down Madeline was talking to David. They seemed a perfect match, she had often wondered if one day Madeline might become her sister in law.

David turned to her "No one was there, I looked over by the field, and it could have just been someone taking a short cut home." He said, his dark eyes softly assuring.

"Probably, it's me I expect, getting a little jumpy after the long miserable trek home."

Madeline nodded her head in agreement, smiling she said. "Sometimes, bad weather, especially sleet and heavy rain distorts things"

"Yes, you're probably right." But her mind was still on the figure by the edge of the field.

"You're okay now?" David asked.

"Yeah fine, I'm just a little tense." She gave him a confidant smile as she crossed the room to look out of the sleet splattered windows to see if the storm had passed.

"Sorry about earlier." David said.

"It's okay." Amanda replied but she still felt a small degree of humiliation at the thought of her brother seeing her naked in the bath.

She sat down on the couch beside David, listening to the sleet pinging the windows and the wind huffing under the cracks in the door, wondering if they should call a cab. "We need heavy coats it's just coming down in buckets."

"I only have a rain Mack but its heavy enough to keep out the cold." Replied Madeline as she carefully filed a jagged fingernail.

"I could give you a lift if you like?" David offered. "I'm going that way."

Amanda smiled warmly. "Oh that would be great David thanks a lot." She grabbed her coat.

David could hardly see a foot in front of him, he flicked on the wipers at full speed, and they hummed and thumped in unison in an attempt to clear his vision.

"Why don't you come in and have a drink with us?" Madeline asked.

"I can't, I promised to meet someone."

"Would that be female or male?" Amanda asked; she saw the look of disappointment on Madeline's face.

"Mind your own business; you are such a nosey parker!" David laughed.

"You'll never get a thing out of him." Amanda grinned.

"Anyway, I'll see you back home later." He leaned over and opened the door for Amanda.

"Okay, take care have a great evening, see you later, if you get any problems call me."

They watched David's break-lights disappear into the sleet drenched night.

Stones nightclub was hot and cloying despite the foul night and the cold air that drifted in from the open door. Cigarette smoke hung in the air in a pink hazy mist channelled from the lights. People stood in groups talking loudly above the music, with their heads bent together trying to hear their own conversations; their voices sounded like a flurry of bees.

Amanda asked. "What do you want to drink?"

Madeline looked around her as she jostled for a place to stand. "Gin and Tonic if you can get near the bar."

The place was packed to the brim with bodies, and with only two nightclubs in the whole of the village, was all you could realistically expect.

As she got to the bar, that was when saw him; dominating the whole space where he stood, an Adonis of a man standing so tall and erect, a man so handsome he could make an angel's heart beat faster; his hair was a shimmering blond under the lights and he struck such an arrogant poise as he raised his hand to attract the barman. It wasn't just his good looks or tall lean body that attracted her and it wasn't his age either because he looked a lot older than her. It was just one of those things that happen from time to time. The strobe lights couldn't disguise the vivid blue of his eyes with each white flash. Suddenly he turned, his eyes locked onto hers hypnotically, until she was forced to look away. Her heart beat fiercely, her pulse rocketed and a flush spread across her delicate features. Although she had never been the type of girl to deliberately attract the attention of a man, she wasn't about to let this moment slip by unnoticed by him. She pushed her way towards him at the bar intending to strike up a conversation. As she got closer to him his aftershave or body spray was so familiar to her it was 'Kouros' she knew it anywhere, it was David's favourite aftershave. But the aroma didn't remind her of her brother, it was specific to the stranger, it was an aroma she would never forget. He was so broad shouldered that it occurred to her that he obviously did a lot of workouts in the gym! And he looked as if he was capable of breaking a man in half. The stranger smiled down at her. She wanted to ask him if he wore contact lenses, surely no ones eyes could be that blue? Where had he come from? Amanda knew nearly everyone in the village but she hadn't seen him before. He looked kind of haunted, uneasy as if he was carrying a hoard of bricks around with him, and the burden had become unbearable.

Already she had forgotten what Madeline wanted and plundered into a whirl of alternative drinks. Her mind seemed to become fuzzy, she mumbled to the barman, and now she could feel her face flush. "Gin and Uh…"

She knew it wasn't orange; Madeline didn't like any kind of orange drink.

"I think you mean tonic? It usually goes with gin" The stranger replied.

"Yes, that's it, thank you." She smiled avoiding his eyes; the barman popped the top of the tonic bottle and placed it on the bar beside the small glass of Gin. She took her drinks and headed back towards Madeline.

"Did you have to wait long?" she asked.

"No, once I got to the bar they are fairly quick." She placed the drinks on the window ledge. It had become oppressively hot, beads of perspiration broke out on her brow, she took out a tissue and dabbed her forehead, and then she felt a soft tap on her shoulder.

"Would you like to dance?" It was the tall fair stranger. For seconds Amanda stood there staring at him, his request had been so directly stated as if he was sure she would say yes. He held out his hand and she took it, following him into the pink hazy light that had now turned into a twilight shade of blue.

"I'm going to be cheeky and ask you your name?"

She looked up at him and smiled "I don't think your being cheeky at all, it's Amanda; and while we're on the subject of cheeky what's yours?"

"Paul, Paul Marriott. Are you here on holiday?"

"Oh no, I live here with my parents they are local; but I was born in London and we moved to North Wales two years ago, I'm studying Law at Bangor University."

"Good for you at least you'll have a career, the way things are going these days I think Lawyers will be the only ones employed. I used to live in London; I guessed we had at least one thing in common, you don't have a Welsh Accent." he smiled.

"Where did you used to live, what part of London?" Amanda inquired, not that she had much idea where towns and cities were in London anyway.

"Mile end, it's in the East End, not that far from Hackney, do you know where that is?"

"Yes, I know where it is, I'm not that familiar with it, but I have been there on one or two occasions. What are you doing in North Wales?"

"I work here, I'm working for a company that do all the electric supply for the power plant."

"How long will you be working here? "

"Oh, I have another two years at least, who knows maybe I'll stay here, make a new life it's a lovely place."

The night seemed to hurry on like an intercity train, she was afraid if she blinked he'd be gone and she would never see him again. She took the time to look behind her, Madeline was still standing where she'd left her in the corner by the window, she saw her and held her drink in front of her in a contemplative gesture, and Amanda smiled and gave her a wave.

Madeline returned her glass to the window ledge, she had never been much of a drinker anyway and one drink could last all night if she wanted it to.

Amanda had dreamed of this moment, she had never felt safer than she did right now in Paul's arms, she wanted to stay like this forever, she knew the night would end soon enough, and she wondered if tonight would be the last time she would ever see him again, or could this be the start of something more. Paul's eyes fixed on something behind her, he was smiling she turned and saw Madeline standing there with the drink still in her hand.

Amanda Looked surprised and she asked "The same drink?"

"It is the very same." Madeline replied. In her other hand she held another drink. "You should never leave your drink unattended Amanda."

"Oh, I'm sorry, I didn't realise how long I've been gone." She looked at Madeline and felt guilty; it had been almost an hour since she'd left her standing in the corner alone.

"Uh, let me introduce you." She turned to Paul and smiled. "Paul, this is Madeline." He nodded politely. "Madeline this is Paul."

Madeline gave him a warm sincere smile. "Hi, pleased

to meet you." Then she turned to Amanda, "I thought you had forgotten all about me."

"Oh Madeline I'm sorry, we'll come over and sit with you, grab a table, there's one free over there." She pointed to an empty table near the door.

"I'll get it and wait for you." She hurried towards the table placing her bag and her Mack on the chair opposite. It was a matter of seconds before friends from work spotted her, they moved her things, sat down, and took up residence on the two chairs she had saved.

Paul kissed her softly at first then with more urgency, he looked at her questioningly and smiled at her, his fingers trailed circles down her back then travelled slowly up to the nape of her neck as he nuzzled her hair. For those few moments it was as if there was no one else in the nightclub except them, the lights were low, softly shimmering as the mood changed. His hands worked gently through her hair, the white bow slipped between his fingers and her hair fell free lying gently around her shoulders like dark velvet

The gentle tap on her shoulder made Amanda smile; she knew who had administered that gentle tap she turned to see Madeline waiting patiently. "Did you want something?" she grinned.

"No, I was just wondering if you would you like to come to a party?"

Amanda turned to Paul. "Would you like to go?"

He smiled warmly." No thanks, I have work in the morning, I'm up at the crack of dawn."

"Its some friends from work, they asked if we would like to go, but if you rather stay, I'll go on my own."

Amanda replied. "Do you mind if I don't?"

"How will you get home?"

Paul answered. "I'll see she gets home alright."

"Are you sure Amanda?"

"Yes, of course she is." Paul smiled. "I promise to get her home safely."

"Okay, if you're sure, thank you." She looked behind her to the table her friends were just vacating. "Hang on; I'll keep the table for you, I'll put your coat on the chair."

She felt uneasy, had she done the right thing to leave Amanda to go home in the company of a total stranger? She swallowed a big despairing lump in her throat. Her instinct was to follow them and she almost did, until she heard her friends calling her to hurry, she wasn't even sure she wanted to go anymore. She turned anxiously towards Amanda, and then finally headed towards the door. Amanda stopped and pulled back from Paul's grip, she ran towards the exit just as Madeline disappeared from view. Paul called her but she ignored him.

"Madeline?" She shouted above the noise, Madeline

stopped and looked behind her. "Will you be okay?" she asked.

Madeline waved her hand indicating she would be fine.

"I'll call you tomorrow."

Madeline waved again then vanished into the cold night air, leaving Amanda and Paul sitting alone on the table she had kept for them.

Paul handed her a Bacardi and coke then hung his jacket over the chair.

"Don't worry about Madeline, she'll be okay."

"I know she will; I just felt bad about leaving her like that."

He took out a packet of cigarettes, lit one and blew smoke into the already suffocating air.

"So, you live with your parents then?" he asked.

"I could never afford to live on my own; everything is so expensive, besides I go to Uni."

"So where's home exactly?"

"Not far from here, it's the next village, Bedgellert do you know it?"

"I think so," he answered.

"It's such a small place; you must get bored on your own? There isn't much to do around here is there?" she said.

"Not a lot of time to do anything by the time I finish work."

"Does your mother live in London Paul?"

He took a sip of his drink. "No, I was put into care, my mum and dad died when I was three, and as far as we know I don't have any other family. When I was seventeen I was shoved out into the big wide world on my own."

"Oh, how sad, I'm so sorry." her face screwed up in an expression of sympathy.

"Oh don't be, I don't even remember her, it's a long time ago now."

Amanda sat silently, thinking how terrible it was not to have any one in the whole wide world.

It was then she looked at the time, it was almost two thirty in the morning.

"Paul I have to go." She was already heading for the door with her coat draped over her arm.

Paul snatched up his jacket and hurried after her.

"Hey! Wait I'll take you home." he shouted.

Outside he took her hand and they walked to his car.

Although the sleet had lifted the night air was cold; a freezing damp fog had descended from the Mountains making visibility almost impossible. In the distance they could hear the sounds of sirens, lots of them and they were heading towards the small Village.

"That is unusual." Amanda remarked with a soft frown lining her brow.

"What is?"

"Sirens, emergency vehicles, lots of them too."

Paul grinned "What's so unusual about that?"

Amanda listened they were getting closer. "You don't hear so many all at once, I wonder what's happened?"

He slipped his arm around her waist "Maybe it's a fire?" he said pulling her closer. .

"Maybe." she replied.

CHAPTER TWO

"Come on Muff! Hurry up laddie I'm bloody freezing here." The elderly man clapped his hands together several times, stamping his feet in unison to keep the cold from getting to his chilblains and arthritic bones, while the large fluffy brown mongrel sniffed for a place to do his business. He cocked his leg and scraped his back paws on the ground throwing up bits of grass and mud like a man frantically digging for gold. He glanced over at his master and then trotted off to check out the trees and the pond. The man followed with a degree of impatience. The dog's beautiful Amber eyes looked like two glowing orbs in the dark, gazing inquisitively from a face of brown and white warm shaggy fur. His nose twitched at the new smells he picked up from the damp grass. The man followed; hands behind his back as he waited for the dog to finish. After another round of leg cocking and earth scratching Muff suddenly stopped still, head slightly bent, tail stiffly erect; he growled low and menacing, hackles stood up on his back, his muzzle drew back to reveal sharp white teeth, nose pinched as if he was going to let rip one almighty sneeze.

"What's there Lad?" The man hurried toward him his hands moving from behind his back to his sides for balance. "What have you found boy?" he asked warily, knowing something was up by the tone of the dog's growl.

The dog pawed at something, it was lying at the edge of the pond, at least half of it was, he barked and drew back with a snarl and then his head vanished into the soil as his front paws dug into the earth to retrieve it; the man hurried across the muddy grass. As Muff turned his head the two glowing orbs fixed on his master. In his mouth was something red and sinewy, a sticky Port Wine substance leaked from the object and dripped thickly to the ground. The man studied it for only a second as his heart lurched and his stomach turned over violently before he yelled. "DROP IT LAD NOW!" The dog tilted his brown fluffy head in surprise his soft liquid eyes looked questioningly, and obediently he dropped his catch to trot towards his master.

The hand with ribbons of flesh flopped onto the bank; the man grabbed the dog's collar and slipped his lead on. He didn't stop to see where the rest of the body was; his haste almost sent him tumbling headfirst as he hurried as fast as his old legs could carry him.

Paul stopped the car and turned to Amanda. "Well, you're home safely."

"Thank you." She said.

"Can I see you again?"

She didn't delay in answering him, she almost answered too quickly. "Yes." She replied, "I'd like that."

"Would tomorrow be okay?"

"Yes, tomorrow would be fine."

"Where will we meet? What time?"

"Seven o'clock by the old quarry line."

Paul frowned. "Quarry line? Where's that?"

She realised he had no idea where that was. "Oh, over there, can you see the little bridge?" she pointed towards the small humped bridge two hundred feet away from where Paul's car was parked. "The quarry is over the bridge, you can't miss it."

"Alright, I'll see you there at seven." Paul took her face in his strong firm hands and brushed her lips gently with a warm moist kiss. "See you tomorrow." he murmured.

She got out of the car and stood at the side of the road watching his taillights vanish into the fog. Wrapping her arms around her and shivering in the freezing night air. There was no sight of him now only the lingering aroma of his body sprays and the memory of his vivid blue eyes and soft moist lips that she could still taste. She walked up to her door with just one thing on her mind, she hoped that he would turn up tomorrow, or she may never see him again.

She knew there was something wrong the minute she opened the front door. There was nothing unusual about the soft shaded light from the lamp stand in the living room, except that it was still on instead of usually being turned off when everyone went to bed and the dancing embers of shadows from the fire were still burning in the hearth. A terrible trepidation shrouded her as the silence of unnatural proportion descended upon her.

She closed the door and stepped into the hallway. She had an overwhelming feeling that something was about to happen, causing her to shudder visibly. She didn't take off her coat but walked across the hall towards the living room. The warm glow was usually a welcoming sight especially when you came in from the cold, but tonight, the cold overpowered the warm cosy glow.

Flames danced in the fireplace lapping at the chimneybreast with hot fiery tongues of bright vivid colour. The silence almost deafened her; except for the coal that spat and hissed as it leapt from the grate like the sharp short crack of a whip.

Amanda's eyes fell on the silent figure huddled in the armchair; dim shadows displayed the haunted face of her mother.

Megan sat as still as a freeze-framed picture. Her hands were folded in her lap over the apron she wore. A hairnet held her almost grey hair in place except for a few wispy strands that hung around her face. At first she turned her head and she frowned deeply, then a look of concern appeared as Amanda crossed the room.

"What's the matter mum? Is there something wrong?"

She got up from the chair; there was a look of relief in her eyes. "Oh, thank the dear lord! Where the hell did you get to Amanda? I thought it was you when Madeline called to see if you had got home okay. Amanda didn't you hear the sirens?" Her voice was louder than usual, with a note of hysteria in it.

She felt as if she'd dropped from a sudden height. "What do you mean thought it was me? What is it? What's happened?"

"A young girl was found dead, she had been murdered, they found her by the pond surely you must have heard all the sirens?"

Amanda nodded her head numbly; she remembered the wailing sirens they had heard in the distance.

"My God!" she murmured. "Do they know who she was?"

"Not yet, she was too badly mutilated. A man found her, he was walking his dog after midnight, in the little field by the pond and it was the dog that found her, the dog picked up her severed hand she was battered beyond recognition.

A look of disgust masked her face. "But, how did you find out about it then?"

"I heard the sirens, everybody went out to look, it was only a few feet away, so I went too, I didn't see the girl, the police had everything sealed off in tarpaulin but her description was the same as yours, she had long dark hair and for one terrible moment I thought it was you!"

She couldn't sleep trying to focus on Paul's handsome features; but all she could see was the vision of the young girl floating face up in the pond. Amanda realised that they had passed it earlier on that evening, and that poor girl must have been lying there then! She saw the blood that gushed from her severed hand turning the water crimson, and the girl, her eyes staring up into the black abyss of nothingness, eyes like glass orbs, vacant and empty with the clear rivulets of water rippling across the unidentified girls face. She imagined her long hair floating out behind her and then her vision changed to one of fixed frozen horror. She sat up quickly shaking her head to clear the awful vision of her overworked imagination.

The slamming of the front door brought her quickly back to reality. She was familiar with David's stumbling gait as he made his way drunkenly to his room. He paused briefly at her bedroom door, Amanda pulled the covers up to her neck and sucked in a painful breath, she hated it when he came home drunk, he always came into her room to tell her with slurred speech and clumsy movement what an awful night he'd had, then he'd garble on for hours until she was forced to escort him like an inebriate Muppet back to his room. Thankfully she heard him stumble away from her door and head up the hallway towards his bedroom. Glancing at the luminous clock she was surprised to see it was four a.m.

The next time she woke it was twenty past eight. She pulled herself up with a stiff unpleasant headache that travelled from the bridge of her nose to the back of her head. Amanda put her hand across her thumping forehead, promising to get it some pain killers immediately she could drag herself to the medicine cabinet. Sluggishly, she forced herself out of bed wincing at the jackhammer that pounded away inside her head and then slowly, very slowly reached for her bathrobe, slipped it on and pulled herself to her feet. She really felt like an old worn out dish rag this morning, She had not had a headache like this one for years, but at least she was grateful for one thing, this was not a working day, it was a Saturday she didn't have to rush about to get ready for university. Gliding across the room she made her way downstairs for the aspirin bottle.

"Good morning." She groaned, planting herself slowly on the chair with a glass of water in one hand and two painkillers in the palm of the other. David looked as bad as she felt, he didn't glance up from his coffee cup but she could see the deep bags under his eyes. He reached for the sugar bowl and heaped three spoons into his cup. The constant stirring and jangling of the teaspoon grated on her raw nerves, it seemed to replicate every sound louder. Her mother came in with a tray of plates, her hands shook and the plates clattered onto the table with a crack of china and glass splintering into a million pieces, scattering the salt and pepper pots, with grains spread in a mixed heap all over the table cloth. When everything came to rest in a jumbled heap they were surprised to see that not one plate had smashed, apart from a glass and two cups. Megan's hands trembled even more after the accident; it was evident that she had not got over the shock yet. Amanda wanted to yell at her to be more careful; it could have been a scalding cup of coffee or tea! Her eyes travelled from the plates to Megan's tired face, and then to David who was still playing around with that damn spoon! And her head was still pounding. At that moment she wanted to scream. The anger was building up inside her like a bubbling volcano about to erupt; but instead of yelling, she sucked in some deep breaths.

Reece Williams was how he always was first thing in the morning, clean-shaven, dressed and alert, especially alert this morning after hearing about the girl in the stream. Usually he was a quiet unassuming man who would just sit quietly relaxed in his chair with a pipe dangling from his mouth, eyes fixed intently on his newspaper. But this morning he was far from relaxed, he was angry, his eyes were as dark as Amanda's and this morning they looked sombre.

He watched his daughter silently behind his newspaper, coils of smoke emanated from his pipe, as he puffed hard on it while trying to play down the events of the night before. Even though Amanda was old enough to decide the time to come home at night, she should have come in at a reasonable time. He was angry because she didn't call them to let them know she was still alive and breathing and it wasn't her that had been found hacked to pieces in the stream. He sniffed loudly then went back to reading his paper. He heard the distant echo of his wife's voice in the background of his thoughts, and her voice reverberated through his head, he tapped his pipe noisily on the ashtray.

"How thoughtless you are Amanda! We were so worried we thought something had happened to you!" Megan shrieked. "Can you imagine how I felt?" She rested her hand on her chest. "No one knew who the murdered girl was! She was mutilated so badly you couldn't see her face!"

"Ok Mom, stop fussing for God's sake! If I'd thought you were that worried I would have phoned, honestly, you panic for nothing!"

Her words forced Reece's sudden anger. He put down his paper. "Oh, I see! We're not important enough to call us and tell us you were safe." He took his pipe from his mouth and slowly got up from the chair.

Amanda paled significantly. "No dad, I didn't mean it to sound like that. I didn't know anything about it until I got home!"

"No? Well you just listen to me young lady, while you live in my house you will abide by my rules, from now on I want you in this house no later than eleven, is that clear?"

"No it isn't! I'm nineteen, not nine years old, what the hell is wrong with you dad?" she yelled.

"I don't care how old you are! If you do not keep to the rules around here, then I suggest you find a place of your own."

The blood drained from her face at her father's sudden outburst, they were a loving family, a close family always able to talk things over, and why should he suddenly lose his temper with her? She had done nothing wrong.

"Dad, please, I'm sorry, I didn't think, I love you both so much I should have called, I had no idea anything so dreadful had happened how could I have known? I wasn't even around here last night."

Reece picked up his pipe from the ashtray and struck a match, and then he relaxed and was instantly sorry for snapping.

"Oh, for goodness sake, I'm sorry too, I shouldn't have reacted like that, of course you weren't to know, how could you possibly know someone had been murdered a few hundred feet from where we live?"

Amanda said anxiously. "I just hope they catch him quickly, it's so unusual for a murder to take place in this small part of the world."

"Things happen everywhere today love, just promise me something Amanda."

She smiled at her father as she lifted her coffee cup. "Of course I will."

"You'll stay out of dark secluded areas until the bastards caught, it's so very remote around here, don't put yourself in a vulnerable position okay?"

"Okay dad, don't worry, I'll be alright."

By the time she had walked up the path to Madeline's house, the ground was iced over and the sky looked like the upturned belly of a dead fish, grey and dull.

"Hi." Madeline called from the doorway, her hair hung over her face in dull and lifeless strands and her eyes looked glazed as if she had been up all night. Amanda could almost see the words on Madeline's lips before she spoke them.

"I know exactly what you're about to say, and I wish you hadn't called my parents last night, they almost had a fit!" she followed Madeline inside the house.

Madeline turned halfway down the hall, looking at her in total disbelief.

"I was worried about you, when that girl was found my heart almost turned over, I called your Mum and she said you hadn't got home yet. You didn't even know the guy did you? Why on earth did you let him take you home?"

She knew the answer before Amanda opened her mouth, and continued towards the kitchen, taking two willowed patterned cups from the cupboard

"He was okay! I knew I was safe with him."

Madeline tightened the belt on her housecoat and looked at her uneasily.

"Amanda, how the hell can you be safe with a total stranger! The murder took place yards from your home, and you can't blame me for worrying besides, I felt so guilty leaving you with him, and you hadn't come home then, and I knew I should never have gone to the party and left you."

Amanda lowered her head, but she could see her point.

"Okay, I suppose you're right but I had no idea, we did hear the sirens. But nothing like that has ever happened around here before. Did they say who she was?"

"On the news this morning they said her name was Mary, I don't know her second name but she was a local girl." Madeline put two steaming cups of coffee on the table.

"Madeline?"

"What?" she replied taking two elastic bands from the drawer to tie her hair back from her face.

"Yesterday I walked home from work and a man jumped out on me, scared the shit out of me."

"What do you mean jumped out on you? Did he threaten you?"

"No, he never said a word, he wore some kind of hood, then at home just before you came, someone was looking up at my bedroom window and it was the same person who jumped out of the alley."

"Why didn't you go to the police?"

"Because I wasn't sure, it could have been a tramp or an old man trying to find shelter for the night it was pretty bleak and gusty."

"You should have phoned the police."

"I couldn't do that, supposing it was an old man looking for somewhere to shelter for the night?"

"Then you would have done him a favour, wouldn't you?"

"Madeline, that wouldn't have done him much of a favour would it?"

Madeline pushed the paper in front of her pointing to an article on the front page.

"In the papers it say's the dog picked up the girls severed hand."

Amanda grimaced. "I know, my mother told me, how disgusting! I bet he scrubbed the poor dog's mouth out well, that must have been horrible."

She pictured the dog with the severed hand in its mouth.

"Exactly, it would have been worse if it was your hand, and it could have been."

Amanda said "Oh you are so bloody minded and gruesome this morning, what's wrong with you?"

Grimacing she took a sip of her coffee, then put the cup down and missed the saucer completely; the edge of the cup cracked off the side.

"Look what you made me do with your gruesome thoughts."

She turned the cup around to check it wasn't chipped then placed it carefully back down again.

"Can you not see I'm making a point Amanda? You went off with Paul what's his face last night without even a thought for your own safety, he could have been a serial killer."

Amanda almost choked on her coffee, the liquid spilling down her chin as she wiped it away with the back of her hand.

"And you are nuts!" She laughed. "Serial Killer, Oh how sad are you!"

"Yeah right, you laugh Amanda, but the police are warning woman to stay off the streets after dark."

The fog had lifted from the night before and a glimmer of moonlight propelled its head through the clouds. Amanda thought about Madeline's words, they spun around in her mind like tiny carousels, Madeline was usually right, she was wise, level headed, but that still didn't stop her walking towards the quarry; Madeline's warnings didn't make her turn around and go home, forget she ever saw Paul Marriott. Even the shadows that flickered in front of her looked grim, and they were only harmless shadows thrown down from the bright street lights onto the lime trees that lined the road. Her hands moved to her neck to pull her scarf tighter around her from the cold. Her hands were like blocks of ice even though she wore sheepskin gloves. She longed for the summer when the evenings were lighter, it didn't really matter whether they were warm or not, everyone preferred the lighter evenings to the dull cold ones. House lights went on at four o'clock in the late afternoons and all you had to look forward to were the cold dark nights and coal fires with little else to do in such a small country village.

Ahead of her something caught her eye, it was so quick she hardly saw it move. A shape scuttled into the darkness. It turned briefly to look behind and then stood as still as a mannequin in a shop window. She stopped where she was and edged back towards the tree. She couldn't see it clearly but was aware of a long black cape that hung almost to the ground. "HEY YOU!" she called, but she made no attempt to approach him. It was the same figure she had seen by the bridge and outside her bedroom window, and now she was certain it was 'the grim reaper', that was the nickname she had found for him. He turned to face her and a long black arm snaked out from beneath the cape, rising in a gesture as if he was beckoning her, it wasn't one of friendliness but of menace. She no longer wanted to call out to him to find out who he was, it didn't seem to matter anymore, and her instincts told her to avoid him at all costs. She looked again something slipped from his hand and floated to the ground Amanda hid further behind the tree.

She waited and checked he had gone. Her eyes searched the darkened street. Carefully she stepped out from behind the tree, still watching the street for signs of him but she was almost certain he had gone. When she gets home tonight she intended to call the police, it could be the man who murdered the girl in the pond and it could also be the hooded figure that jumped out on her last night? She lifted her hand and peered at her watch, holding it close to her face so she could see the time; it was hard to see under the trees that hid the normally bright sodium light but she could just about make out the big hand that had just passed the seven, now she was late; to call the police now would just detain her further! Checking from side to side she crossed the road and ran to where the figure had stood. As she looked down there was something lying on the ground, it was so easy to spot on the crisp white pavement, the thing she had seen slip from his hand was a single red rose! Was this meant for her? Why? She stooped to pick it up, and as she held it in her hand she noticed the green leaves had been crushed but the Rose was in full bloom, where would he get a Rose at this time of the year? There was something bad about the rose she could feel it, it felt bad in her hand, like some evil essence that was pouring from its sap. Amanda dropped it to the ground and walked on, stopping. Briefly to look behind as if the rose would suddenly get up and disappear.

Paul leant over the bridge chucking stones onto the railway line below.

"Aren't you a little old for that?" She smiled walking towards him; he looked like a handsome carved statue that had been sculptured and erected there by an Alien culture. Her heart pounded a little at the sight of him, and as she watched him she wondered why he didn't seem to feel the cold because he never wore an overcoat.

He turned towards her and rested his hands on the railings of the bridge, and she could tell he was a little embarrassed that she had seen him throwing stones.

"Hello." He said. "I didn't think you were coming."

"Sorry, I'm a little late I got held up."

She thought of telling him about the hooded black caped figure, but decided now was not a good time, perhaps she'd tell him later.

"Oh, by the way." He said turning back towards the bridge. "No trains pass through here do they?"

Amanda laughed at him. "No, not anymore, the railway shut down a few years ago; it belonged to the coal mining industry."

She climbed into his Explorer and sank back into the seat, at last she felt relaxed. She watched him as he started the engine; his handsome profile and tousled blond hair were shaded by the confines of the car. But the visible sweetness of his features was there, he resembled an innocent little boy. She almost laughed aloud at the thought of Paul being a vicious killer, he looked no more of a killer than father Nathan did at the local church her parents attended; and she hoped that for once in her life Madeline had got it wrong!

They stopped outside an old pub that was familiar to her; it was a local area where lovers met for the seclusion of the woods. The 'Fisherman's Rest' was used in the earlier century for fishermen on long trips. Old heavy fishing nets were draped across the windows to give the place authenticity and theme, most of them were deteriorating with age and left to hang in dusty shreds of mere cotton, paper thin and very unimpressive.

A large metal swordfish hung on an old weatherworn sign outside, creaking on its rusty hinges each time the wind blew. Inside the pub it was warm and welcoming.

The food was good in here with a varied selection for various tastes from Steak to Chicken to Fish and pasta. Paul led her to a table in the far corner of the room where a soft flickering candle shimmered invitingly from a brass candle holder shaped in the petals of a Rose.

Madeline became increasingly agitated. She had always been of a nervous disposition anyway and the murdered girl weighed heavily on her mind. She had always lived in this tiny Village and had never heard of a murder being committed before it was the kind of place where everyone knew everyone else, intimately. Looking towards the book shelf at the photo album lying on its side she decided to look through the photo's of her deceased father; that might help to take her mind off things. Her legs felt like leaden weights as she crossed the room to retrieve the album. The sudden shrill ringing of the telephone almost made her drop the album. She laid it on the coffee table as she hurried to answer it her hands shook as she snatched the receiver from its cradle.

"Oh Mum." She breathed, yet relieved to hear her mothers soft voice.

"Madeline darling, are you okay?"

"Yes I'm fine I thought you would have been on your way home by now."

A deep anxious frown shadowed her soft pale features.

"I've missed the last bus, I'm going to have to come back in the morning will you be alright alone?"

"Of course, I will, I'm old enough and ugly enough to take care of myself."

She could hear her mother laughing softly in the background, and imagined her Uncle standing beside her while she made sweet innuendoes of endearment towards the telephone.

"I know darling, but I wondered if you were nervous after the terrible murder of that young girl."

"No, of course not I'm okay, everything's locked up; it didn't happen around here anyway."

"Okay then darling, as long as you don't see any 'Ghosties' or Demons."

This was her mother's way of treating her like a child, and it angered her, especially in front of other people! Why did she always have to poke fun at her?

"No mum." She replied. "I don't see Ghosts, never have."

"I'm sorry sweetheart, look I could get a cab home if you like?"

"No, no don't do that its late I don't want you walking about in the dark, stay with your brother and come home in the morning ok?"

She blew a kiss down the phone and said goodnight. Kicking off her slippers she settled down on the sofa, it was absolutely no use looking through the album now it would only depress her anyway so she decided to read her book instead. She opened her book at her marked page and started the first sentence, and then noticed a cold chill rushing up her legs and for a moment she looked puzzled, Madeline frowned, where was the draught coming from? She sat forward with her book in her hand, and gazed down the hall towards the back door. The curtain fluttered from a draught as a blast of cold air sifted through the open door.

Her eyebrows rose curiously, why was it open? She had closed it earlier when she went out to bring in the washing from the line; she knew she had! She had definitely remembered kicking it shut with her foot while carrying the heavy burden of clothes and towels in her arms. Maybe it had sprung open? Madeline shook her head and glanced towards the door again. It was a mystery but one she needn't bother her head with right now. She shrugged it off as a coincidence and then got up to close it.

She went back to her chair and curled her feet underneath her. She was tired yet comfortable; she reached for her book then laid her head back and started to read. The house was as silent as a Pharaoh's tomb, except for the clock that ticked loudly on the shelf by the fireplace. She found herself reading the same sentence two or three times until the words echoed in her mind, and then she lost the plot altogether as her concentration vanished. She couldn't keep her mind off the dead girl in the stream, and Amanda's new boyfriend. It wasn't that she disliked him exactly! She could hardly judge someone she had only just met on one occasion. And he was at least fifteen years older if not more. That didn't matter of course many relationships worked out perfectly well with a large age gap, although she couldn't quite see Reece and Megan being too happy with that! She uncurled her legs and sat forward with the book in her hand hanging between her knees; she looked around anxiously; her head tilted slightly upwards as she sniffed the air.

She could smell something strange! It was unfamiliar to her yet there was definitely a strange odour coming from somewhere. She sniffed a few more times but couldn't smell anything alarming, so decided to make a coffee, perhaps it would come to light later. Madeline laid the book on the coffee table and went out to the kitchen. As she switched on the hood light over the cooker, her eyes widened. The gas taps were on! For a second her breath caught in her throat. They had been turned halfway just enough to let out a steady flow of gas that would have been a silent and deadly killer. She turned them off quickly realising that must have been the odour she could smell, she opened the window to let out the fumes and waited a few minutes before switching on the electric kettle. When she came home that afternoon she remembered making a coffee and hadn't touched the cooker at all, so how could they have turned themselves on? Impossible! Unless someone had turned them on! She would never leave gas leaking like that! Pouring the water into the cup, she put the kettle down and closed the window tightly making sure all the latches were secure and then went back to the living room.

She started to worry about the open door and the gas

taps; she could have been guilty of leaving on one of the taps, but not all four! Instead of reading her book she sat on the edge of the chair. Unless she was losing her mind she remembered the click of the door as the latch engaged and the cooker had not been used since yesterday.

He stood at the sidewall of the house; there were no lights in the back garden only one large tree and beds of stocks and shrubs. The machete swung slowly back and forward as his hand tightened its grip on the handle. A smile sneaked across his face as he studied Madeline's puzzled features, he was having such a fun day tormenting and terrorising her.

'Think you can keep me out by nuts and bolts do you? Oh, how wrong you are!"

He would like to bury that machete in her head, see what colour her brains were? If she had any! He pulled the hood over his head and moved silently towards the back door, his hand reached out for the doorknob.

Madeline was restless, she imagined she could hear every Ant that passed in or under the floorboards, and the ticking of the clock seemed to be much louder than it had done before. She picked up her book and started reading again trying hard to concentrate on the novel, but still the same sentences repeated in her mind and it began to annoy her. The silence was impenetrable and restlessly she got up and went back to the kitchen.

She stood at the door for a second, clasping her hands

in front of her in an anxious knot, imagining that the taps would be on again and the door would be open, but they weren't. She went back for the cup, she was sure there was nothing to worry about.

Putting her cup in the sink she glanced up at the window, the circling darkness held no comfort for her so she closed the blind half way.

She tried to tell herself she was being silly and she was going to force herself to pick up her book and read the rest of the chapter, even if she had to plug her ears with cotton wool and put headphones on, she was determined to finish her chapter. She went back into the living room and sat down again in the armchair; she put her feet out in front of her and got to page two of chapter five. It was no use! And it would have been no better with cotton wool or earphones either. She closed the book; her mind just wasn't on it. Madeline glanced at the clock, her eyes following the second hand as it spun around the dial, now it was ten past two in the morning. There was no way she was going to get any sleep tonight and the night was going to be one endless drag, never ending and terrifying! She began to wish her mother had got that cab home after all, at least she would have felt safe now. After laying her head back and taking a few deep steadying breaths she started to relax, Her eyelids got heavier and suddenly they closed, she slept.

The next thing she was aware of was the thudding of her heart, it frightened her so much that she sat bolt upright in the chair, for a moment she struggled to breathe and then relaxed, she had been dreaming and they must have been nightmares that she no longer remembered.

Glancing at the clock again it was almost three thirty in the morning. Feeling like she had been weighted down with lead she pulled herself up and stretched, then placing the guard around the fire she headed for the stairs.

As she got to the fourth step up from the bottom she heard a noise, it was a chuckle that sent hairs on the back of her neck standing up on end as stiff as if they had been plugged into an electrical socket. She froze! Her eyes searched the darkness, like a Fox that had been caught in the glare of a car headlight she couldn't move. A hot flush of fear spread through her and her mouth felt as dry as sand, her throat constricted. With one hand she held tightly to the banister while the other cupped tightly to her mouth. She knew she hadn't imagined the sound, because she had heard it so clearly.

She wanted to get to the phone to call the police! But what if he had cut the wires? That's what happened in films, and who was HE? How did she know it was a man? But this wasn't a film it was real!

She heard it again, a childish giggle, hoarse and squeaky at the same time. Madeline turned her head in the direction of the sound; her long auburn hair fell over her shoulder as the moon cast a bluish hue over her shockingly white features.

She seemed to stand there for ages listening for sounds; rooted to the spot so afraid to move, but the only sound she could hear was the thumping beat her heart made in her ears.

Sensing movement, Madeline cast her eyes towards the back door handle, they widened in shock, it was turning, she was sure it was! Perhaps only one or two degrees, but she definitely saw it move. Someone was out there. She felt a clammy sweat spreading under her arms and then running down her back, it broke out on her brow, fine streaks ran down from her hairline and a thick lump in her throat stopped her swallowing. As she studied the door once more she realised the bolts were not in place and the key was still in the lock, she had been so sure she had locked that door earlier and taken out the key! Suddenly she darted forward slamming both bolts into place and snatching the key from the lock.

She stepped back and waited. She was going to call the police and tell them there was an intruder outside she didn't really care if they thought she was a little unhinged, she was going to call them anyway, at least she would know then that there was no one outside, once the police had checked the place thoroughly. She crept toward the kitchen a few yards ahead and looked out through the half open blind pressing her face to the glass. Outside was an empty black space with no shape or substance and no light. She wondered why her mother had never installed one, she knew what she was going to do first thing tomorrow; she was going to buy a security light and get someone to fix it!

She placed both hands on the sink and pressed her face further towards the glass.

Something scuttled under the window, Madeline moved back slightly as a soft worried frown creased her features, a small scratching sound followed, and she craned her neck forward just a little to see what was scratching under the window. Something flew at her hitting the glass at such force that she thought it would shatter. With a startled scream Madeline threw herself away from the window.

A large black prominent shape with eyes that were deep yellow and baneful glared back at her, light from the reflection of the cooker hood bounced off the pupils making them huge and round, then retracting to slits like the thin edge of a razor. Her terror raised a whimper in her throat, and her hands curled into fists at her sides as she pressed herself tightly to the wall. The resentful angry gaze lasted only a moment. Madeline saw the expanse of hot angry fur as it skidded down the wall; its claws scraping on stone, then the clattering of dustbin lids; and then the enraged mewling of the huge black Tom Cat as he vanished off into the night. Madeline almost cried out in relief as she stumbled away from the window shutting the blind tightly, after all that, it was the local Tom Cat.

The range Rover cruised at a slow steady speed, it carried video equipment used mainly for car accidents, but tonight it was on the lookout for potential killers, especially the one who murdered the young girl in the stream. The radio crackled and Quince picked it up, his eyes darting around while he held it to his mouth.

"Nothing yet, no one suspicious, in fact it's quieter than a cemetery after a funeral."

He put the radio back and turned to his partner.

"Control Reckon he's long gone now, besides, where would you seek refuge in a small place like this."

"Someone must know who he is just keep your eyes open."

Taylor gave him a weary grin, his eyes looked lifeless and dull, and he felt as if he was coming down with something. Suddenly he saw something move on his right, a large shape emerging from the darkness over a wall leading to a back garden.

"Hang on!" Taylor shouted. "Over there!"

He brought the Range Rover to an abrupt halt. They jumped out and gave chase running towards the figure that was flying almost literally towards the crossroad.

"Hey you stop where you are!" Quince shouted.

The figure kept running, a black cloak flapping in the wind, Quince was after him in seconds, the figure ducked sideways and leapt over a fence. Quince stood for seconds unable to believe how he had leapt over a fence of about five feet in height as if he had springs on his heels.

"Did you see that?" he called to Taylor. "He shot over that fence like fucking superman!"

Taylor got on the radio and called it in. Quince jumped and somersaulted over the fence, he landed on the other side, but there was no one in front of him the figure had just vanished into thin air.

"Did you see what house it was he came from?" Taylor asked.

"I think it was the one with the red brick front on the right."

The bell chimed and Madeline ran to the door. "Who is it?" she frowned looking at the clock on the wall; it was almost five in the morning.

"It's the police miss, could you open the door?"

"Can you show me some I.D? "

Looking through the spy hole she saw him hold up a warrant card. Once she had confirmed they were who they said they were she slid back the two bolts and opened the door.

"What is it?" she frowned.

"Have you seen anyone lurking about in your garden tonight Miss?" Quince asked her. She shook her head.

"I thought I heard something a while back, but it was the local Tom Cat prowling his territory."

"Well, can we come in Miss, because what we have just seen didn't look much like a Cat to us?"

They searched the garden, looked over the fence but they saw no one.

January brought an avalanche of snow. It was the first bad winter of the New Year and it did

Seem like a blizzard was imminent by the storm clouds that were gathering in the sky.

Amanda struggled through the snow, her flat snow boots made crunching noises on the crisp white ground. She could feel the eyes boring into the back of her head and she smiled, she knew it was her brother and as she turned around she could see him at the bedroom window with a pair of long range binoculars hoping to get a glimpse of Paul. If Paul had agreed to meet her family there would have been no need for David to stand at the bedroom window with a pair of binoculars, besides it was so important to her he should get on with her family. Perhaps now would be a good time to invite him back home, even if it was only for a coffee. She didn't really want to go out in bad weather like this. The shops had closed early and the streets were deserted due to the extreme weather conditions. It wasn't usually this bad in North Wales, but this year had been a record breaker. Snow had now piled up on the roadside making the kerb invisible, and the weather stations had been reporting severe weather warnings all day. Amanda shoved her gloved hands into her pockets and pulled her scarf over her face to shield her from the sharp biting frost as she walked as quickly as she could towards the bridge.

Paul saw her and waved; she waved back struggling to keep her balance where the snow had fallen thickly on uneven ground. She was more than pleased to get inside the explorer in the warm welcoming heat.

"Where are we going?"

"You'll see I have a little surprise planned for you."

He slipped the gear in first and released the handbrake.

"The pub is over there?" she said pointing to the small inn half a mile away.

"We could walk?" she said.

"We're not going to the pub."

"Paul, I don't think we should drive in this, it's not a good idea."

He laughed. "Have faith my little bunny. "

She sat back in her seat, his words did little to comfort her and she could feel the pull of the car as it skidded on the snow.

"This is a four wheel drive you can't get a safer vehicle in the snow." He took his hand off the wheel to squeeze her leg. "These cars climb mountains, so don't worry."

But she did worry, especially as they started to climb the mountain road, it was rapidly becoming invisible through the thick flurry thundering down. The windshield wipers moved back and forward sluggishly as they tried to clear the snow, it was building up as fast as the wipers were clearing them.

"Paul! Paul please, let's go back its too dangerous."

She couldn't see now, and if she couldn't see then neither could Paul. Terror was mounting inside her, she braced herself against the seat because she knew these roads and the dangers they held; they were bendy and windy and just a little further ahead, there were ravines.

A smile nudged the corners of his mouth, he glanced at her confidently.

"Don't worry; I wouldn't let anything happen to you."

A bend came into view; Amanda stiffened and shouted a warning but it was too late. Paul slammed his foot down on the brake sending the car on a sideway slide towards the barrier and a two hundred foot drop.

"Paul!" she screamed bracing her both hands on the dashboard.

Paul turned the wheel in the direction of the skid, the car went slamming to the right, churning up snow under the wheels as they whipped up fresh white sludge that hit the side windows like hurled snowballs, it felt to Paul like a Jumbo Jet speeding down the runway, he saw the edge of the barrier which looked like the top of a roller coaster before the long drop on the other side, he braced himself for the impact. With a tortured screech the car stopped inches from the barrier.

"OH Fuck!" Paul said, his voice subdued yet thick with fear, beads of sweat lined his brow despite the cold.

Amanda was numb, she felt sick inside, and her hands were still braced tightly to the dashboard.

She looked up slowly. "I think that could definitely be described as a positive near death experience!"

He turned to her. "Are you alright?"

"Just about, I do believe my heart is still beating, because I can feel it!"

She was so angry; he should have listened to her in the beginning. "I'm sorry, I'm sorry."

Amanda didn't reply, she folded her arms across her chest and stared straight ahead of her. The mountain to her left was now only a blur. At first she thought they were unshed tears of terror that was clouding her vision until she realised she was staring through a blizzard of thick snow. Somehow it had become worse up in the mountains than it would've been in the Village. Her breathing was still very much fast in tune with her heart. She sat still for a moment quietly containing her anger, while she waited for her heart to resume its normal rhythms.

Paul switched off the engine and turned to her. "Look, I'm sorry, you were right, I should have listened."

"You already said sorry three times, too late now."

"Amanda, I just wanted to see you, I was planning on giving you a surprise."

"Oh you certainly did that alright!" she shrugged.

"I wanted to see you."

"What was wrong with the pub? Or even my parent's house?"

"I'm sorry."

"Oh you keep saying you're sorry, but sorry doesn't do it, are you aware that we are going to be stranded up here all night?"

He nodded. "Maybe we can get help?"

She looked at him angrily. "Are you serious?" she said. "Are you really serious?" she repeated. "Where are we going to get help from? Do you see anyone around here that could help?"

"Well, they can't leave us here!"

"Can't they now! Who do you think is going to be stupid enough to drive up a mountain in thick treacherous snow like this? Mountain rescue?"

"Oh don't be so patronizing Amanda! We'll phone someone, the police, or the fire department."

She let out a long patient sigh. "Have you got your mobile?"

Paul looked at her with a pained expression and she already knew what he was going to say before he even opened his mouth.

"You left it at home?" she murmured, he nodded miserably. "Oh well, it looks like certain death for both of us then doesn't it?" she replied sharply, her dark eyes flashing angrily.

Amanda looked out of the window; her breath misted the glass as she watched the mountains disappear as darkness started to descend on the road ahead. She knew there was no way they were going to drive back down that road tonight, visibility was down to ten feet and it was getting colder. She lifted herself from the seat to look behind and saw that snow had piled up behind them in the direction they had come.

For a moment Amanda thought she was feeling giddy, and then with a crystal clear clarity almost slapping her in the face she realised the car was moving. "Oh Shit!" she exclaimed. "Paul, can you feel the car rocking?"

Paul looked out of his side window, they were nearer the edge than he first realised, it only needed another strong gust to push them further towards the barrier and send them plunging down the ravine.

"We're too exposed here, lets try and move the car over to the verge under the mountain; we are far too near the edge of the barrier."

Paul was already out of the car slapping his hands together and stamping his feet, already numb from the cold. Together they struggled to push the explorer but gave up after a couple of minutes. The wheels were stuck fast, the snow too thick, and for now they were in no danger of being pushed over the edge, it was wedged tightly; the car would just have to stay where it was.

Amanda worried about her parents. Madeline would be sure that Paul had murdered her, dismembered her body and left her lying in a ditch somewhere! Although the thought was absurd she knew how Madeline sometimes let her imagination create havoc.

Amanda hugged herself and stood there like a lost child, she wished he had brought his mobile with them at least she could have called her parents and let them know she was safe. She could hear Reece's angry voice; they had already argued and she had promised him it wouldn't happen again, and now she was about to break that promise; only this time she was going to do the job properly and not come home at all! Oh Bollocks she thought angrily.

"Amanda, you okay?"

Paul's voice sounded so distant as if the wind had snatched it and hurled it towards the mountains.

Amanda shook her head. "No, not really, you remember the night you took me home?"

"Yes of course I do."

"My parents almost freaked out because of the girl who was murdered by the stream, they thought it could have been me! The situation was made so much worse because her description matched me perfectly, and when I didn't come home they worried sick, I can imagine how they're feeling now!"

"Amanda, I'm sorry, look, maybe we could walk back down I know it's quite a way…"

"Forget it, we'd never make it its too cold, we'd die before we reached the bottom."

"Ok, well let's go back to the car at least we can shelter."

Paul glanced at the car, it was already covered in a foot of snow, he reached for Amanda and wrapped his arm around her tightly as the wind tried to force them back, and together they crouched and stumbled towards the car.

As Paul opened the door of the Explorer wads of snow that had bunched up on the roof and windows; came down like a tiny avalanche and piled up in front of him.

He shook snow from his hands. "I'll keep the engine running that will keep us warm."

"And when the fuel runs out what then?"

"It shouldn't, I filled it up yesterday."

They sat in the back of the car, her head resting on his chest. She complained of feeling drowsy and cold and he held her tighter wrapping her in a deep and meaningful embrace.

She felt afraid, it was creepy and dark on the mountain she had never been so scared in all her life before. The thing foremost in her mind was freezing to death, of being found in Paul's arms, stiff, blue, and very dead! People died in cars in extreme weather conditions like this. Her eyes wandered towards the sky; there were no stars on view only an empty blackness and a sea of heavy thunderous snowflakes.

"We're going to die here, it's so cold." she sniffed.

Paul looked down at her, moved his head slightly so he could see her. "No we're not." he said sincerely. "I'll never let anything happen to you."

He brushed hair from her eyes and kissed her brow softly. From the heat of his body, and his positive thoughts, hope lifted her and she relaxed. The night was spent in his arms ensconced in the warmth of his love, his soul reached out and touched her, and it was the first time for her and it felt so right, and she knew in that moment that she wanted to spend the rest of her life with him.

The night passed, it seemed as if they had been up here on this mountain for days instead of hours.

Amanda shifted awkwardly, eyes opening slowly then closing against the glare of the early morning sun. Stiff muscles complained bitterly as she lifted her head; it felt as if she had been resting against concrete. With a groan she sat up. Paul was lying at the side of her, his princely features relaxed in slumber.

"Paul! Wake up, it's early morning."

Paul's eyes opened, his hand rose in front of him in a contemplative gesture not really sure he wanted to wake or stay where he was.

"At least we're still here." he grinned.

Amanda was already out of the car. "Come on, lets start walking, I need to get home, I can imagine the chaos."

CHAPTER THREE

Lana was a plain simple girl who liked ordinary plain simple things. The only thing in her life that was not ordinary was Richard. They got married four years ago, and it was a marriage made in hell, the biggest craziest mistake she had ever made in her whole life. That was how Lana viewed it anyway, a marriage of pure living misery and hell. Richard had not been her ideal soul mate, they were two different characters in looks and attitude, she knew only too well she had not been made to be blond and beautiful; and often wondered what had made Richard marry her in the first place? But now after four long years of misery, she couldn't care less anymore.

She knew they were a mismatched couple like Beauty and the Beast with the roles reversed. He had destroyed what little confidence she had possessed in the earlier days; at the start of what she thought was a blissful romance. That little bit of confidence that she used to have had been so brutally destroyed that it made her think she was less than useless, which of course was stupid. Lana was as good as the next person, what she lacked in beauty she certainly gained in personal quality. Her self-esteem was often so low that sometimes she felt she needed a shovel to scrape her confidence off the ground.

She was always looking in the mirror and guessed she could have done a lot with her appearance, because she had a sweet and gentle face; her flecked grey oval eyes had a wizened expression, as if they had been crammed with the knowledge that was equivalent to a master's degree. Her short brown hair was layered thickly across her forehead in a straight unflattering fringe. If she had worn a little make up at least it would have added some colour and a little panache to her pale uneven skin tone. Richard was a handsome, clever and witty son of a bitch! (She didn't mean that in the literal sense of the word, or to cause any offence to his mother, who was equally sweet) But he had it all. When they married Lana had made a painful transition from dumb (as she thought) to bright in a matter of a few months. It was hard and arduous keeping up with Richard and his affairs, trying to keep one step ahead of him was slowly wearing her down. She had always wanted children it was her goal in life as is every woman's, her commitment would have been total if she had adhered herself to becoming a mother. But Richard was too selfish! He had made that clear from the beginning. Children were not part of his plans either now or in the foreseeable future, they made too much mess, they cried constantly and he could never stand all that noise! And besides they smell! So that ended her dreams of becoming a mother.

When she first met Richard she had found him funny, loud, charming and sweet, (If you can call a man sweet) She could hardly believe it when he began to take such an interest in her it was far beyond belief, but he did, and he couldn't have made it anymore clearer in his attentiveness towards her. But not being one to look a gift horse straight in the mouth she let herself be dragged into a web of lies and deceit.

Lana sat at the table near the door; her eyes fixed on Richard whose attentions were on the barmaid with the yellow straw hair and make-up that reminded her of Cruella-de-ville!

The moment they had entered the pub he had left her on her own while he trotted off to chat up some bimbo! Anger stirred inside her like a raw open sore. Richard was right about one thing, she was so glad they didn't have kids because she didn't fancy the thought of bringing a child up on her own, and that was the one thing Lana was quite fanatic about; children need both parents and no kid of hers was going to be brought up without a dad!

She didn't really care who Richard slept with anymore, but the thing that had made her angrier than ever was the fool he made out of her in front of the whole village! That's what made her so pissed off with him, like what he was doing now! This was not the first time she had been humiliated by him; it had happened on several occasions and tonight was going to be the very last time, she'd had enough. As she glanced around she saw people standing at the bar, sitting at tables, she watched the glares of the local people who frequented this pub, people she knew; and she saw the pity in their eyes and she felt instantly degraded.

Lana lifted her glass with a double Brandy and touched the warm brown liquid with the tip of her tongue; she held the glass tighter, then she saw Richard leaning over the bar, and the straw haired barmaid bending forward with a low cut top that revealed a perfectly moulded cleavage, an enticing avalanche of warm flesh. She was sure if Richard moved any closer he would fall in and suffocate. It was obvious by the blank look on her face she was hanging onto his every word. As ever, Richard was the perfect charmer.

Lana felt as if she had sunk to the lowest level of pecking orders, and the feelings of humiliation swelled inside her as if she had been pumped full of helium, and she knew this night was going to explode soon enough. Lana looked around at the people who were watching her, their gazes switching to Richard, heads together in deep conversation. Conversations about her! She gripped the glass tighter as her tension mounted, she was not even aware of how firmly she was holding the glass, until the loud muffled 'crack' alerted her as it shattered into a million pieces, slicing a deep gash in the centre of her hand. Blood trickled down her arm staining her jumper and onto the floor. Instinctively she opened her hand and let the glass fall. The gash was deep.

"Oh SHIT!" she cried grabbing a tissue from her bag and pressing it firmly to the wound, the throbbing pain adding insult to her rage as she watched him; He hadn't even noticed her she got up and walked towards the bar.

"We need to talk." she said.

He looked at her irritably. "About what?" he snapped.

Her eyes held his in a hostile conquest, an angry little flint had struck a flame deep within her, it didn't help as she glanced towards the barmaid and noticed she had a smile on her face it made Lana want to slap her, rake her nails down the side of her face, grab at the girls cheap peroxide hair and drag her across the bar.

"Are you going to talk to me or not?"

"Lana, I talk to you all the time, I live with you." he replied smartly, turning to the barmaid and grinning at his clever remark.

"I'm leaving."

"Oh wait a minute, I'll get my drink." He said impatiently.

"No! Richard, I don't mean I'm leaving the pub, I'm leaving you!"

He followed Lana as she sat down and placed his drink on the table. "Leaving me?" he laughed. "And where do you think you're going?"

"I don't really have to even tell you."

"You are behaving irrationally Lana."

"Am I? Have you got any cigarettes?"

"Do you want me to get you some?"

He reached into his pocket for some change, Lana

watched him carefully counting out every penny. Is this what I'm worth? She thought; all his small change? She wanted to punch him, hard! The urge was so great that she clamped her hands tightly together on her lap wincing as the pressure hurt her wound. A piece of paper fell from his pocket and fluttered to the floor, he went to retrieve it but Lana was quicker.

"What's this?" she said, waving it in the air, she turned it over. It didn't take her long to realise whose telephone number was written in spidery handwriting on the back.

"Lana, it's not what you think! She asked me to do some plumbing for her."

Lana looked at him in disgust. "I bet she did! Considering you don't know the difference between a washer and an elbow joint! Why don't you hire yourself out as a stud? That's about all you're good for Richard." She got up and snatched her coat from the chair.

He looked shocked, stunned at her outburst, she had never spoken to him like this before. "Where're you going?"

"Not that it's any of your business, but I'm going to my brother."

"Don't be so stupid, your brother won't keep you."

Lana ignored him as she headed for the door, Richard was on his feet following her with her drink in his hand.

"Wait! I bought you a drink and you haven't even touched it." He held it towards her.

Lana turned around. Finally, she thought, after four years of sacrifice this is all she was worth to him, a wasted drink! And some small change! She smiled at him, raised her eyebrows took the drink from his hands and said. "So I didn't!" She tipped the glass over his head, and the amber liquid spurted like a small fountain down his face staining his suit that he was so meticulous about. "There!" she said. "Now it's history, like you!"

Outside in the cold night air Lana slumped against the wall, the tears that she had stored inside her all night now fell from her eyes. At least she was happy that she hadn't cried in front of him. She took the last tissue from her bag, blew her nose and dried her eyes.

The voice was friendly, it was soft and assuring. Lana looked up into his warm brown eyes.

She sniffed and tried to hide her embarrassment. "Hi, how're you." She smiled softly.

"I'm okay, but your not; anything I can do to help?"

Lana dried her eyes, she felt stupid. "Thanks, I'll be alright once I get home."

"Where is home?" he asked, handing her another tissue.

"Over the other side of the field, where all the lights are shining." She pointed across the field.

"You're not going to walk across the field alone are you?"

"Oh, no." she laughed. "I can go through the village; it's probably safer, especially with the murderer in the village."

"Would you like me to walk with you?"

Lana hesitated, she felt uncomfortable. "Uh, no thanks, I'll be okay."

"I saw you in the pub, was he your husband, or boyfriend?"

"Husband, unfortunately."

"Marriage problems?"

"Severely." She smiled. "Are you married?"

He grinned at her. "Not that stupid, I have many years to go before I think about marriage."

"Can't say I blame you, how's the job going?"

"Oh, not bad, interesting." he smiled warmly.

Lana looked down the long winding road it would take her at least three quarters of an hour to get home if she took the long route, darkness had become a huge cavernous mouth; It would surely be safer to take the longer route home.

"I think I had better be going." she said.

He fell in beside her. "Let me walk with you, I can be really good company."

Lana gave him a warm generous smile, at least she knew him, he was sweet, and a real gentleman, and she'd be safe.

"Oh, alright then, am I putting you out of your way?"

"No, I live in the same direction I have a room not far from here."

In the distance Lana could hear the haunting cry of an Owl. She searched her bag for her small pocket torch, she loved Wildlife and thought there was a good chance she'd see it if she trained her torch into the tree ahead of them.

"What's the torch for?" he asked frowning.

"An Owl, look, over there he's somewhere in the tree." She pointed above her.

"Do you like birds?"

"I love all animals."

He smiled warmly "So do I, sometimes they are better than people. Do you work?"

"No, I used to but gave up when I married Richard."

"Got any kids?"

"No, Richard doesn't want any, doesn't see the need for them, he's selfish really."

"Why do you stay with him then?"

"Habit I suppose."

"If you try hard enough you can break bad habits." He grinned.

Lana laughed at him, she liked him, and he was good company.

They reached the side of the field one hundred yards from Lana's house.

"Well, this is it." She smiled. "Thanks for walking with me; maybe I'll see you again in the week."

He didn't reply.

She turned to walk away.

And felt a sickening blow to the back of her head sending her crashing to the ground heavily, her mouth opened in shocked surprise, hands pushed her face into the earth as mud choked and gagged her, a thick rush of blood to her ears drowned out her muffled desperate cries. Cruel hands lifted her onto her back as iridescent colours and patterns danced before her eyes, and she found herself looking up half dazed into a featureless yet terrifying face, a face that had changed in a heartbeat from one of kindness to one of cruelty. Lana thought of just one thing at that moment, she was never going to see Richard again.

The machete rose high above her then fell with a swishing sound as it cleaved the air; the sickening sound of something wet hitting a jellied surface, like that of a large jellyfish being split in half was the last sound she heard, as her head exploded from the impact of the machete.

Blood, bone, and viscera accompanied by cerebral fluid sprouted like a fountain into the face of her killer, he huddled over the broken body; smiling in morbid fascination. He snatched up Lana's small torch from her bag to shine it in her mutilated face; and then watched her body jerk and twist in the last of its death throes.

Amanda walked into the police station in Bedgellert she wiped her sweat damp hands on her coat. The station officer looked up and put his pen back in the holder by the desk.

He smiled at her. "Morning, can I help you?"

"Yes, I hope you can, I thought I should come in and report an intruder, well, not an intruder actually, but a person who I have seen twice in the last two months, he could be the man you're looking for regarding the murders?" she looked at him sheepishly. "He looks kind of weird." she added.

A frown now replaced the smile. "What do you mean

weird?" he asked picking up his pen again.

"Weird, in the sense that he was weird." she scrunched her face into a grimace and a frown as an image formed in her mind, wondering how she was going to describe him.

"Well, he wore a hood."

"You say he had a hood over his head? What's weird about that then?"

"Well nothing I suppose, but have you ever seen Dennis Wheatley Grim Reaper? That's the only way I could describe him, he just didn't look right!"

The officer frowned; she could see this conversation was going nowhere.

"The first time I saw him he jumped out on me as I was coming home from University, it was sleeting quite bad so I couldn't see his face, I thought he might have been a tramp or someone looking for a place to stay for the night, that's why I didn't report it before, but then I saw him again, he appeared outside my window later in the evening, and I have seen him again, the other evening."

"Did he follow you home?"

"I don't know, I don't think so, he vanished in the opposite direction."

"And then you saw him again?"

"Yes, near the Quarry line, he dropped a red Rose; there was blood on the crushed leaves."

"Did you happen to keep the Rose?" He asked her.

Amanda shook her head "No, I wouldn't keep a rose with blood on it."

"And you haven't seen him since?"

"No, I haven't, not since the other night."

"Right, I'll get someone to see you Miss, take a seat shouldn't be long."

Amanda sat down on a long bench.

A crowd of inquisitive people had gathered at the edge of the field, their necks craned to see what was happening over by the big Oak tree on the far side of the field. Their voices rose in unison in excited chatter. They had been prevented from going any further by the police ribbons that stretched between them and the outer edges of the field. Photographers from the daily newspapers scrambled for a place, but even they were not allowed near to where Lana's body was covered in tarpaulin. Three police officers stood in front of the police cordon; their boots were caked in mud as they watched silently stamping their feet and rubbing their hands together from the cold.

Detective Inspector Ray Collins stood with his younger partner almost beside the body of the mutilated girl. He looked at his watch it was only seven fifteen in the morning yet the crowd at the edge of the field had swelled to something resembling spectators at a football match. Bad news travels faster than the speed of light! He thought grimly. Even so, he was shocked at the brutality of the murder itself.

Both men turned their attention on the Coroners black van as it came towards them flattening the blades of grass as the muddy tyres rolled over them. Collins turned up the collar of his coat and moved to the side of the tree as the wind tore past him, he reached into his pocket for a wad of tissues to wipe his runny nose, and coughed as a tickle started in the back of his throat. His head felt thick and heavy, he knew he was coming down with a cold.

"Is there anyone taking care of her husband?" D.S Pete Haldane asked.

"I think there are some friends with him, the guy is devastated."

Haldane rubbed his hands together.

Collins watched as the pathologists started to prepare Lana's body for removal.

"He should never have let her walk home on her own, they had a row, and she stormed off; he wished he had gone after her.."

Haldane frowned. "Did anyone see him leave?"

"Oh yes, Lot's of people saw him leave, it was a really

bad fight, but he's got a rock solid alibi a neighbour walked home with him, and the neighbour was there when he found her body and apart from that he was in the pub all evening."

"Did they have any kids?"

"No." Collin's replied.

Haldane sighed. "That's a blessing; imagine explaining to your kids how their mother died."

They watched as two men took a metal coffin from the van and laid it beside Lana.

Collins felt his stomach convulse as they removed the tarpaulin, and between them they carefully lifted her. Both men wore white surgical gloves and Collins noted with disgust that one mortuary attendant held each side of her head, instead of her shoulders, so her head didn't split completely in half with the pressure as they lifted her. Her Jumper and jeans had turned an insipid dark brown and Collins felt his stomach tighten in readiness to spill this morning's breakfast.

"You okay sir?" Haldane asked with concern as he noticed Ray's features turn from an Ivory shade to pale.

"Uh? Oh, Yes, Yes I'm fine." He replied, feeling slightly embarrassed, as if he was a new recruit at an Autopsy; not that he'd seen that many!

"I've got a rotten bloody cold coming I just feel a little sick that's all."

His tough urban image had not stood him up for this kind of brutality; this was the second violent murder in less than three months.

Haldane shoved his hands in his pockets and looked around at the crowd gathered at the edge of the field.

"So now we have two victims, both murders replicated, Mary Saltash was killed almost the same way, mutilation also, I only hope we have not got a serial killer what do you think Guv?"

Ray Collins frowned; he turned and looked behind him as the coroners van headed towards the road.

"Possibly, But that's two too many, we had better get more patrols out on the street, especially late at night, make sure every young woman is aware of the dangers, get the news channels involved, make sure they warn woman to stay in brightly lit areas, and if they have to go out at night, take someone with them." Collin's said.

"There could be a link to the guy Quince and Taylor spotted the other night, going by the description Amanda Williams gave, it looks very much one of the same man. He had a long black cloak and a hood."

A gust of wind ruffled Collins hair as he turned to look at Haldane.

"It's a possible link, it's a shame they never caught him though, maybe he was looking for a victim that night but he was disturbed. Quince said he sprinted over the fence like superman, and he was right on his tail, when Quince jumped over the fence the bastard had vanished."

Haldane said "Great, we're looking for a man around six foot tall wearing a long black cloak and a hood, should stick out like a sore thumb, we'll find him in no time." he said with a little sarcasm. "Right, I'll get the media sorted out, at least people will be aware of what we're dealing with here."

Apart from the drifting fog, the night was quiet, Paul was going to ask Amanda to marry him, But he needed to get past her parents first. He had got on extremely well with Megan and Reece over the past few months, he liked the feeling of family, of warmth and love that emanated from them. But Paul was never a one to do things in short measures, he was going to make a dramatic explosion of feeling in front of Reece and Megan, he felt secure enough to know they liked him a lot. It worried him at first that the fifteen year age gap between him and Amanda would be a bridge too far to cross for Amanda's parents, but they took it all in their stride and as long as he loved their daughter then they were sure it would be fine.

He took a large bunch of lilies for Megan and a box of cigars for Reece. He smiled as he walked up the small drive to the house; confidently he rang the bell and waited. His heart leaped when the door opened and Amanda's mother stood there.

"Oh?" she exclaimed when she saw the lilies. "You must have something pretty important to say, you must be trying to impress me, come in." she laughed.

Paul blushed as she took the lilies from him. "Would you like something to drink?"

Megan opened the wrapping and took the flowers through to the kitchen to find a vase for them.

Paul followed her. "You can read me like a book Meg." he laughed. "I'm going to ask Amanda to marry me."

Megan filled a vase full of water and put the flowers on the kitchen sink. She turned around and smiled at him.

"Well now, I can't say I'm surprised, at least I won't have to worry about her anymore."

She came over and gave him a hug. "I wish you all the happiness in the world, I couldn't think of a better person to become my son-in-law."

The wedding was a fairytale occasion, in a tiny church in the tiny village, Madeline felt a little sad as she wondered if she was losing her best friend and she resented Paul but liked him a hell of a lot. But Amanda's happiness was the main focus in her life and as long as she was happy, then Madeline was to.

Paul found a small one bed-roomed flat, or perhaps a Rabbit hutch would have been a better description.

"Amanda, I want you to come and see it, it's not too bad for our first home."

It was not exactly what she had hoped to start married life in, but for now it was all they could afford. It stank of fungus and decay; of mould and mildew, the wallpaper peeled and hung like a dirty banana skin. Amanda looked miserably at the walls, narrowing her eyes and pinching her nose at the sights and smells. "And all these added extras for one hundred and forty five pound a week. A bargain at the price, I don't think!"

"I know sweetheart, it's not the best of places, but it was the better of three I looked at."

"Not what I expected Paul, in fact it is dirty and dingy, but on the other hand we could paint it up and make it look something. Besides, we will need a lot more room soon."

"Soon?" Paul looked at her questioningly "Why, what's happening SOON." he gave her a playful jab with his finger.

"We'll just need the extra room, a place to put a cot for instance!"

Paul's eyes almost shot out from his head, his eyes clouded for a moment.

"You mean?" he stuttered the words folding them into unclear sentences. "You mean! You…Are Pregnant?"

She laughed and nodded her head. "Yes, the babies due next October, late October."

Paul lifted her in his arms and kissed her, tears sprung into his eyes and fell like transparent dewdrops off early morning leafs.

"Oh, have you told your parents yet? And what about Madeline? Have you told her yet?"

"No, I thought that seeing as you are the father its better to tell you first."

"Well, that is so thoughtful of you! This is the best thing that could ever happen to me I am so happy, at last, my own little family I love you Amanda."

"I love you too." she smiled, "Paul, there's something I need to tell you."

"About what?"

"I went to the police about the murders in the village."

"The murders in the village. When?"

"I popped into the police station the other day."

"Why, what's the murders got to do with you?"

"Nothing, but, I think I saw him, or thought I did."

"But, how did you know it was the killer? It could have been anyone"

"I didn't, it's just that he was acting strange, and dressed in a strange array of clothing I just thought it best to tell someone."

He took her by the shoulders and sat her on the chair.

"Okay, well I'm glad you did, has he made any threat towards you?"

"No, no, but in such a small place it is not the usual thing to see someone dressed so weird I just thought I should let the police know."

"I told you, you did the right thing. Listen, I don't want you walking about on your own, do you hear me?"

"Oh Paul, I'm not that stupid, besides, where do I go at night?"

Collins and Haldane waited until the pathologist finished his examination on Lana. Ray wrote in his notebook, and a quick glance at the trepan in the pathologist's hand diverted his attention to other things. Instruments set down on metal made him shiver; it was something he had always hated. It was the same routine at the dentist. He turned his back on the autopsy table and walked over to the display cabinet under the window; where volumes of pathology books were kept.

"Inspector Collins?" The pathologist called.

"What have you found? " He said turning around sticking his pencil behind his ear.

"I have to make my report in full of course, but this young woman was attacked ferociously with a machete or wide bladed knife."

Doctor Max Forman peeled off his surgical gloves and scrubbed his hands right up to the elbows.

"The blows were sufficient enough to fracture her skull in three places and drive fragments of bone into her brain; whoever did this Inspector would have been literally covered in blood." He dried his hands; threw the paper towel into the bin and walked over to the Inspector.

"That's stating the obvious." Collins replied. "Is there anything else?"

"I found grass and mud down her throat, it looks as if her face was pushed down hard into the ground, and there is another deep cut to the palm of her hand, it is not what we call a defence wound, it looks more like a cut from a glass, it might have happened earlier on because it wasn't a completely fresh wound, it had been attended to."

Haldane moved away from the autopsy table to join Collins and Doctor Forman by the display cabinet.

"Funny how no one heard or saw anything?" The Pathologist said thoughtfully. "You wouldn't miss someone running from a field covered in blood; even in the dark it would be so noticeable."

Collins blinked then frowned. "I really don't know, but it was in the middle of the night, and there are not many people around that area, and it happened near the field, he must have dragged her there so she must have struggled and screamed even if anyone heard her would they bother to investigate? I don't think anyone would to be honest, not in this day and age, people have changed I think they're too scared."

Collins eyes were stinging from the formaldehyde and the chemicals in the room. He looked up at the frosted glass in the high window at the onset of darkness that was quickly descending through the misted panes.

"Well, then, I'll make my report, you'll have it on your desk first thing Monday morning. If there is anything else I'll let you know".

By the time they had left the mortuary Ray Collins felt sick, the stench of decay clung to his clothes and hung in his nostrils. He was glad they were out in the open. Swallowing hard he took a deep breath, fumbled in his pocket for a packet of mints then popped one into his mouth. The back of his throat was sore and the cool temperature of the mortuary had left him feeling chilled. Haldane peeled the wrapper off a mars bar and started to eat it, Collins watched him with astonishment.

"What's your stomach lined with; Lead?" he grimaced.

Amanda loaded her shopping into the Explorer and looked up at the pale clouds that were holding back a warm amber sun as the early evening filtered in. She hated the thought of going back to that small cramped flat.

The best thing she had done since their marriage was learn to drive, she couldn't imagine being stranded in that pokey hole that Paul called home and rotting away like the fungus that grew up the walls. She opened the driver's door and eased herself in. There was stiff competition between her and her bulk for room at the wheel. It was only two weeks before her due date now, and she felt an eager anticipation at the thought of being able to sit normally without shuffling herself about. A dull ache had started in her lower back in the last hour and she shifted in her seat to ease it.

Amanda hadn't noticed the single red rose that was stuck to the left side of the windscreen until she switched on the ignition. "What the hell?" she mumbled struggling out of the car once more. She snatched the rose from under the wiper and noticed a small note wrapped around the stem. "Hi there, remember me?" It read. She glanced around the car park expecting to see that creepy character in that long black cloak and she shuddered. But there were few people around as they got into their cars after loading up their shopping, and they were so busy humping heavy bags to notice Amanda staring dumbly at them.

For a Wednesday it was almost empty, only a couple bays were left that were full of cars. A small frown lined her face causing her a few worry lines. She didn't recognise the handwriting, she stared at the solitary rose lying in her open palm and noticed that the leaves had been crushed like the single red rose that the figure dropped when she was on her way to meet Paul; but this time as she looked closer there was blood on the stem and the note. Without touching the Rose she turned her hand over and let the flower fall quickly to the ground.

"Are you okay Miss?"

Amanda turned around quickly. "Uh, yes, fine, have you been standing here long?" she frowned at the dark haired young man.

"A little while, why?"

"Did you see someone put this Rose on my car windscreen?"

"No, I have been in the store, is there anything I can help you with?"

"Uh, no, no thanks."

She went to get back in the car and the stranger held the door open for her.

"When is your baby due?" he smiled.

"I've got two weeks yet."

"Do you know what you're having?"

She found it strange that a person she had never met before would ask her such a personal question; she looked directly into his dark eyes.

"No, I didn't want to know." She replied.

She slid as gracefully as she could into the seat and fired the engine.

He smiled and closed the drivers door for her.

Amanda turned out of the car park. She was heading for Madeline's, she could call the police from there, this was the second time he had left her a blood stained rose. Why he was leaving her a single Rose, and who was he? Was he singling her out? Could he be the serial killer?

Her thoughts had been filled with the birth of her baby that she hadn't bothered to listen to the radio; her only worries lately were of birth, pain and discomfort, so when she heard the news she turned the radio up.

"Another mutilated body was found earlier on today. She was named as Lana Templeton a local woman, and as yet police have no motive for the vicious attack. This is the second violent murder in a matter of months. Police are warning young woman to stay off the streets and not go out at night unless accompanied by someone else. And now for the weather report"

Amanda had lost interest in the weather instead she leaned forward as much as her cumbersome body would allow, to ease the nagging pain in her lower back.

It could be no coincidence that Lana Templeton's body was found not far from where Mary Saltash had been murdered, her eyes were fixed intently on the radio. Her fingers touched the dial and moved on to another channel to see if there was anything new on this latest murder. While she was fiddling with the dial she almost missed the turning off the motorway, glancing quickly she checked her centre mirror, then the left side wing mirror, flicked down the indicator and moved into the left hand lane.

Madeline had seen the car from the kitchen window and ran down the drive to meet her.

"Oh it's so good to see you." Madeline laughed. But the laughter faded when she saw the look of worry on Amanda's face. "What's wrong?" she asked cautiously.

"Grab my hand." She said sticking her hand out, Madeline gripped it firmly. "Someone left me another rose on the windscreen of my car, can I call the police?"

"Of course you can, call them now."

It didn't seem long since she'd made the phone call that the police were ringing the doorbell.

Madeline answered the door and led them into the kitchen where Amanda waited anxiously sipping the last drop of her coffee.

The young police woman smiled at her. "I'm PC Rosie Bartlett, and this is my colleague, Simon Millington, you reported a stalker?"

"Not a stalker as such, but this is the second Rose he's left me; he seemed to know where I was today."

"And you didn't see anyone lurking around Mrs Marriott?"

"No, no one, I went into the store, did my shopping and came out again."

The young police woman took the note. "It looks like you have an admirer." She smiled.

"Not the sort of admirer I want." Amanda replied. "He's spooky, why doesn't he say who he is? He could be the guy that's killed these two women."

The police officer frowned. "Unlikely, but I suppose it's possible, but this note doesn't indicate anything sinister, as I say he could be an admirer, there is nothing of a threatening nature about the note."

"There's blood on the stem, I kept it this time."

Rosie Bartlett took the rose and carefully examined it.

"There is nothing to indicate this is anything sinister Mrs Marriott, the person who placed it on your windscreen could have pierced themselves on one of the thorns, I can't really do very much to help I'm afraid, he hasn't made any threats towards you has he?"

Amanda shook her head.

It was almost seven by the time she arrived home. She struggled out of the car the dull ache had now turned into a throbbing pain and it was everywhere. She took her time climbing the two flights to the flat, stopping to take a deep breath as each wave intensified with every step she took.

Paul had heard her; he helped her with the shopping. His face drained of colour when he saw her face that looked as white as freshly fallen snow, her lips were bloodless.

"You look very pale darling are you okay? I've been worried where have you been?"

"To Madeline's, I'm so sorry, I should have called you. Someone left me a Rose on the windscreen of my car with a note."

"They left another Rose With a note attached?" Paul's eyes darkened, his usually soft and reassuring face, now became creased with worry. "What did the note say?"

"Remember me, with a question mark."

"Did you go to the police?"

"Yes, that's why I'm late."

"It must be some lunatic you knew once."

"Lunatic? I'm not in the habit of making pals with lunatics." she laughed, "At least not yet, that comes later after I've studied law, when I take my forensic psychologists degree."

"Just relax, you're all wound up, I'll put the kettle on, you sit down and take it easy."

He turned to reach for the tea bags from the shelf, and then studied Amanda's white features again.

"You're looking tired honey, you alright?"

"I am having pain in my lower back, after tea I'll go and lie down."

"Is it the baby, or the stress of the idiot that left the Rose?"

"Probably 'Braxton Hicks' if anything." she grinned.

The kettle started to whistle, he turned, and tripped over the worn carpet as Amanda spun around in sudden surprise and watched him plunge toward her, everything seemed to stop, it was as if she had been watching a slow motion picture, arms flaying, feet stumbling, Paul staggering as they collided and she went sprawling to the floor. The impact was severe as her head hit the side of the worktop; the kettle slipped from his grasp spilling boiling water towards her. Paul yelled a warning; he tried to grab her away from the scalding liquid as the kettle landed a foot away from her.

Amanda was aware of Paul screaming for help, she floated on a sea of pain and confusion and then darkness clouded her vision.

Bethany was born at five twenty a.m. October the twenty six. The birth had been difficult, something she wasn't about to forget in a hurry, but she was so grateful that she hadn't been burnt. She lifted her hand gently to her head and felt a lump the size of a golf-ball.

She picked up the baby from the cot and held her in her arms, tears rested on her long dark lashes. Bethany's hair was light brown and her features were like Paul's. She had the same beautiful countenance that Paul had been so lucky to be gifted with, and she knew that one day Bethany would definitely go far with her beautiful looks.

Paul waited in the corridor while Amanda was cleaned up; he had felt every pain, and every suffering she had gone through. A bouquet of flowers was clutched tightly in his hands. He felt angry with himself for being so careless, angry because at every good opportunity in his miserable life he always seemed to screw it up! He hung his head, he didn't even have time to tell Amanda how sorry he was, and he hadn't meant to fall on her she could have been scarred for life because of him. Even the flowers that he clutched so tightly couldn't stop his hands from shaking. The door opened suddenly and a midwife popped her head around the door, smiling she said. "Mr Marriott you can come in now."

He grinned broadly, yet blinked back tears and followed her through the swing doors.

She looked disturbingly pale. Her long dark hair spread out on the pillow, damp strands curled around her face that made her features even paler. His awkwardness made him fingers and thumbs as he sat down beside her bed. The baby lie in a cot beside her, and his eyes travelled towards the tiny bundle wrapped up in a white cotton blanket. Paul smiled and reached out his hand his fingers touched her tiny face, her little fingers curled around his thumb. "Oh, she is so beautiful." he smiled.

"I know." Amanda answered. "She's so tiny and precious."

Paul studied her for a second he could not find the words to say very easily.

"Amanda I'm so sorry."

Her eyes softened. "I know you are." She smiled.

"It was an accident, I tripped over the carpet."

She grasped his hand and held on as if she never wanted to let go, his eyes held hers.

"It's okay Paul; don't blame yourself it was an accident."

"God I am so glad its over, thank god you didn't get burned and the baby is safe." He held her in his arms for ages planting warm kisses on her brow.

For once the sun was out, shining like a huge yellow sunflower, and dazzlingly bright when Madeline arrived to take Amanda and the baby home, the taxi pulled up right outside the Maternity unit. "I won't be a moment; I'll just collect my friend and her baby." The cabbie smiled, "No rush my love."

It felt strange arriving at Megan's with a tiny baby in tow; Amanda carefully laid her precious bundle into the crook of Madeline's arm.

"Oh I have been waiting so patiently to get my hands on this beautiful child she is gorgeous Amanda. She looks a lot like Paul,"

Amanda nodded. "Never mind." She laughed, "She has time to grow out of it."

"With two good looking parents, she has been gifted don't you think?"

Amanda smiled. "Thank you for your prayers and praise."

She glanced towards the kitchen. "I hope he doesn't mind me staying with Mum at the moment, only it's pretty scary being alone with a new baby."

Reassuringly Madeline said. "Oh no of course he won't mind, he's at work all day so I suppose he's relieved you won't be left to manage alone."

"Paul will come here straight from work for a few days, and once I feel more capable we can go home, by the way, where is my mother?"

"Oh she won't be long she just popped to the shop to get a few more baby things." Placing the baby on the sofa she smiled.

"You know what new Grandmothers are like! Never sure they have enough to start off with."

Amanda nodded with a weak grin. "Thanks for picking us up, Paul is so grateful."

"It's okay." Madeline grinned, by the twinkle in her eye Amanda knew there was something she wanted to tell her.

"What?" she smiled.

"I could be joining the ranks of motherhood soon."

Amanda looked at her with shocked surprise. "You're pregnant? With whom?" her voice raised a crescendo.

Madeline laughed, her eyes seemed to radiate a bluer shade than normal, and Amanda guessed how happy she was.

"No, I'm not pregnant, but I really like him a lot, I'm just kidding you, I would have to be very sure before I even took that step, he's kind, considerate, and a gentleman, you don't find many of those these days."

"You know you should work for the security services, you keep everything to yourself, where did you meet him?"

"In the café, he asked me out, and I've been seeing him off and on for the last two weeks."

"Is he local?"

"No, he works in the café in town, his names Evan."

"I'm so pleased for you Madeline, just take it easy though, don't jump into anything you might regret."

"Amanda, you know me too well to see me jump through a hoop that has only one side."

Bethany whimpered as if she sensed her new and unfamiliar surroundings. Amanda lifted the baby into her arms.

"No more Roses on the windscreen then?" Madeline asked.

"No, I never heard anymore about it, Paul is very angry though."

"I'm not surprised, it's probably someone playing a joke on you, I bet it's somebody you know, Halloween is in a couple of days, maybe it's their idea of a spooky joke."

He crouched low watching her in the long grass, the cold never seemed to bother him; he had become acclimatised to bad weather over the recent months. It was his feelings that were cold; because it was ice that ran through his veins instead of blood. He saw himself as a conquered spirit whipped and beaten but not discouraged. His hand dropped to his side, releasing a thin sharp skewer to nestle in the grass beside him, he laid himself flat to the ground like a commando on surveillance, and his legs stretched out flat behind him as he waited.

In the distance he saw the flashing lights of a police patrol as they passed slowly up ahead of him and he ducked low. He was facing the back of the house so he had a clear view of what went on in the kitchen where they had gathered, fussing and cooing over this new baby. He had watched Amanda over the last year or so.

CHAPTER FOUR

It was seven thirty on a Friday morning that Amanda awoke to the muffled sounds of Paul's voice. She sat up quickly rubbing her eyes, and looked at the clock on the small table by her bed, it was gone eight' clock, "he's late for work" she mumbled. Amanda ran her hands through her hair brushing the tangled strands from her eyes; swung her legs over the side of the bed, pulled on her dressing gown and hurried out the door along the landing and down the stairs.

"You're late for work Mister?" she kissed him lightly.

"I know I've just bought a house." Paul beamed.

"You bought a house?"

"Yes, you got it right first time angel, it's a surprise, I have been saving hard, and that's why I've been doing all this overtime. To get the deposit together."

Amanda's eyes flew open. "You're kidding me? Where?"

"Tynant."

"That's miles away; it's up in the mountains."

"I know it's a bit too far, but I got it at really great price, it's what you always wanted isn't it? We couldn't live for much longer in that little box flat, not now with the baby; besides all that fungus growing up the walls is not healthy for a new born child."

"Oh my God!" she cupped her hand to her mouth and laughed.

"Amanda, it has four bedrooms, a massive lounge, a reception room, and a basement that runs right under the house, I got it at a bargain price, it's repossession I paid a hundred grand for it, and I got the freehold."

The explorer climbed the mountain road easily, she found herself gazing out over endless spaces and fields with giant trees that lay silently back from the road, some congregating in places others segregating as if they had become an exclusive set. A slight chill brushed through her as she watched the mountains disappear under an eerie mist at their peak, and she noticed with some concern that there weren't any other houses or farms around. She wasn't sure she wanted to live in such a lonely place, like she was the only woman on the planet it was the most desolate part of the country she had ever seen. What would happen if an emergency occurred?

"You must be careful if you're driving on these roads, they are full of rocks and stones, and if your wheels get stuck in one of these ditches you'll need a crane to lift it out." He hit the brake as a narrow bend appeared in the road. "See what I mean?"

Amanda nodded.

She suddenly saw the huge house appear out of the mist. It was a great big rambling place with big bay windows, and it looked like there were so many rooms by the amount of windows on the ground floor, and that was before you even got to the top of the house.

The building was only one story high. Ivy crept up the walls and under the windows. The sloped roof had a lot of tiles missing that had obviously loosened the guttering on the way down, leaving it hanging by a thread of rusty bare metal.

Paul stopped the car just over the hill.

"It's a wonderful view in the summer." He smiled striding towards the big arched oak door. It reminded Amanda of the Church door in the village.

Amanda followed him. "Paul why do we have to close all the gates? There are four on the way up."

She felt her feet slipping on the sodden ground and held her hands out in front of her to keep her balance. Once she got to the house she found the driveway had been coated in gravel.

"Sheep I think." Paul slipped the key into the lock.

"Sheep, I don't see any. Where?" She looked around searching for a white woolly face.

"Somewhere around here."

"Are there any farms nearby?"

"No, I don't think so, the last farmer sold up a few years ago."

"You mean a few sheep reside around here, and that's all?"

"Oh I expect there are a few farms around, probably over the hill somewhere," he said gesturing with his hands, and then he struggled with the lock.

"It's got a bit rusty, I suppose I'll have to change the lock, I'll try oil and W.D forty first."

He put his shoulder to the door and pushed hard, it opened stiffly and they found themselves in a very large hallway. To the right was a reception room, it was dirty and dull shadows crept through the dusty windows throwing thin reams of light over the room. It was decorated in shades of grey that had deteriorated over years, and it wasn't a nice light grey but a drab dull dirty colour. An old bureau stood against the far wall, it was a beautiful piece of furniture but like everything else it had also deteriorated. Amanda had already decided that she was going to restore it to its natural beauty. An old grey leather armchair rested in a recess and above it was a wall light that looked like it had been wrenched from the wall and just left there with all the wires exposed. Next to the chair was an old coffee table; on its chipped wooden surface was a stone grey table lamp, remarkably like quarry slate and the lampshade's frills hung in ragged loops like dusty cobwebs. Amanda crossed the room to open the curtains wide and let some light into the room, as she did so a cloud of dust escaped almost choking her, she coughed loudly. "Jesus! Wasn't this room ever cleaned?" She wiped her hands down the front of her jeans.

"I think it's been empty for a couple of years. Come, let me show you something."

She followed him down the hall towards the living room, her mouth open in wonder at the pure size of it.

"Wow, Paul, this is a mansion, not a house."

The room was big enough to hold a seminar in. An oatmeal sofa and two armchairs surrounded a beautiful white marble fireplace; the ashes still lay in the grate. Amanda lifted the big brass poker from the bucket containing tongs and small shovel.

"Wouldn't like to get whacked over the head with this." she laughed, placing the heavy poker back with its companions. "I wonder why the tenants didn't clean out the grate before they left."

"I don't know, perhaps they didn't have time before the removal truck came."

He smiled confidently; he knew she liked the place, and for once he felt he had done something right.

Amanda tilted her head slightly as she looked across the room.

"I don't like these low bay windows, makes me feel vulnerable."

She went over to the window and closed the curtains.

"Your pretty safe here, no one comes up the mountain, it's too far and too bloody awkward especially at night in the dark, you couldn't be more safe anywhere."

Amanda gave him a sly little grin. "You mean Vampires and Werewolves don't get the time to get up here at night?"

He joked, "Haven't seen any recently."

He led her through to the kitchen. It was an immense dream, something she would never have thought she would own, at least not for many years yet. It had been fitted with every kind of facility you could think of, a dishwasher, washing machine, tumble drier, built in oven and hob, funnel cooker hood with lights, light oak fitted units, even the cupboards were occupied with plates, cups, saucers, china, all kind of cooking utensils, even a swan electric kettle. "Isn't this strange! They left everything behind; it's like a fully furnished kitchen with all utensils thrown in with the price."

"Perhaps it is?" Paul said. "I didn't ask the agents about that."

"Oh, well, never mind, we needn't buy a thing, everything looks to be new."

"Do you like the colour scheme?"

"I love it!" She said glancing around at the light cream walls. She noticed a dark stain on the wall by the door it looked like a handprint. "What's that?" she said, running her hand along the mark.

Paul bent down to study the stain. "It looks like a tomato sauce stain, perhaps someone got careless with the bottle?"

"If it doesn't clean off I can paint it with some cream coloured paint, never mind." She said absently.

Opposite the kitchen was a door. "What's down there?" she asked, turning the handle.

"Oh, that's the basement I was telling you about. It runs all the way under the house. We could turn it into a play room for Beth when she's a little older, or perhaps make it into another room you could even turn it into another three or four room's."

"Shall we go and look?"

"There's no light down there at the moment and there are about twenty two steps, you won't be able to see much anyway, wait till I fix a light."

She smiled at him and followed him back down the hall.

"Who owned this house Paul?"

"I think he was an architect and she was a doctor, or the other way round."

"Why did you use the 'past tense' are they dead?"

"I have no idea, that's what the estate agents told me."

"They must have had money, I mean look at all this furniture, it must have cost a fortune there is nothing cheap here."

"I suppose so; they obviously ran into trouble and left the house as it was. Shame really." He said shaking his head.

"Something must have happened to make them just go, and especially to leave all their stuff behind."

Paul put his arm on her shoulder as they mounted the stairs to the bedrooms. "I guess so, could be anything, well, it's their loss and our gain, the estate agent told me he had trouble selling the house only because it was in such a remote area."

Amanda stopped and frowned. Something worried her.

"Paul, why do you think a wealthy couple that could afford such elaborate fixtures and fittings, and a big house like this should suddenly leave and let the house be repossessed? You would think they would have at least sold the furniture first?"

"I don't know, are you allowed to do that? Don't forget they couldn't have kept the payments up."

"It's pretty weird." Amanda replied.

Two of the guest rooms looked out onto the back of the house, they were as big as the rooms downstairs and both had separate showers, and there was one bathroom just down the hall. The master bedroom had an en-suite shower and was only slightly bigger than the other two. The last room had obviously been a child's bedroom, it had been decorated in the Disney theme, and a fantastic wonderland for a child that it almost brought tears to her eyes. She sensed that a little girl; and also a baby had occupied this room. There was a brass cot in the corner its once beautiful lace hood and coverlet now grey with dust. She looked towards the other corner on the other side of the room, which would be the little girl's bed with 'Barbie' duvet, sheet and pillowcases.

Amanda suddenly felt a rush of deep sadness, why didn't they take all their possessions? She couldn't understand it, but she would pack everything in boxes until they came back to collect them, she was sure that one day they would.

She studied the room carefully, gazing intently at Trixie bell, Peter Pan and Pluto as she walked over to the cot. She ran her hand along the edge, it came away covered in dust and she wiped it down the front of her jeans. The Disney mobile was still hanging above softly turning in the mild disturbance of her movements.

"I find this really peculiar Paul, they have even left the children's toys behind, how long ago did they leave, did he tell you?"

"About two years ago, they had stopped paying the mortgage about a year before that, the bank said they tried to trace them but no one seemed to know where they had gone."

She turned back to the cot, deeply unsettled at the mysterious disappearance of the previous tenants.

"Well." Paul said holding the door for her. "Let's just hope they don't turn up and ask for their possessions back, at least until we buy our own."

He meant it with humour but Amanda couldn't shake off the feeling that there had been something darkly disturbing to cause their sudden departure. Amanda closed the door silently.

She looked through the living room window at the vastness around her, and then turned to Paul. "Why couldn't we fence some of this off?"

"Why? The view is magnificent."

"It's also bloody creepy."

Paul laughed at her. "Ok, if you want, but Halloween is passed now and everyone has gone back to the graveyard."

It was early November by the time they moved into the house. Peace at last was hers.

She had decided to turn the reception room into a study/reading room where she would put a computer. She bought a lovely shade of deep blue curtains and a new table lamp for the little coffee table, and they painted the room cream with a blue border around the middle and top of the walls to break the colour down a bit, at least it didn't look too clinical for now. She found herself to be a better organiser than she had been in the tiny one bed-roomed flat that they had rented.

By December the weather had turned exceptionally cold, and she found a remarkable difference living high up on a mountain to a small flat in the Valley. It took a long time to get used to the strange sounds, like the wind soughing fiercely past the house uttering a melodic sound like the huffing of breathless banshees gathering together for some awful ritual, but after a while, she had got used to it, and hardly noticed it anymore.

She lifted Bethany from her pram and laid her on the changing mat in front of the fire. The doorbell rang startling her, she got to her feet and hurried to answer it.

A large bunch of red and white roses lay on the doorstep, they had been perfectly wrapped in metallic red paper, and she lifted them up carefully parting the paper to get to the card inside. "FROM PUNCH TO JUDY." It read. Amanda shook her head. Who could have left them here? She looked out and saw no one. Who the hell is Punch? She wondered as she closed the door with her foot. Paul couldn't have sent them he would have either brought them home with him or had them delivered by inter-flora! For now she would have to wait until he got home late tonight. She hurried back to Bethany; changed her and dressed her for bed. The flowers played on her mind. Maybe they had come to the wrong address?

The shrill ring of the telephone disturbed her thoughts. She picked it up, and noticed her hands were shaking.

"How're you doing up there in the outback?"

She laughed with relief at the sound of Madeline's voice.

"Good, everything's fine, I'm so pleased to hear from you, how are you?"

"I'm ok, miss you a lot, I can't get to see you much these days it's so far away, not even a bus comes that far."

"Madeline, you need to learn to drive."

"Yep! Looks like I'm going to have to if I want to see you and Bethany."

Amanda knew Madeline would never drive she was too nervous.

"Madeline, did you send me some flowers today?"

"No, why, have you received some then?"

"Yes, a lovely bunch of red and white roses, the same as I got before."

"Perhaps Paul sent them?"

"But they usually knock on the door and hand them to you don't they?"

"Usually they do, why?"

"They were left on the doorstep."

"Maybe you weren't in when they called?"

"No I was here, they rang the bell."

"Oh, how strange, perhaps they were in a hurry."

"I wouldn't have thought so." Amanda replied.

"Was there a card with them?"

"Yes, there was a card; it read 'from punch to Judy' I certainly don't know anyone called Punch!"

Madeline laughed, "Perhaps Paul sent them, you'll probably find out later when he gets home."

Amanda suddenly felt herself perspiring, her palms became moist, the underarm of her sweater damp, her skin turned cold and clammy, yet sweat stood out on her brow.

"Amanda! Are you still there?" Madeline called anxiously.

"Yes, yes, just a minute."

Laying the phone on its side she glanced toward the big bay window she was almost certain she saw a shadow pass. Crossing the room she pulled the curtain wide, her eyes searched the black beyond and there was nothing in sight, she checked to the right and left of her scrutinising each corner until she was satisfied there was no one out there. And then she went back to the phone.

"Ok?" Madeline asked.

"Yes, I thought I heard the Explorer pull up, it's a little early for Paul."

"Well for one moment there I thought you had seen the 'bogeyman' you sounded so scared."

"I am so together Madeline you have to be, especially living in a big old creepy place like this." She laughed.

"So, you like the house then?"

"Yeah, as I said it can be a bit lonely and scary at times but you get used to all the strange sounds; Hey why don't you come up for dinner Saturday, bring Evan with you, you can stay over night and Paul can take you back in the morning, we could get a couple of bottles of wine, what do you say?"

"That would be nice; Evan has a car anyway what time?"

"Let's say about seven?"

"Ok, seven it is, see you then."

Madeline held the phone in her hand for quite some time, she could sense there was something wrong but couldn't make out what it was, and it could even be something Amanda wasn't even aware of.

Amanda busied herself tidying up after little Bethany and then she heaped more coal onto the fire prodding it with the poker, the shear weight of it in her hand made her arm ache.

The sharp bang on the door shattered the silence, her head turned towards the sound; her eyes opened wide, her heart pounded with the sudden fright. For seconds she couldn't move, and then as if a giant hand pushed her forward she headed to the door.

"Who is it?"

"It's the Police; could we have a word with you?"

Her fingers curled tightly around the key as she started to turn it in the lock, it creaked stiffly as it opened. A tall dark figure stood behind the heavy oak door she looked up at him and could barely hear his voice from the thunderous roar of her heart.

"Are you ok ma'am?" He frowned with concern.

"Uh, yes, absolutely, why wouldn't I be? What is it you want officer?" Her hand had moved to her throat.

"We've had reports of a prowler around these parts, I wonder if you have seen anything unusual?"

Her heart thumped against her ribs; maybe it was him who had sent the Roses?

"Yes, a little while ago I'm sure there was someone outside my window, could you take a look?"

He smiled. "Of course, we'll take a look around."

"Where was this person seen?" She asked anxiously. The flowers came into her mind, should she tell him about them?

"Just at the bottom of Tynant highway, take it easy miss," he grinned, "you're probably safer here than anywhere it was quite a long way from here."

She watched him disappear, he seemed to be gone a long time, and then he appeared to her left. "All clear, we circled the house there was no one around, do you have an outhouse?"

"Oh, no, just plenty of open spaces." She smiled.

"Ok then ma'am, just make sure everything is locked up, you don't live here alone do you?"

"No, my husband will be home shortly he's at work at the moment."

"That's fine, sorry to bother you, goodnight."

She almost called him back; the police visit had unnerved her. She watched him get into the car the flashing blue and red lights created a kaleidoscope of colour as it headed toward the road. She knew it had something to do with the killer, they were still hunting him. She knew the police would not drive all the way up the mountain at this time of the evening for nothing. Suddenly her thoughts turned to the roses. They had arrived at five thirty five, a little late for the florist to deliver? They usually close at five. She almost laughed aloud at her crazy thoughts. Serial Killers do not send huge bunches of flowers to their proposed victims!

She walked slowly towards the kitchen hearing sounds accentuated by the deadly stillness of the house, and her own irrational thoughts! The entirety of the darkness outside with one stupid street light that had faded almost to a 'bleep' was accentuating her fears, she had asked Paul to put up some security lights, if there had been anyone lurking in the darkness they would be announced by the powerful arc lights! But as usual it took Paul a long while to do anything. She closed the kitchen curtains shutting out the marauding darkness of a thousand eyes; and then took down a pan; her unsteady hands shook as she filled it with water splashing it all over the floor. Placing the pan on the cooker she snatched up the dishcloth and bent down to wipe up the mess.

Suddenly an intense vibration shook her, someone was standing behind her and the intense sensation of a hostile presence standing there silently behind her was so strong she could almost feel his breath on her neck; she was too terrified to turn around. For a moment her eyes closed, her lips parted, and her breath stuck in her throat. And then a hand clamped her shoulder.

CHAPTER FIVE

He was already thirty seven, and now the years were flashing past like an intercity express train. He had familiarised himself perhaps too quickly with the house and its occupants, trying to solve problems that he should never have tried to solve in the beginning.

If things had never gone wrong in the first place then he would still have been living there. Instead of that, when father left, Mother, struggled on, placing him in the care of the local Authority. HE had felt so angry and now he was homeless again! There hadn't even been a For Sale sign on the property. And where was mother?

When he saw the estate agent arrive; he could hardly believe it had been put on the market after all this time! The house was empty, since the departure of the last residents and now someone decides to buy it right under his nose! He was the rightful owner anyway! Now he would have to start all over again!

He had never been close to his mother, but she was all he had. She had been a detached kind of woman, never wanted kids, so she told him often enough. She had never been the type of mother to show affection or love in any way towards the boy. His father was the product of an incestuous relationship between brother and sister, and he was more aware of that as he grew up. Father ruled the house with a rod of iron and a thick leather belt with a hard buckle to match, he had felt the weight of that many times across his buttocks and his bare legs, and he still had the scars to prove it.

He carefully laid the rucksack under the bed and scrubbed his hands with carbolic soap, carbolic gets rid of all the nasty stuff. He looked at the clock on the wall. My how time flies!

Madeline came in and sat at the last booth near the door. Evan watched her, slowly lifting his dark hooded eyes to study her amazing features. Her hair was Auburn, her eyes the colour of a calm blue sea, and felt a stirring inside him he turned his head towards the counter. She looked up and smiled, a beckoning nod of her head brought him quickly to her table.

"Evan, I'll have an iced bun and a cup of coffee please. What are you doing Saturday?"

"I'm going to London to see my mother; she's not too well, why?"

"Oh, its okay just that my friend asked us over for dinner, you'll really like her, but, if your mum's not well, then we can do it another time."

Evan smiled warmly; he reached out for her hand. "Sorry Madeline, but I need to see my mother; she's got really bad flu." He turned to check the bun situation, smiling when he saw there were three left. "I'll bring your bun over."

Madeline gave him a generous smile; she liked his soft accent, "Thank you."

Madeline watched him; he was handsome and had an air of helplessness about him. She took out her paper and started reading the headlines.

His eyes were on her while he made the coffee, heating up the milk in the machine and absently reaching for the bun from the display cabinet. He brought over the coffee and iced bun and put them in front of her.

"You don't mind then?" he asked with a half hearted curl of his upper lip.

"Of course not, your mother is more important than a dinner party, I hope she get's better soon Evan, besides, there's plenty of time to meet her."

"Does she come here? To this café I mean? Maybe I've seen her?"

"No, not a lot, only when she meets me from work, she has a baby now."

"Oh, lovely I suppose you will be Godmother now, what did she have Boy or Girl? "

"A little girl, she called her Bethany. "

"That's a nice name, I'd better get on, see you tonight."

She ate her bun and drank her coffee, watching Evan as he walked away with a teacloth slung over his shoulder.

Amanda felt the cold dread of fear that had rooted her to the floor, her heart felt as if it was skidding against her ribs. Slowly she looked behind her.

"JESUS! WHAT ARE YOU PLAYING AT!" she screamed, her face relaxing slightly, the tenseness fading like softened wax.

Paul withdrew his hand and stood behind her, his arms hanging loosely at his sides his face almost as pale as a cadaver.

"What were you trying to do, be a catalyst for a heart attack?" Amanda got up slowly leaving the rag on the floor. Her eyes filled with tears at the sudden shock of seeing him. "Make a noise when you come in, let me know you're there for Gods sake don't just creep up behind me like that!"

"Amanda, I'm so sorry, I didn't mean to scare you so bad."

Amanda wiped her dampened palms down the front of her jeans. She looked at him and smiled, instantly sorry for snapping at him

"It's ok darling, you gave me quite a shock that's all, anyway everything alright?"

Paul nodded his head eagerly. "It's more than alright; I've got the management job. They told me today."

"Oh, you never said anything about it?"

"I just wanted it to be a surprise, not a disappointment

if I didn't get it. It means we can pay off the mortgage quicker."

"You know." She said putting her arms around him and resting her head on his chest. "I was so lucky to find you; I don't know what I'd do without you."

"Oh, by the way, talking about the insurance on the house, if by any chance anything did happen to me, the insurance would pay off the mortgage."

She looked up at him. "Nothing's going to happen to you."

"I know that honey, but I just want to make sure you know everything, I wanted to make absolutely certain you and Beth never suffers any hardship."

Paul kissed her and his eyes wondered to the worktop. He saw the flowers lying still wrapped in their red cellophane packaging with a red bow tied around the stem.

"Who sent you those?" he asked frowning. He walked over to read the card that accompanied the flowers.

"You did, didn't you?"

"No, why would I send you Roses when I could just as easily bring them home with me."

He looked at the card.

"Who the hell is Punch?" he asked bemused, his eyes crinkled up at the corners as he laughed.

"I have no idea; I thought you had sent them."

"Well who delivered them?"

"I don't know that either, the bell rang and there they were, on the doorstep."

"Madeline must have sent them then? She must have."

"No, it wasn't her either; I've spoken to her this afternoon."

Paul scratched his head. "Someone's having a laugh, unless you have a secret admirer?"

He looked at her doubtfully.

"Oh Paul, No, definitely not, I would have told you."

"I don't even know what shop they were ordered from." Amanda checked the card again.

Paul felt uncomfortable knowing someone had sent his wife flowers, and not cheap ones either, they must have cost a lot of money because there were at least three dozen of them. He couldn't sleep it played on his mind, and got up to watch television.

The next time he woke it was six a.m. he had slept nine solid hours in the armchair, and now he felt as if an unforeseeable force had beaten him up during the night. He got up from the chair stretching and yawning, fists punching the air to bring life back into his numb limbs.

Paul poked at the dying embers in the grate, and then he snatched up the bucket and headed for the coal shed. He could hardly wait until he had enough money to install central heating. He could only but guess why the previous owners had not bothered to install it, they had two small kids and such a big house to heat, and both with top class jobs they must have had the money to do it!

He had just heaved a sack of coal over his shoulder when Amanda came down with Bethany in her arms. She brushed passed him as he stepped forward almost tripping on her pink housecoat.

"I thought you'd left me, had enough and gone!" she teased.

"I'm sorry, couldn't sleep so came down to watch T.V. then must have fallen asleep,"

Paul squinted through clenched teeth at the weight as he lifted the heavy coal sack.

"And this is a damn nuisance humping coal about, no one wants to deliver anything these days it almost breaks your shoulder!"

Amanda didn't reply and the pain in his shoulder made him mutter a curse. The morning was crisp with a smell of damp earth that hung in the air, and outside a mist like a transparent blanket covered the peak of the mountains.

Amanda looked at the kitchen clock it was already

seven a.m. Paul came into the kitchen breathing hard from his efforts with the coal sack, rubbing his hands together before coal dust settled into the crevices, and reached under the sink for the Vim. As he ran the hot water tap, he sneaked a sideways glance at her; his eyes rested on her, her long raven hair shimmered like black silk from the early morning rays of the sun, and he knew why he loved her so much, she mesmerized him.

"What are you doing today?" he asked.

She turned to face him, she looked pale, her skin made her almost black eyes stand out in stark contrast, and her lips had a slight hint of natural colour to them. She turned away from him for a moment and put Bethany in her high chair, and when she looked at him again she was smiling.

"Going shopping with Beth and Mum, should be back at around four though."

"Right then, I can't sit here grinning at you like a Cheshire cat all day, I've got to get to work."

He grabbed her roughly in his arms; she threw back her head and laughed. He kissed her and then hurried up to the bathroom.

Outside as the early evening arrived; he crouched behind the tree, the machete swung lazily at his side. In his free hand he took out a picture of the young woman inside the house, it was a recent picture he had managed to snap of her as she came out one sunny morning.

His eyes narrowed maliciously, his head tilted slightly to the right as he hugged the photo close to his chest, and then grinning sheepishly, he ran his fingertips over the glossy picture, tracing the outline of her lips. He would like a family of his own; he would like THIS family perhaps?

It was gone six by the time they got back from shopping, Amanda put Bethany to bed and then started on dinner, she closed the kitchen curtains shutting out the darkness, then hesitantly stood as though pinned to the spot with her back towards the empty kitchen, she felt a presence so strongly that for a moment it made her wonder if Paul had returned and she hadn't heard him come in, just like earlier on. She turned quickly glancing around to see if there was an intruder behind her. Moving slowly towards the hall she called. "Paul is that you?" Shadows crept and fluttered across the ceiling sending small tremors of shock waves flooding through her. Her hand found the light switch in the hall and flooded it with light, glorious bright light! "Is someone there?" she called again, walking towards the front door with her hands curled into fists by her sides.

The figure backtracked now circling towards the front of the house, pausing briefly to check no one was around. His eyes were sharp and clear in the silvery moonlight. It seemed in the eerie radiance that another-worldly presence was waiting for the countryside to sleep, as the stillness surrounded him. It had started to unnerve him he clutched the machete tighter and approached the front door, his strong cruel hand reached out for the handle.

Amanda moved hesitantly, her eyes fixed on the door, her right hand reaching for the keys on the hall table. "Is there anyone there?" her voice sounded weak. And then she took the key and slipped in into the lock turning until she heard a 'click'

A sea of darkness greeted her, but it wasn't the darkness that scared her it was something worse, much, much worse. It was a force so strong that raced so quickly through the darkness that she expected it to appear at any moment and do her irreparable harm, and with her breath catching in her throat she slammed the door hard. How could she be so stupid? A knife could have slashed her throat in a second if someone had been outside. Her breath came in gasps and on weak and trembling legs she leaned against the door listening to her heart thundering in her ears, something was out there she had sensed it so clearly. Her lips parted as she gulped in air. Perspiration clung to her, dampening the hair that now fell over her eyes. She took a few deep breaths, wondering if perhaps she had suddenly developed a death wish the way she had opened that door. What the hell was the matter with her! There was a killer on the loose, and police still hadn't caught him. She headed for the living room her mind clearly set on calling the police; her uneasiness was out of proportion as she stood there with one hand over the phone, hovering like a descending parachute. "What do I tell them?" she said aloud, "Someone is outside?" she shook her head doubtfully, they would think she was one hysterical female living in a remote place far from anywhere on top of a mountain! And with all the talk about serial killers, she had let her imagination run away with her. She hadn't seen anyone about; it was her imagination that was in chaos! It was Her mind hat was in turmoil.

Amanda hurried around the house making sure all the windows were locked and the curtains drawn tightly so not even a gap appeared. She picked up her notes from University and sat in the big armchair curling her feet underneath her, she tried to relax lying her head back, trying to study. The house was silent and nothing moved; her eyes closed as the sweet scent of calmness softly washed over her senses, and then she heard the scuttling of feet outside, feet crunching gravel. Her eyes flew open, she dropped her notes and her hand moved to her chest to still her painfully beating heart, the door opened slowly, she heard the familiar creak on one rusty hinge that Paul was supposed to fix. She knew the door was closed properly but couldn't remember locking it. 'OH GOD! I didn't lock the door!' and then footsteps slowly walked down the hall. For a while she thought she was in the Amazon rain forest on a hot clammy day, sweat poured from every crevice, and a giant hand held her to the chair as if she had been glued there. With her feet still curled beneath her she stiffened. Her eyes fixed on the door to the hall. "Paul?" she called, as the footsteps continued to walk the length of the hall without stopping to hang up a coat, and then a tall shadow emerged.

"PAUL!" she gasped.

"Amanda." The look on his face brought her quickly to her feet, with a flood of relief that was so welcoming, that she almost threw her arms around him and hugged him.

"Oh, I'm sorry I scared you, are you okay? You look really rattled."

He looked parched, washed out.

"Yes, didn't hear you come in."

"I need a drink." he said.

She followed him to the kitchen. Paul poured a large glass of water and downed it in a couple of gulps, then patted his pockets and looked agitated. "I need to buy cigarettes; I thought I had a packet in my jeans."

"I wish you could stop smoking, it's so bad for you, that's why you look so worn out." She had noticed that recently he had developed a cough, and sometimes he was breathless.

"I know, I will try and stop, I get very thirsty recently, look, I won't be long." He said taking his coat from the hallstand and quietly closing the door behind him.

Amanda fell into a deep exhausted sleep. At first the moans were soft, barely audible. She turned in her sleep and heard her name, "Amanda?" It was just another dream, a voice echoing from the backdrop of her mind. Her eyes flew open and she sat up, her mind a foggy haze from her deep and troubled sleep. She groped the space beside her Paul was not there, she looked towards his side of the bed, where was he? Her eyes felt so heavy as she squinted at the clock, but she was wide enough awake to know it was three a.m. in the morning, and the noise was not just in her groggy mind, but coming from the hall downstairs. Brushing hair from her eyes she grabbed her housecoat and stumbled from the bed. Amanda felt as if she was floating in slow motion towards the foot of the stairs, the moans got louder and then she began to run. It was Paul! She could hear him calling her! And a chill settled in the pit of her stomach.

"Amanda.... please.... help." The voice was garbled, the 'please' sounded like 'pees'

She ran to the top of the stairs and peered over the banister to see Paul lying at the bottom. "PAUL?" she gasped snapping on the light switch. At first she thought he had fell down the stairs, stumbling, she almost fell as she reached the bottom. For seconds she stood there unable to take in the sight before her, *was this a dream?* She wondered. She stared in horror at the blood that seeped rapidly from an ugly head wound. A trail of blood led from the door to where he lay, bloody handprints splashed the wall. She wanted to pinch herself to make sure this was real and not a part of her dream, and how she had wished it was! But Amanda knew this was no dream.

"PAUL! Oh darling what happened to you?"

"Nooo.Tooo...Hurts" His words were incoherent. His shirt was covered in blood. She had no medical knowledge, but it didn't need a surgeon to tell her that the grey area around the deep gash on his head was exposed brain tissue, and she had no idea how she would stem the flow of blood. She looked frantically around the hall afraid to leave him to get a clean cloth for the wound. The first thing she needed to do was call an ambulance, she glanced at the front door it was open.

"Stay still Paul, I'll call for an ambulance!"

She left his side for a moment and rushed towards the telephone, panic had taken away all reason and her fingers shook badly in the dial, she found herself garbling out the address, begging them to hurry he won't last long! And then she raced back to his side.

"What happened to you? Where were you when it happened? How did it happen?"

But of course he couldn't tell her. She looked into his eyes they were vacant, distant and she knew he wasn't even on this planet at this very moment! This added more terror than she could ever imagine. She saw the grey area pulsing and knew Paul was almost embracing death.

"Stay with me!! Don't close your eyes!" her words were sharply spoken with a degree of hysteria. She cradled him in her arms praying that he wouldn't die, but if he did then he would leave this world safely ensconced in her arms and at least he would feel her love; the love that he would take with him.

Her tears fell, dripping down her face onto his almost still chest.

"I love you, I love more than you could ever know Paul, so please fight this, please fight for me and Beth!"

As she watched him his eyes started to close, he was shutting down.

"OH NO PAUL! DON'T GO TO SLEEP!" Her voice sounded hoarse.

She knew it was fatal to let him sleep with such a terrible head injury but felt so helpless, she couldn't shake him, and neither could she lift him and walk him about. Was this the end of everything? "OH DEAR GOD PLEASE?" she squeezed her eyes shut and her teeth gripped her lower lip in anguish.

"Paul? Don't close your eyes darling, please stay with me, the ambulance will be here in a moment, Paul please hang in there!"

She knew he was slipping away from her and all she could do now was hold him in her arms and comfort him. Her words came out in a flurry to let him know everything she should have told him before, she needed him to know it now!!

"Do you remember the night we were stuck on the mountain in the snow storm? You were my first Paul I loved you from the first time I saw you in 'Stones' and you have so much to live for darling."

She felt his hand clutch her own hand weakly, a cold almost freezing hand but at least she knew he understood; and her tears flooded down like a waterfall. His breathing had become a loud snorting sound and she knew he was so close to death and all she could do was sit here and watch him die!

Suddenly her drive was lit up with light, a helicopter hovered overhead and she turned her head and saw the shadow of blue beacons flashing in the dark. It seemed as if half the emergency services had turned up with an entourage of paramedics.

"Please hurry he's lost a lot of blood and he's not breathing properly."

She hadn't realised it was her own voice she was hearing, It was like a dream nightmare; everything was so unreal! Paul had now lapsed into a coma, and he still sounded as if he was snoring loudly, it was a sound she would never forget. The house shook as the air ambulance circled around for a place to land and then she heard it coming down in the field at the back of the house. She stood up straight and erect her hands curled at her sides as the doctor and paramedics worked on Paul, her eyes were like two dull globes as she watched Paul's life slipping away from her. The rasping got weaker, and his chest was finally still, he had ceased to breathe.

The night was calm, and for a change silent, no wind howled through the trees and no rain drummed on the windows. It was almost as if the whole town had taken a deep breath in eager anticipation of warm summer nights to come. This night should have been named 'Sleepy Hollow' because that was the way he liked it, staid and silent with no one to bother him. And soon he could move into the house again and make everything okay! He had removed one obstacle tonight, it was the other one he wasn't too sure about, he didn't know how he was going to deal with her yet, she was nice, a kind person, he liked her a lot it would be such a shame to waste her!

He sat on the floor with his Art book open on his lap; his ambition one day was to become a painter; but not just (a Painter) but a famous one of great and wonderful talent that would shake the Art world to its canvases. He did have talent of course (one of many things) his paintings were always in bright vivid colours, scenes of countryside, mountains, (That was one of the reasons he moved to North Wales for inspiration) hills and Valleys. He had exhibited some of them and done reasonably well, a few collectors had bought some of his work and this gave him a tremendous boost!

A noise distracted him from his painting; it came from the skirting board. As he got up, he smiled, he knew exactly what was needed, opening the fridge door he took out a chunk of cheese, cut it into neat little squares, and tossed it to the little brown mouse that was sitting patiently in the corner washing its tiny whiskers with minute dainty paws. "Here you go little fella." He grinned broadly. The mouse regarded the cheese for a moment its nose twitching as it sniffed the air suspiciously before darting forward and snatching the cheese morsel, then darting back to the safety of the skirting board, where a hole accommodated his living quarters. He watched the mouse for a moment and then went back to his studies. He came to a picture of the 'Mona Lisa' and took in every detail, because he planned to paint her again, perhaps he could capture some of the magic Leonardo did? He laughed softly to himself.

"Why don't you come and sit down, he's in good hands, the best in fact."

She looked up half dazed into the eyes of Ray Collins; He could've been an alien for all she knew because she hadn't noticed the two plain clothed officers before, her eyes had been fixed on Paul.

"Have you any idea how it happened?" Collins asked quietly.

She gazed at him distractedly as Paul was wheeled past her, his words sounded distant.

"No, I, I've no idea." And then she called to the paramedics. "Where are you taking him?"

"St Andrews, they have a good Trauma unit there, he's going by air ambulance."

Collins asked. "Would you like us to take you by car Madam?"

"Uh, I have a small child I need to wait for my mother, I can call her now."

Collins nodded and turned to the young police officer beside him.

"Ok, I'll go with them you can stay with Mrs Marriott until her mother arrives."

P.C. Tom Page smiled. "Would you like me to make you some tea?"

She looked at him as if he had become transparent, with no substance or form, wondering why she would want to sit here drinking tea while her husband was fighting for his life.

"No, no thanks." She murmured shaking her head.

"It might help steady your nerves?"

"No, honestly, I'd rather get ready to go to the hospital when my mother arrives, it shouldn't take her longer than half an hour to get here."

By the time she finished her garbled conversation to Megan, her face had become as white as a freshly laundered sheet.

"Are you ok?" Tom asked. "Why don't you sit down, maybe I could get you a Brandy or something?" Again she shook her head.

"He only went out to buy cigarettes, how did he end up in that state?" She mumbled.

Tom looked at her with deep sombre eyes, "Sometimes these things happen." He said.

"How the hell did he get such a terrible head injury like that?"

"In the dark it is so difficult to see where you're going, he must have fell off his bike and hit his head on a rock." he replied.

Amanda said absently. "Some rock to cause that much damage."

"Probably happened because the mountains are very unstable, sheep get up there and dislodge the rocks and they come tumbling down, it's a course of nature." He smiled. "How long have you lived here?"

"About six months, I'm beginning to wish we had never bought the place, it's too remote; that's why they called the air ambulance, and they don't come out for nothing."

"I know it looks bad, they called the helicopter because the road going down is too dangerous for someone with a head injury as bad as that. But these things often look worse than what they are, but at least they got him breathing again, and he is in the very best care I can assure you." He said softly, reassuringly.

For the first time she smiled weakly. "Yes, I know, and thank you for your company."

"That's ok, you're more than welcome." He turned towards the cellar door. "What's down there?"

"Oh, it's just an unused cellar Paul was going to make it into a play area for Bethany when she gets older."

"That's a good idea, great for a small kid."

She led him through to the kitchen. "You're not from here are you?"

"No, I was born in Kent, my parents came here to live when I was sixteen, then I decided to join the police force see what I could do to stop crime, which up to now I haven't been able to do."

"Well, that's a good as excuse as any I suppose." She said, suddenly she remembered, he looked just like the guy who came up to her in the car park the day she got the rose on her windscreen. "I remember you; you spoke to me the day I found the rose on my car."

Tom smiled. "Yes I was off duty then; but you looked so worried I wondered if everything was okay."

She was just about to thank him when their conversation was interrupted by the sound of David's car and the flickering shadows of sweeping headlights; that could just be seen from the kitchen.

"Ah." Tom said rising to his feet. "Your mother has arrived." He picked up his hat and headed towards the door.

"Thanks for staying officer, you were a great help."

"No problem Mrs Marriott, I hope everything turns out okay for you."

With a nod of his head he took her small hand and shook it gently, then walked towards the police car.

David helped Megan from the car; her face was slightly pinched and drawn in the pale moonlight.

As David stepped inside he was shocked at the amount of blood.

"Fucking hell! It looks like a massacre has taken place in here, God Amanda, what's happened?"

Megan stood at the door, her face turned ashen. "Oh Jesus." she breathed. "Poor Paul."

"I know I can hardly believe it myself, come and sit down." Amanda led them through to the kitchen away from the sight of the blood.

"How was he knocked down? How could he possibly get knocked down up here?" Megan asked; a deep frown edged along her forehead from the shadows of the dimly lit room.

"I don't know it still isn't clear if he was hit by something or he hit a stone and crashed into a ditch."

"What was he doing out so late?" David asked.

"He went to buy cigarettes." She suddenly looked behind her. "Just a minute." She said, and went out to check the front door was closed.

Megan clasped both hands together as she sat at the kitchen table. Amanda came back into the kitchen, she looked far worse than Megan had expected her to look, tears streaked her face her hair hung in damp untidy strands, and at that moment she wanted to take her in her arms and smooth the hair from her eyes and try to comfort her.

"Had he been drinking?" Megan asked.

Amanda looked at her mother in agitated surprise, her face darkened.

"NO, he hadn't had a drink at all; he had an accident! Why do you always look on the dark side of everything Mum? He has had a terrible head injury, they called the air ambulance to ferry him to hospital, for god's sake."

Tears spilled from her eyes and she almost fell into the chair, Megan got up and put her arms around her while David shot his mother a look of angry despair.

"I'm sorry love; I didn't mean it to sound like that, if he'd had a drink it could have explained why he fell, I'm so sorry darling; go to the hospital now we can stay till you get back." Amanda squeezed Megan's hand. She looked at her mother and instantly felt sorry for snapping, Megan loved Paul like a son and it was a perfectly logical question to ask.

"I know mummy, it's alright." she replied.

David said, "I'll clean up the blood while you're gone."

After walking down endless corridors, Amanda stopped at the intensive therapy unit; she rang the bell and didn't wait a second before a young nurse opened for her.

"You've come to see Paul Marriott?" she inquired.

"Yes, yes please could I see him now, I'm his wife."

"Yes of course you can, come in, I don't know if you are aware but he is on a breathing machine, a life support system I'm afraid it doesn't look good at the moment the next few hours will tell us more."

She led Amanda to the fifth bed along and for a moment she held her breath. Paul looked so different he was as grey as death and looked so artificial. For a moment Amanda thought it could not possibly be him.

"I know he looks terrible, not at all like the same person you know." The nurse said as she put her arm around her, rubbing her back gently.

"But as I said its early day's yet, no one looks the same on life support." She gave her a warm smile. "Are you ok?" she inquired.

Amanda nodded.

"The doctor will be here shortly to talk to you."

"Ok, thank you."

"If you need anything just give me a call, I won't be far away." smiling again reassuringly as she walked down the ward.

Amanda sat down slowly she needed to take the weight from her body before she collapsed. The shock was just beginning to hit her.

It seemed as if she had been there for hours, caught in a time warp until a voice spoke from behind her. "Mrs

Marriott?"

She turned, not even aware that anyone had entered the ward behind her, she was too absorbed with Paul, but it was the doctor she had been waiting virtual seconds for, he was young but he gave her a feeling of security in his warm smile.

"Uh, yes." She murmured getting to her feet. "Is he going to be ok?"

Suddenly the doctor's face darkened, he frowned slightly.

"Well, it's too early to say at the moment, he has sustained a very serious fracture to the right side of his skull, his injuries are quite severe I'm afraid, it wouldn't be fair for me to tell you he is going to be fine because I just don't know."

"But you must have some idea?" Amanda persisted.

He shook his head. "Mrs Marriott, I wish I could tell you he will be coming home next week, but he won't I'm afraid, as I explained his injuries are very severe, do you know how it happened?"

"No, I have no idea, he said he was going out to buy cigarettes and that was the last I saw of him until I found him."

"You see the injuries are fairly consistent with a whack on the head."

"What do you mean 'a whack on the head'?

"It looks like he was struck with something."

"Struck with something?" She was beginning to feel like an African grey Parrot learning to talk the way she repeated everything he said to her and she looked at him stupidly.

"Yes, had he been in a fight?"

"No, No, of course not, as I said, he only went out for cigarettes."

He smiled. "It is possible he could have fell and hit his head."

"Maybe you should tell the police?"

"Well, I'm not a pathologist, and unless there was reason to believe your husband was assaulted it wouldn't do my career much good to surmise." He smiled at her.

"I'm sorry; I didn't get your name."

"Julian Richards, I'm the neurology consultant for this ward, I will be looking after your husband."

"I, I don't know what to do doctor, I can't believe this is happening to me, it's a nightmare." She flopped down onto the chair.

"Can I get you anything?"

"No thanks; just make him better."

"Oh, you can bet on that, we will just have to see what happens in the next twenty four hours." He turned to go, and then stopped suddenly at the door.

"The up side is, we got to him in the golden hour."

Amanda frowned. "Golden hour?"

"That means he was given immediate attention within the hour of the accident, or he wouldn't have stood much chance otherwise."

Amanda leaned closer to Paul, she brushed hair from his eyes and planted a soft kiss on his cheek; he looked like he was never going to return again. His face was cool yet damp at the same time, his eyes were closed, his lips had no colour, and no warmth. She touched them gently.

"I love you darling, please fight this for me, please fight for me and Bethany, we love you so much."

His cheek became wet and she took a tissue and dabbed it gently, and only then did she realise that the wetness were from her tears.

Amanda stayed until the shadows took their place in the early evening. She left the hospital in sombre mood. How could this happen to her now? A heavy mouldy lump sat in the pit of her stomach as she walked towards the car. Amanda looked up at the dirty grey cotton coloured clouds and her despair thickened. She slid sluggishly into the car and switched on the ignition, her intentions were clear, go home have a sleep, get her head in order, and then take her back to the hospital.

Madeline waited at the door. Amanda pulled into the drive, her eyes flooded with tears as Madeline hurried towards her.

"I'm sorry, I should have called you."

"Its ok love, I'll stay for as long as you need me."

By the time she got in the house Megan had Bethany dressed and ready to take home.

"I'll take her back with me until you sort things out, she'll be fine."

"Thank you Mum." She leaned forward and kissed Megan on the cheek. As she turned and looked around the room, she had noticed almost immediately it was something she had never been used to living with until today; all the blood had gone.

"David?" she called. David came in from the back garden. "Thank you for cleaning all the blood for me."

"Its ok how was Paul?"

"Not the best I've seen him, in fact he could have been better."

CHAPTER SIX

Melanie had waited for ages at the bus stop frowning sourly distorting her sweet features as she looked at her watch. She knew she should have left the party earlier. She studied the timetable and realised she had missed the last bus; it had gone half an hour ago. She looked around her; if she wanted to get home tonight then she was going to have to call her father to pick her up. He was going to be absolutely furious with her! She would hear his angry voice in the car in Dolby surround until they got home, because she hadn't done what she was told. She felt fuzzy headed and tired, it was a long walk home, and with a man on the loose that had already killed two women she would rather swallow her dignity and get Dad to give her a ride home. Besides, police had warned women to keep off the streets until he's caught. She took her mobile out of her bag.

"Hi Daddy, its Mel, look I know you are not going to be pleased but I have missed the last bus."

"Oh Melanie, I told you to leave earlier, where are you?"

"By the woods on the Freemantle road, about a half mile from shopping city, will you pick me up? I am standing near the phone box, the one that never works."

"Melanie, you were told not to walk on your own, don't you kids ever listen?"

Here we go! I just knew it she told herself. "I'm sorry dad."

"Right, can you go back to the house?"

Melanie hesitated. "I could, but it's a bit far to walk I might as well walk home in that case."

Her father sighed impatiently. "Oh, alright, just stay on the main road I'm on my way it will take me at least twenty minutes, don't talk to anyone."

The phone went dead and Melanie knew he was on his way and angry as hell with her for putting herself at risk.

She was the one who always went on about having her own independence, and now she felt as if she hadn't proved a thing to her parents at all. The only thing she had achieved tonight was making them realise how irresponsible she is by missing her last bus!

Melanie had always been a submissive little creature, a girl of sweet nature and quiet disposition, and they trusted her. She had been the produce of a twenty five year old childless marriage, and then when her mother was in her late forties she discovered she was pregnant with Melanie, "you were a gift from God" her mother told her. That was why she wanted to do so well in life; at least she could pay them back for the years of sacrifice they had made for her.

Bunching her shoulders against the chill night air, Melanie started to walk downhill so she would see her father's car as it came up the hill. She wasn't dressed properly for the cold because today it wasn't cool to wear heavy coats when you went partying; so all she wore was a light jean jacket.

She could hardly wait for Monday to arrive, it was her first job after leaving school as an assistant to a fashion designer, well, it was office junior really, she just liked the way 'assistant' sounded, it made her feel just that little bit more 'important' In a couple of years from now she would really BE the business. That was her dream ambition; she wanted to be a top fashion designer, meet all the celebrities; mix with all the top people in the industry. Melanie grinned at her thoughts, she was quite proud of herself really. She had managed to get two 'A' levels in Textiles and Ceramics. She had everything planned for her future, after working to gain experience in designing she would go to university or the Royal College of Art.

She was a bright vivacious sixteen years old with the face of an angel and a personality to match. Even the world's best hairdresser could not be able to create the red streaks in her golden hair, they were a natural part of her beauty, and her green eyes were like emeralds. Her one purpose in life was to climb the ladder to success, (as far as she could at least)

Now her pace quickened. Glancing at her watch, the face peered back at her. In fifteen minutes Dad would be here.

Melanie was only two hundred yards from the call box when she heard the chuckle from her left. At first it sounded like a naughty child up to mischief, and it was then that the first tingling of fear crawled up her spine.

"You shouldn't be out so late on your own; didn't your mother ever teach you that?"

The voice was friendly, soft and comforting, Melanie turned in the direction of the sound.

"Who...who's there?" She squinted, and became rapidly aware of the darkness around her the silence, the loneliness, there was no one walking around to be of any help to her, the streetlights had now diminished to almost a glimmer, and the countryside had started to look more like a hushed graveyard.

A dark mass poured out from behind the tree, a smiling grotesque form with a white face and thin bloodless lips.

"Oh come on girl! Why are you afraid?"

Melanie's heart beat at an alarming rate. "Please...I don't have any money."

"Money! Oh don't be so daft, I have enough money of my own."

"Then what is it you want?"

"To talk to someone."

"Who are you? Why are you dressed like that?" She moved back edging towards the road.

"A kiddie's entertainer…who did you think I was?"

"I, have no idea."

"I have just come from a kiddie's party; I have lost my bearing, that's why I'm dressed like this."

Melanie started to relax she took a deep breath and moved a step towards him.

"Where do you want to go?"

"The village, could I walk with you?" He tilted his head slightly to the right.

"Um, no not really, I'm waiting for my father to pick me up, he should be here any moment now."

She gave him a half uncertain smile. He reminded her of 'Punch' from 'Punch and Judy' He was at her side before she realised it, he seemed to leap at such speed that she began to wonder if he had springs on his heels, he moved with cat like grace and bat like movements and it unsettled her.

"What's your name?" he asked falling into step beside her.

"Melanie."

He took her arm, she pulled away.

"I'm not going to hurt you."

"I don't know you so don't grab my arm like that!"

He stopped and turned to face her. His face looked more grotesque than it had before and now there was a menacing vibe in the way he grabbed her arm. She could see the whites of his eyes through the mask, and the deep pools of black that were his pupils, they looked soulless and deeply penetrating; unnaturally black as if she were staring into a never-ending pit.

"Now what is it with you? Why are you so scared of me?"

Melanie almost laughed, how could anyone not be scared of such a macabre person in such a frightening costume? Even the kids he said he entertained would be terrified of him, which came to her second question.

"Why are you still dressed like that? Surely the kid's party finished ages ago, they must all be tucked up in bed by now."

"Oh, you are so smart!"

His voice had now become menacing, and Melanie knew she had to get away from him as quickly as she could.

"My father is waiting for me."

She turned to run but he held her with a grip of iron.

"Leave me alone!" she wailed. "I want to go home!"

Her heart thumped against her ribs, she tried to prise his fingers loose but the more she struggled, the tighter his grip became, until she could feel his nails piercing her soft tender skin. All she could think about at that moment was where was her father? It seemed ages ago she had made that call, where was he!

"Well, that IS a shame! Perhaps you should have thought about that before you started wondering about in the dark so late at night!"

He drew her closer and that hooked nose almost touched her face, she felt his warm sour breath and she squirmed.

His voice had grown cold and detached as if he was speaking from another dimension. It all felt so unreal Melanie began to wish this was just some terrible frightening nightmare, but she was only too aware that it was really happening it was now and it was real and she could hardly contain her terror.

What made her befriend this man in the first place? It is not usual practice to meet someone in the dead of night near a wood, especially dressed the way he was and walk off with them as if you had known them for years! God in heaven! WHAT WAS WRONG WITH HER? Why didn't she bolt the minute she saw him? At least she would have had a fighting chance.

Melanie stared at him, she kicked out, her shocked terrified eyes were as wide as saucers, and in her own way she knew who he was! He was the monster everyone had been looking for, and now she had found him after all the warnings on the T.V. and radio to keep off the streets. She also knew that her brief life was coming to a very swift and very violent end!

Panic caused a huge rush of adrenalin as she twisted her arm from his grip, furious that he had the audacity to hold her against her will! She was free. Melanie ran and she ran anywhere as long as it was away from him. She found herself running towards the road, but the town was a virtual ghost town at this time of night, there was no one to help her. How she wished she had called her parents before, and to hell with independence, she could have been sitting in her fathers car safely in his care on the journey home by now.

She screamed as loud as she could, until her throat felt like it was on fire as she raced across the grass. His hand snaked out and grabbed at her jacket spinning her around to face him. Her little praying hands medallion flew from her neck, her brief thought was how she was going to get it back, and it had been given to her by her dead grandmother. Her hands flew out to protect herself; too late she saw the machete cleave the air and slice off three fingers of her left hand, she put up her right hand to save her face and four fingers flew through the air. Her shocked terrified eyes almost bulged from their sockets, and for one crazy moment she wondered how on earth she would become a fashion designer with no fingers! She felt no pain only a sense of sadness and helplessness, knowing that she would never see her beloved parents ever again; and the strangest thing of all was, she worried how her mother would cope with the heartache, and then she screamed pitifully. "MUMMY, DADDY!" as the machete came down a third time; shattering her skull.

Amanda left the hospital a little after eight o'clock there was no change in Paul's condition so her mood remained the same. She felt as if the nightmare would go on and on and never seem to end. A steady roll of thunder bounced off the mountains humming steadily like a drum roll in the distance. She knew it wouldn't be long before it hit the mountains and she hated the thought of being alone in the middle of an electric storm.

As she got near to the treacherous bend to Tynant, the windscreen wipers flew back and forward to clear the rain that was now coming down in a torrential flood. She heard it lash the windscreen and the 'thrup, thrup' of the wipers as they tried to clear her view. By the time she had got to the last gate she began to feel an all-consuming dark depression hanging over her. She leapt from the car to open the gate, cursing silently as the lock stuck fast. Finally she kicked it and at last it gave way on its rusty hinges. Her hair was plastered to her head, dropping wet strands down the back of her neck as she shivered from the freezing rain. Jumping back into the car, she released the handbrake, slipped into first gear, and then eased her foot off the clutch. She didn't bother to lock the gate, there had never been any cows or sheep in the area, and as far as things go, it was just another stupid regulation to make life that much harder!

The shadows of trees mirrored and distorted giant

puddles with a kaleidoscope of reflections and images ahead of her. She felt there was someone watching her; she thought she could see a movement to her right, like something scuttling behind those humongous trees. She slowed the car and quickly glanced behind her, but there was no one there, probably a distortion of shadows with the heavy rain creating an illusion in her already troubled mind.

She turned into her drive and was more than a little relieved to see the two figures huddled in her doorway.

"Oh Inspector, what a night you picked, I've just come from the hospital, come inside." Amanda opened the door and flooded the place with light.

"Have you come about Paul's accident?"

"Just dropped by to see how things are actually. You have a nice place here." Ray Collins commented as he looked around at the vast hallway.

"Not bad once you're inside." She replied.

"Don't you like it here?"

"I don't like being so far away from everything and everyone; otherwise it's a very pretty place to live. I am just so grateful to whomever it was who had the good sense to install a telephone; the night Paul had the accident."

"Well, you would be mad not to have some kind of line, even a mobile in such a dense area as this."

"Yes, you would be." Amanda smiled, nodding her head. "And it's so kind of you to come all this way to find out about Paul Inspector, but he's still the same; it's not looking good at the moment although the doctors are holding out more hope now than they were before."

"At least that's something." He smiled warmly. "We found your husbands bike not far from here, in fact it was near to the last gate as you get to the house."

Amanda stared at him, at least she had now begun to realise the implications of what he had said.

"I am so grateful that he didn't get further down the Tynant road, he wouldn't be here now, coma or not."

"That's very true; he had a lucky break there. Mrs Marriott, did the doctor talk to you?"

"Yes he did actually, about his injuries."

"Did he tell you he thought he had been attacked?"

"Yes, but not in so many words he said it looked as if he had been hit by something."

"We examined the bike there isn't a scratch on it, if he had hit a stone or gone into a pothole there would have been signs of that."

She turned suddenly. "What are you saying Inspector?"

"It is possible he could have been mugged, did he have any money on him?"

"Well, yes of course, he was going to buy cigarettes."

She looked at him thoughtfully for a moment and then added "Let me tell you something about my husband Inspector. He is a strong able bodied man he could take two or three men on at once if he had to, and believe me if someone was going to rob him, they would have been the ones to end up in hospital where Paul is right now, That, I can assure you of. If anyone attacked him they must have got him from behind"

"I'm sure you are right Mrs Marriott, although possibly he could have caught the front wheels on a large stone or a brick."

Amanda sat on the kitchen chair gripping the arms, feeling the cool wood under her fingertips.

She wanted to tell him about the intruder but wasn't sure if she should or not, and she certainly didn't want them to see her as a hysterical woman. Haldane stood at the kitchen door with a pencil clutched between his teeth; his eyes were fixed on the cellar door. Collins looked at him and followed his gaze.

"What's down there?" Collins asked.

"Oh, that's just the cellar, everyone asks me that."

"Is there any access in from the outside?"

"No, it's all sealed up, Paul would have secured it if there had been."

"Have you ever been down there?"

"No, Paul is going to turn it into a playroom when Bethany gets a little older."

"Well, as long as it's sealed up, do you want me to check for you?"

Amanda sat nervously, rubbing her hands together then placing them between her knees.

"No, its ok, I know it is secure Paul would never leave it open, there is not even space enough for someone to crawl through."

The pencil was no longer between his teeth; Haldane put it back in the top pocket of his jacket. "I did check it the other night, there is no opening for anyone to climb through only small slatted slots I doubt even a mouse would get through there, and I also checked it from the outside."

Amanda suddenly felt more secure now, her mood had lightened slightly and she found herself shedding a smile.

"Thanks for taking good care of me."

"Well we must make sure you are alright here alone." Collins smiled warmly.

"Inspector." Amanda said sitting forward her hands still tucked between her knees. "What made you say you thought Paul was attacked?"

"I didn't say he was definitely attacked, I said it was a possibility he could have been mugged, he could also have hit a rock gone down in a heap and hit his head on a hard rock or large stone." He grinned at her amiably. "Now don't you start worrying about that ok?"

"Ok." She smiled.

"The important thing is to get Mr Marriott well."

"It's made me think about moving from here, I have to make a list of everything I need, there is no little corner shop just down the road, if you forget things you have a long drive to the shops."

"Well." Collins said rising from the chair. "It is a remote place for a young woman to live on her own with a young child, I just want to make sure you are both safe."

"Don't worry Inspector, I will keep all my windows and doors locked I promise."

"Well, I suppose we must be going now, if there is anything you need please don't hesitate to call."

Amanda closed the door and made sure it was locked. Inside she felt inexplicably lonely, she wished they hadn't gone. His words had unnerved her about Paul, and it made her think, that perhaps she would be better off staying with her mother until Paul gets out of hospital. Bethany was not the easiest of babies to get to sleep at night and her crying would probably get on her fathers nerves, she would end up keeping the whole house awake, maybe it would be better to stay where she was for now. It would have been the answer to most of her problems, but unfortunately this was one of the sacrifices she had to make for being a mother.

The air was thick and clammy; a sure sign that the storm hadn't passed yet. She heard the roar of thunder bouncing heavily off the mountains towards the valleys; and hopefully in an hour or so, it would've burnt itself out. It was way past eleven the next time she looked at the clock, and early evening had melted into late, late night.

Outside the night was foul, and the thought of driving back down the mountain at this time of night would have been a very unwelcoming thought. She knew she had made the right decision to stay here, a cup of coffee and a hot bath would be a much better option, and then she could lie in bed listening to the gentle swaying of the leaves as it was fanned by the wind. She loved to listen to the rain gently pattering on the windowpanes; it never failed to lull her to sleep.

She had only been in the bath ten minutes when she got the irresistible urge to get out, fast! The house seemed to rock on its foundations; it was too quiet and unsettling. Reaching for her bath towel she dried herself quickly, so quickly that she almost tripped on the end of the bath towel. She threw on her robe and then raced along the hall towards the stairs, taking them two at a time as if she was expecting someone to be there. Amanda stood at the bottom of the stairs looking around her, there was nothing wrong the lights were on; everything was fine. She moved into the living room, then back out to the hall and down towards the kitchen, she snapped on the light, her eyes travelling around the kitchen, the curtains were shut; everything was in the same order as she had left it.

It had to be her own imagination-playing tricks once more, especially after what Collins had told her about Paul's supposed attack? She wished he hadn't said anything at all; subconsciously, it had made her nervous, she had checked all the windows and locks, so why the hell were she so jumpy? She went back to the living room and poured herself a large Brandy, gazing up at the high ceilings as if she expected something to be hanging there, like a vampire from Bram Stokes 'Dracula' The curtains were tightly shut, not even a gap appeared. As she stared at the big bay windows that stood so far back to where she was standing, it made her wonder why they needed such a big house like this? She sat down in the armchair and swirled the brown liquid around the crystal cut glass.

The reception room for a start was never going to be used, she grinned to herself, they could always rent it out to the local undertaker all they needed were a few candle shaped wall lights and an organ playing 'Ave Maria,' and there you go! A fortune made in no time. It has potential, good potential for a library and closet room. Paul could fix it up, he could smarten the whole room up to be a nice restful area to read or to write; or what ever you wanted to do in there, even if you just wanted to sit there and think in restful surroundings. And then her mood changed. Paul couldn't smarten anything up at the moment; it was going to take all his efforts to smarten up his own poor mind. Her eyes filled with tears, it had only been a few hours since she was last at the hospital, but to her it felt as if she hadn't seen him in days.

Leaning forward Amanda put the glass on the table; at least the Brandy had relaxed her; but her head swam, and exhaustion overwhelmed her. Yawning she cupped her hand to her mouth.

Stretching, she got up from the chair and looked towards the big bay windows. Outside a midnight ocean filled the room like an invisible fog. Slowly, Amanda's eyes searched the room; then tentatively she moved towards the window. Tension mounted as she drew back the curtain; she only drew it back slightly, an inch or so, but enough to see outside, the moon hung in the sky like the grim reapers scythe. It looked like a crest of shimmering brilliance. It was almost as if someone was breathing down the back of her neck, so she closed the curtain as the wind came howling around the house shaking the trees violently as it past. Pouring another Brandy she wondered what she was going to do with the rest of the night, because sleep had slipped down to the bottom of the list for now, no matter how tired she was, sleep would slip from her grasp the minute her head touched the pillow.

She sat in the chair with her legs out in front of her as if she was ready to bolt at any moment and race for the door.

Trying to steady her nerves was harder than she thought

as a bolt of lightening lit up the room, sending a hue of white blue light streaking in its midst. Taking deep steadying breaths, she curled up in the armchair her feet tucked beneath her. Thunder roared above her, she expected a giant fist to pound through the ceiling at any minute and split the house in half. A cold draught filled the room but she was too scared to get up from her 'safe' place to put coal on the fire, instead she wrapped her arms around her and lifted her head towards the ceiling. Rain came down in torrents pinging and bouncing off the windows with a dull pattering thud, the storm had hit the mountains full force. Amanda bit her lip; a tight anxious frown masked her face. How she wished she had driven down to her mothers in the first place instead of sitting here scaring herself half to death. She didn't even have her baby for comfort.

Suddenly her head spun towards the hallway, her eyes widened, *'Was that a knock?'* She listened trying to hear above the raucous storm and then she heard it. CRACK! It was coming from the back door. Uncurling her feet beneath her, she rose steadily from the chair and her thundering heart seemed louder than the storm. She moved on weakened legs towards the hall. Her hand slithered around to the light switch and she plunged the hall into darkness. The few steps she took were like walking a mile as she passed the staircase; and then very, very slowly she lifted her head, and her eyes travelled towards the back door…There in the darkness faintly silhouetted by a dull moonless glow was the shape of a large grotesque figure, a figure of childish nightmares that the dark moulded into a person, she could only just make out the large object he held above the powerful shoulders, it was an axe!! The object came down in a shattering blow crashing into the door, sending splinters of wood flying in all directions. Her eyes shimmered and her skin took on a grey greasy pallor in the little light there was. But she knew in an instant this was the stalker, and he had come to stalk her. Amanda threw herself against the wall, she didn't scream, she couldn't, her voice had been caught in a strangulated embrace.

She turned and ran hitting her leg on the table in the living room, shinning her ankle painfully, she needed to plunge the house into darkness, *'if he can't see me he can't hurt me'* she mumbled. The house became ink black and with it came her worst nightmares, fears she had harboured since she was a child, spiders, and rats being her worse phobia, prickly bodies and cool leathery tails!!

Her eyes were wide but they shimmered with tears even as the light from the moon bounced off her pupils. It had gone quiet, a foreboding silence, a hush that had filled the house and she crept into the living room to fumble for the phone. She felt like a blind person, flayed fingers clumsily scrambling for her only lifeline. Finally she found the telephone, and held the receiver tightly in her trembling hands, praying that she wouldn't drop it and lose herself valuable time, she expected the line to be dead yet the dialling tone was purring loudly.

It rang and rang and to Amanda it seemed like minutes rather than seconds and then a voice answered. "You are through to The Emergency Service and you are held in a queue, please hold until an operator is free."

She almost dropped the phone. "NO…FOR GOD'S SAKE …NO!"

A woman answered. "Emergency which services do you require?"

"Police, please hurry, a man is breaking into my house, he's almost in!" Instinctively she looked behind her.

"What is your telephone number?"

For a second she froze, she couldn't remember her phone number or her address. Her mind had gone blank; a fleeting moment of panic had taken all her memory away.

"Oh, I can't think!" She put her hand to her forehead to calm the pressure that was building there. "Oh yes, it's 32642398, the house on the hill in Tynant, uh, foxglove is the address, you can't miss it! It's the only house on the mountain." She gasped, looking behind her.

She heard the operator talking to the police, giving them her phone number, and then a man spoke to her.

"A car is on the way, in the meantime can you put something against the door?"

"Like what?"

"Can you barricade yourself in? Is he still there?"

"Look, please hurry, I am alone here."

"Stay on the line with me Miss and a police unit will be there very shortly."

"Ok." Amanda sobbed, she put the phone on its side, it was no use listening to a disembodied voice she needed a material presence right now. Creeping slowly back to the hall, her footsteps echoed every creak in the floorboards; it was so quiet it alarmed her more than the banging had done. She got to the staircase, her heart thundered. Was he already inside? Waiting the other side of the staircase? She stood for seconds, her lips slightly parted as small gasps of air escaped in terrified breaths; she bunched her fist with one hand and covered her mouth with the other to muffle any sounds so he wouldn't hear her approach.

Tentative steps towards the hall or maybe towards her death were intensely slow, she bowed her head, and looked carefully towards the back door, and was horrified to see half the frame was gone. *'Why didn't he smash the glass?'* she mumbled anxiously.

The crunching of gravel made her head turn sharply towards the front door, the handle turned slowly but the door was still locked, holding steady. She bolted towards the living room where she picked up the heavy brass poker in less than a second. Grasping it in front of her she advanced towards the door. Sweat trickled down her neck, the poker moved freely in her damp palms, her throat was as dry as sandpaper. Her eyes darted back and forwards wondering why it was so quiet, even the storm had silenced its angry growls. She was waiting to see if he had another little surprise waiting for her.

It seemed to be so long ago that she had called the police, so, where the hell were they? Her neck and shoulders ached with the weight of the poker, but she was ready and well able to use it if she had to.

Suddenly lights flooded the driveway, sirens blared and she thanked God that finally the Cavalry had arrived.

"I can't see anyone out there Miss, he's obviously miles away by now, I've searched everywhere and sent some officers to search over the hills out the back, but I reckon he's long gone."

The officer looked down on her, he was a giant compared to her.

"I don't think it's a good idea to stay here alone tonight, is there somewhere we could take you? A relative perhaps?"

Amanda looked around and rubbed her dampened hands down the front of her jeans, then brushed a hand through her tangled hair.

"There is a friend I could call, I don't really want to scare my mother; at the moment she is looking after my daughter while my husband is in hospital; I'll call my friend if it's ok by you."

"Yes, that's fine ma'am, I just don't think it is safe for you to stay here alone."

"This is the first time I've ever experienced anything like this."

The officer looked around. "Well, he could have got in here easily enough if he really wanted to."

"Why? What makes you say that?" she frowned.

"You have three ways in here, the three ground floor windows, and of course the back door, he could have cleaned the lock in one hit if he really wanted to; or just smashed any one of the ground floor windows, why give himself all the trouble of trying to batter the door down, it's not as if it's a virtual fortress."

"I don't know what you're getting at officer?"

"I think, he was just trying to frighten you, he's really made a mess of that door." They both walked towards the back door, the officer ran his hand along the splintered framework. "What's down there?" he asked pointing towards the cellar.

"Oh that's the cellar, it runs all the way under the house, and there is definitely no way in or out unless it is by this door." She replied pointing.

"You're absolutely sure?"

"Absolutely, my husband checked it out before we moved in the only light is from small air vents, mere slits really." She added.

"Ok, as long as you are quite positive no one could get in from there."

She smiled and nodded her head. "I'll go phone Madeline."

A police helicopter flew overhead she could hear the whirring of the rotor blades and search lights scanned the area behind her, it gave her some comfort.

Amanda stood in the living room, it had become so cold she shivered and wrapped her arms around her before she could even lift the phone from the hook, the experience had shaken her up badly, and as much as she hated to admit it she no longer wanted to stay in the house alone. She told a shocked Madeline what had happened, and she knew that before she replaced the phone in its cradle Madeline would be on her way. Hugging herself again, the room seemed to be getting colder, it had no warmth or comfort, and she might as well have been sitting in an old draughty warehouse.

Tearing up some old newspapers she threw them on top of the coal and lit the paper, watching it ignite until it crackled and spit as the coal caught fire. She looked around gingerly at the walls, at the floor; what had happened to the previous tenants? Maybe they had been murdered and bricked up behind the walls? Or maybe He'd put them under the floorboards. She was so absorbed by her gruesome thoughts that she hadn't noticed the officer standing at the living room door.

"Everything ok ma'am?"

Amanda turned. "Oh yes, she is on her way."

"Good." He smiled. "I wouldn't be happy leaving you

alone up here all night. I will leave a couple of police officers to patrol the mountain tonight just in case he decides to come back, and there is an air support unit flying around with a bit of luck they might spot him."

Amanda nodded. "We have never had a serial killer in this part of the country before."

"Serial killers pop up everywhere; not just in the United States anymore either, we have a fair share of them here in the UK, not that I'm saying for one minute that the man pounding your door tonight was the man we're hunting." He said. "But it is a possibility."

Amanda reached once more for the poker and prodded the coal until the flames got higher.

"I don't think I have ever been so frightened in all my life."

"No, I don't expect you have, but remember to keep everything locked and bolted until he's caught, just in case."

"Officer, do you know who owned this house before we bought it?"

He looked vague. "No idea I'm afraid, I'm not used to this area, and I'm usually based in Port Madoc."

She watched the yellow flames turn to purple, her thoughts turned to the events of this evening, it was as if she had some kind of precognition into what was going to happen, she had been nervous all evening perhaps there was someone out there all the time? Just waiting for his chance. The more she thought about Paul's accident, the more convinced she was that it wasn't an accident at all! This bought her back to her thoughts of what Collins had said earlier on in the evening.

"Amanda!!"

She got to her feet at the familiar sound of Madeline's voice, and David was directly behind her.

"Jesus, what's going on here, there are police everywhere and a police helicopter flying around with search lights! Are you okay?" David asked anxiously.

"OH, I'm so glad to see you." A flood of relief showed clearly on her face.

"Amanda, I don't think it's a good idea to leave you both in the house tonight, you and Madeline come back with me."

Amanda looked at the clock she could hardly believe it was already four in the morning. "Does Mum know?"

"Yes, she's worried sick; she wants you to come home for a while."

"How is Bethany?"

"Bethany is fine."

Amanda looked towards Madeline. "What shall I do?"

"It's up to you, I'll stay with you until Paul comes home if you want, or go to your Mum's, it's entirely your decision, but either way you are not going to be left alone."

David looked at her anxiously.

"Look, let me give Mum a call and then I'll stay here with you both tonight and tomorrow you can work out what you want to do."

"Ok." She said hesitantly. "It is late, and I'm exhausted, besides, I can't leave the back door like that anyone could break in."

The police officer said. "I can get the place policed tonight, and then you can decide what you want to do, I could get a patrol up here every hour, personally I don't think he will be back tonight."

"Ok, that would be great, thanks."

"As long as you let us know ok?"

"Ok, but I can stay here tonight, it's just that I'm afraid he will break in if there's no one about, as long as my brother and my friend can stay with me I'll be fine."

"Right, then I'll be going now, just make sure you lock up."

"Thank you officer."

It had been a long night; a night Amanda would never forget as she sat in the armchair with her feet curled underneath her drinking coffee. Dawn was almost breaking and soon she would be making the long trip back down the mountain to the hospital.

"Why don't you get some sleep?" David asked.

"No point now, I will have to be up again soon, I'll be ok I can snatch a few hours when I come back, besides, I'm too wound up to sleep right now."

She gazed vacantly towards the window.

Madeline sat forward to place her cup on the table. "I'm not surprised; you look so pale it must have been a terrible experience for you."

"The worst, I hope I never have to go through something like that again." She looked thoughtfully. "You know I have been thinking about what the police said to me last night about Paul."

"What do you mean?" Madeline replied.

"I'm not too sure that it was an accident."

"What makes you say that?" David asked.

"After what happened tonight, I'm beginning to think that someone was waiting outside for him and hit him with something."

"Oh that's absurd Amanda, who would do that, and why? It doesn't make any sense at all."

"David, Paul is a pretty tough guy, he hadn't been drinking and he wasn't the sort to fall off his bike, I really wonder if someone was waiting outside for him…Or me perhaps? The doctor thought a blow to the head could have caused his injuries, and when I think logically about it the more possible it seems. It was pitch dark out there so Paul wouldn't see him coming."

David lit a cigarette and blew smoke into the air.

"Could be, then all the more reason why you can't stay here, what if he comes back?"

Madeline got up and started to clear away the coffee cups.

"If he does then we will be here to fight him together won't we?"

"Madeline." David snapped. "You're not training for the SAS, so don't make silly suggestions, your talking about a madman here, not some stupid little vandal whose best effort is to smash a few windows and run away, I'm worried about my sister."

Madeline put the cups down and faced him, she felt hurt at his outburst.

"I know that! What do you think I'm going to do, leave her to her fate? I wouldn't let anything happen to Amanda, and I'm worried about her too, especially after what she has said about Paul tonight."

David looked down and stubbed his cigarette into the ashtray. "I'm sorry, I didn't mean to snap."

"It's ok." Madeline replied. "No hard feelings."

"Look!" Amanda replied. "I'll see how things are at the hospital and if there is any change in Paul I will come home with you, but David, please understand I need to be home, I feel better here I feel much closer to Paul, as long as I am in the house it gives me some hope that he will come home, and if Madeline stays here with me then we will be fine, he's not going to come back with the two of us here is he? Besides, Mum's house is small, and you know how funny Dad can be at times, I bet Bethany is already getting on his nerves."

David gave her a half smile. "I tell you what, I'll buy you a mobile and you can keep it on you all the time at least I know you are always near a phone, just in case."

"Oh you are a jewel David, it would only be at night that I'd need company, not in the day I'm in the hospital all day and Madeline gets home from work at five so you won't have to worry about me."

"Ok, let's see if that works, but you know you can come home at any time don't you?"

Amanda gave him a warm smile. "Of course I do, anyway, tell Mum I'll come for Bethany tomorrow and bring her home, it might help if I have her at home with me, I can drop her off to Mum in the day while I visit Paul.

CHAPTER SEVEN

Melanie lay still, her eyes open in a soulless vacant daze, she wasn't capable of thinking anymore, and there was no 'anymore' not for her anyway. She drifted on a cloudy horizon, between this world and the next, she had no idea who she was, or what she was, just an inanimate being aimlessly drifting. Little Foxes had scavenged during the night, hungry little foxes, a mother with two cubs had passed by and stopped to inspect the peculiar object that lay motionless on the ground, and innocently; she had found food there for her tiny cubs and she carried the flesh in her mouth to where her lair was.

The early morning brought radiant sunlight to warm the freezing ground that she lay on, although that mattered less to Melanie.

Melanie's father sat on the grass verge, his head in his hands, face as grey as mouldy earth. "What will I tell her mother? Dear God this will kill her stone dead like my Mel."

A policewoman sat with him, she had her arm around his shoulders. "She's not dead sir, she may still have a chance."

He turned to look at her, his red veined eyes watery and puffed. "I got a fucking puncture, I was on my way to pick her up, I told her to go back to the house, but! As usual do they ever listen to a word you say?"

"Don't blame yourself Sir, these things happen, we want you to go to hospital for them to check you over, you've had a terrible shock."

Mr Thomas shook his head.

Amanda parked the car in St Andrews car park; she grabbed the keys, locked the car and hurried towards the entrance. She had been late after the night's events and now she felt as if everything was falling apart; Her studies had gone down, her health was suffering to, everyday she awoke with a headache.

'Keep talking to him' they told her, and she did! She talked and talked but still Paul lay in another world far away from her and Beth. Maybe today would be different, maybe today Paul would open his eyes and give her that glorious smile she had fell so much in love with, maybe today she would see the vivid blue of his wonderful eyes that Bethany had inherited from him, but then again, maybe it wouldn't happen today.

She walked towards the lift that would take her to intensive care. Entering the ward her eyes went automatically to the bed near the door and when she saw that no one was laying in the bed, her eyes widened and panic flashed across her face. She looked towards the nurse's station and a young nurse pointed to the window. Paul's bed had been moved to a brighter part of the ward and sunlight flowed through the window bathing him in warm sunshine.

The young nurse turned towards her and smiled. "We thought it could help if he had some light."

"Good idea, I'm so glad he's not in the darkest part of the ward anymore."

"He will open his eyes now from time to time and if he sees light it may help."

Amanda sat down and watched his pale gaunt features, and the ventilator feeding valuable oxygen to his tortured brain as it inhaled slowly, then exhaled to keep him alive. His hands lay motionless at his sides and dark shadows ringed his eyes. She ran a cool hand across his brow. "Paul." She whispered, his eyes opened, but it was as if a veil had been drawn across them, he could see her but had no idea who she was. Amanda leaned forward and saw blood in the corner of his left eye and she looked around quickly at the nurse who was just behind her, writing notes on someone's chart. As she looked closer blood appeared to be spreading along the lower eyelids making the veins red and prominent.

It didn't look right! It wasn't like this yesterday. And for one ridiculous moment she could hear herself saying in months to come, "Paul you looked like Dracula after his midnight feast." And then her heart thudded and she was on her feet. "Nurse! Doctor! Somebody help!" The young nurse was at her side in seconds and doctor

Richards appeared as if from nowhere training a torch into Paul's eyes.

"How long has he been like this?"

"I looked at him minutes ago he was okay then."

The nurse was calm yet concerned.

Amanda looked frantically at the doctor. "He opened his eyes a minute ago, he, I, noticed it then." Her head was spinning so fast.

"It's a haemorrhage; I need to get him into theatre right away."

She couldn't speak, she felt cold and numb inside, if today had started off bleak, then as the day goes on it will become a dark tragedy, if she didn't ask Doctor Richards how bad this could get, then not knowing would make it not happen, and it would become unreal.

As she watched people running around she saw the two men in green wheeling a gurney. They lifted Paul's rag like body and started to wheel him away with his vacant 'not in' eyes gazing vacantly at the ceiling.

Amanda had never felt so alone in her life before, she could not contact Megan she guessed she had probably gone into town with the baby, and Madeline must have been on her lunch break, so all she could do was sit in the waiting room and pray; pray for all the good it would do her.

A nurse handed her a coffee it tasted bitter but she drank it anyway.

It was four fifty five when she suddenly saw doctor Richards walking towards her in his green theatre clothes, and he had a smile on his face as he made eye contact with her, that dared her to believe that everything was going to be fine. Gingerly she got up.

"Paul is going to be fine, we caught it just in time Mrs Marriott, and he is going to come out of this in one whole piece."

"Oh thank you God! I owe you one!" she said punching the air.

Paul seemed to drift in and out of a pink cloud and reality was never far away, but not near enough for him to grasp hold of. The vision of a beautiful dark haired girl swam in and out of his mind; her long raven hair fell softly over her face, a face that looked pale and drawn. Beautiful intense black eyes that were so full of hurt and pain; with a tear that hid in the corner of those magnificent eyes, like a dewdrop waiting to fall. He had no idea who she was, but somehow she was familiar to him. In his tortured mind he was so terribly afraid. Who am I? What is my name? What has happened to me? Shapes passed him; white fuzzy shapes and a strong smell of ether hung at the back of his throat. Something tightened on his arm causing it to deaden; and then a hiss of escaping air as his arm came back to life. He felt fear and was rendered helpless. He wanted so desperately to get up from his bonds and run away from this place, but he couldn't move. 'Where the hell am I? Please someone help me! Where the hell am I? Who am I? Someone please help me!' But the voice was inside his head, he had a vague recollection of riding a bike down a hill, it was so dark, and then a terrible pain in his head…And then nothing.

Amanda sat by his bed a single tear rolled down her face as she watched his rhythmic breathing; he was now breathing on his own. His eyes fluttered as if they were about to open and she would see the blue of his eyes once again. She lifted his hand and brushed her lips against his fingertips and then softly she held them to her cheek.

"Paul, I love you, I love you so much, so please don't you die on me, although wouldn't it be just like you to die and leave me with a child and a mortgage."

She tried to smile through her tears she couldn't care less about the mortgage, Paul had taken care of that should anything happen to him. She didn't care about losing the house; she'd camp in a field as long as Paul got better and lived with her for the rest of her natural life. "I don't care if we lived in a cardboard box! As long as you are with me." She gazed at him and traced her finger along his bloodless lips.

"What happened to you that night darling? Did someone do this to you? Oh I wish you could tell me!"

Of course, as she had expected there was no response from him, but at that moment there were much more things she needed to tell him; things she needed to say because she wanted so desperately for him to live, because without him there wouldn't be much point to her own existence. She leaned closer, her lips almost touching his.

"Paul I love you more than life itself, you are the reason for my own existence, in fact, I sometimes wonder how I lived before you came along! You must fight this Paul, you must fight it for me and Bethany, Bethany needs you so much darling, she needs her daddy's strength and guidance, Paul; please get well for me." She kissed his lips softly, lingering a while, she could taste anaesthesia very faintly and he had the smell of ether on his breath.

She felt her words had to be said, there wasn't enough time that night for her to tell him how much she loved him, he had to know; he had to know that! She touched his hand against her warm cheek and as she looked at him she noticed tears running down his face.

"You can hear me can't you? Oh God Paul please don't be afraid, you are going to be alright."

Detective Inspector Collins paced the room.

"I don't think there is much chance of Melanie Thomas surviving the attack, it doesn't look good, I want a list of everyone who has recently moved into the area, that means, people who work here but may live outside somewhere, even as far as Chester, Liverpool, all surrounding areas. Also I want the names of anyone who was in the vicinity at the time of the murders. I want names, addresses, anyone who saw anybody acting in a strange manner; he's got to be a local man."

The phone rang Haldane picked it up. "Oh, Okay, I see, when?" He put the phone down and looked at Collins. "Melanie Thomas died twenty minutes ago."

"Oh God bless her." Collins murmured.

Collins sat down and rubbed his chin thoughtfully. "So ,the first Victim, Mary Saltash was killed by the pond in Bedgellert, she was hacked to pieces, the second victim Lana Templeton was attacked by the edge of a field in Manod, almost hacked to pieces not far from a pub where she was drinking and fighting with her husband, now the third victim is the only one that has no connection to the other two because she was only sixteen years old, also mutilated the other two were in their late twenties and neither victim was known to be a prostitute or had anything to do with any sort of crime, they were all decent young women. And, they were all killed, so far with the same weapon, there were no footprints or DNA of the killer left at the scene, he obviously wears gloves, where I wonder, is the connection?"

"There doesn't seem to be one, this is sudden, the guy whoever he is must have recently arrived in the area, I could get on to other police forces in the country and check hospitals, prisons, see if there has been anyone released recently who could have been capable of committing such crimes."

"Well, if there are, they should never have been released in the first place, but it's a Good idea Haldane."

Madeline turned around and stared at the wall, her other hand reaching to pull the duvet over her. The house was so cold at night and her feet had become numb, so she gave up the thought of sleep for the rest of the night, and instead, she sat up and put on the bedside lamp. The rest of the night could be spent worrying about Amanda. Madeline got out of bed, pulled on her housecoat and trotted off downstairs to get a drink. It was now four thirty in the morning. She hurried along the landing as quietly as she could, switching on the downstairs lights, never let it be said that she was the bravest warrior in the world when faced with the dark, she was terrified! Walking down a flight of stairs in a big old house in sheer and unyielding blackness was her worst nightmare! With her hands sliding down the banister as she descended on bare feet that were even colder on the uncarpeted stairs, her eyes moved to the front door where she noticed a large brown envelope sticking through the letterbox. She ran across the hall and snatched the envelope from the letterbox. There was no address on the front so she turned it over and looked at the back, it felt bulky with whatever the contents were inside. She was sure that it wasn't there earlier when they went to bed. She shook the envelope and held it to her ear, Madeline wondered exactly what she thought she would hear, obviously, nothing breakable, or it wouldn't have fitted into the letterbox. Her finger fumbled to open it; and inside it was full of stuffed grey marl paper normally used for padding. Carefully she pulled out the contents, and for a moment the words were not so clear, she held it up in front of her.

'ROSES ARE RED, AND NOW SHE'S DEAD! VIOLETS ARE BLUE, AND SO ARE YOU! WHEN YOU ARE DEAD IN A DAMP DARK COFFIN'

The words were paper cut outs stuck on plain A4 paper. Madeline almost dropped it as if it had become some red-hot object about to catch fire; her instinct was to throw it to the floor just to be rid of it. Her heart pounded so fast it drowned out any other sounds that crept around the sleepy house as she ran up the stairs toward Amanda's bedroom.

"Amanda!" she yelled. "WAKE UP."

"What the hell is wrong?" She was already slipping into her housecoat as the door flung open.

"Look!" she said handing her the paper.

Amanda focused on the clear, bold multicoloured letters, "Where did this come from?" she asked, a deep frown veiling her eyes.

"It was in the letterbox as I went down for a drink, I couldn't sleep, so I decided to make myself a coffee."

As Amanda read the note her eyes widened like globes. "We must take this to the police, it's not a prank, he's been here tonight again, and it's clearly a threat."

Her globe like eyes fixed on Madeline in a terrified glare.

Madeline felt her stomach turn, her eyes widened as she saw blood on Amanda's fingers.

"Amanda! Have you cut yourself?"

"No I haven't, why?" Frowning, she turned the paper around. "Oh, it's on the paper." Amanda gasped.

A vision of a blood soaked hand with newspaper cuttings between the fingers sent a terrifying shiver up her spine; the paper fell from her hands to the floor.

"The note!" Amanda gasped again…. "Has been marked with the blood of his latest victim!"

Madeline checked her own hands, to see if there was blood on them. She had been the first to open the envelope and take out the paper, but there was nothing on her hands at all; there was not even a speck of blood. Why was it only on Amanda's hands and not hers? She followed Amanda towards the bathroom, watching as she turned on the taps, snatching the nailbrush from the sink and scrubbing at her hands as she drowned the tiny brush with liquid soap. Fortunately Madeline had recovered enough from the shock to pull Amanda's hand from the gushing water. "You're burning yourself!" She said turning off the taps and reaching for the towel on the rail.

"He could have aids?

"Yes, he could, but you'd need tons of it and a really serious cut to catch it from him."

Amanda took another clean towel from the drawer and dried her hands, rubbing them vigorously together as if something had stuck to her palms.

"Are you okay?" Madeline asked softly.

"Uh, yes, I think so, the thought is so sickening." She scowled.

"Yeah, well he's a really sick person Amanda, let's get dressed and take this to the police."

The sun had started to lift up over the horizon as they headed down the mountain with the note tucked safely inside a plastic sandwich bag. Madeline noticed an old man carrying a shovel ploughing his way across the field.

"Hey! Stop hang on a minute, look over there." She pointed towards him; he was wearing an old moth eaten brown coat and Wellington boots and was heading for the thick density of the forest. "Could he be a farmer?"

"I don't know." Amanda pulled on the handbrake, and opened the window. "Hey! Hello there."

The old man stopped, he looked towards them and waved his hand, he walked slowly to the car.

"Morning Ladies, its nice day for a stroll."

Amanda got out of the car. "Yes, it is a lovely day," she smiled.

He looked positively ancient to her; older than the mountains, his skin had a weathered look like old worn leather; his teeth had all rotted away except for two in the front that were greyish black. He looked more like a tramp than a farmer, his eyes peered out of a puff adder face, red and watery, and a face that was bloated and swollen like the alcoholics they had seen at the town centres sitting in doorways with bottles of cheap booze in their hands.

"I hope you didn't mind us stopping you but we wondered if there were any farmers living around these parts."

The old man put down his shovel and frowned with hairy caterpillar eyebrows.

"Oh no lass, the last farmer sold up here about six or seven years ago, there's no one living around here anymore, too remote you see?" He had a strong Welsh accent.

He picked up his shovel and walked away. Amanda watched him as he disappeared into the forest. She now knew for sure, that they were the only living beings up here on this godforsaken mountain. Madeline waited by the car her auburn hair was whipped by the wind, turning it almost golden in the sun.

"Well." Amanda said as she opened the car door. "Paul certainly found a plum place to live didn't he? Smack, bang in the middle of nowhere."

Collins took the plastic bag from Madeline. "Certainly looks like blood, but we will know more when we get it to forensics."

Amanda asked. "Inspector how long until this maniac is caught?"

Collins gave her a wry grin. "How long is a piece of string?" he said.

She raised her eyebrows in question. "So, that could be forever then?"

"Mrs Marriott, he will make a mistake and when he does we will be there waiting."

"Yes, I expect you will! But that doesn't give me a lot of comfort, he has already tried to get into my house, and now he has made threats on my life! What the hell do I have to do to convince you? I am scared! In fact I am so scared that one night I'll wake up to find him hovering over my bed with an axe in his hand!!"

She was almost shouting now at his laid back attitude.

He walked back towards her. "Mrs Marriott, I don't mean to sound flippant, I care deeply believe me, until we catch him I am going to place a twenty four hour police patrol around your property, at least it will make you feel more secure."

"Well I hope you do Inspector, because if you can't protect me I will find someone who can! I will also contact the papers, and your chief of police, even if I have to go to London's Scotland Yard."

They walked to the car in silence, both of them still stunned from the blood on the paper and the attitude of the police Inspector.

"I never thought you had it in you." Madeline smiled.

"I don't usually, but when things get bad and my child's life is threatened things change."

As far as Amanda was concerned the threat was very clear, she had no idea why he chose her, and she didn't need it spelled out for her. Why he chose her was because he had obviously seen her and marked her as his next victim, but from now on they were going to have to be a little more than vigilant, because now she felt she was being hunted, she knew exactly how the Fox felt after it was rooted out from it's lair by the hounds, and she didn't want to end up like that Fox!!

She chewed at her thumbnail as they walked towards the car park.

Madeline glanced at her. "Look, are you alright Amanda?" she asked.

"Yeah, I suppose so, I'm as alright as I can be, and I just feel a little insecure at the moment." Amanda looked doubtful, and then she asked Madeline. "Would you mind coming to the hospital with me?"

Madeline smiled and took her arm. "Of course I will."

By the time they arrived at the hospital Paul was sitting up, his eyes open and his head resting on a pillow. Amanda stood at the door with Madeline at her side, her hand went to her chest to still the enormous excitement that was building there, and she almost shouted her joy but held it back so she rammed her fist into her mouth instead. Doctor Richards appeared behind them.

"We had been trying to contact you this afternoon Mrs Marriott, but couldn't get a reply."

She realised the mobile was turned off, after the scare she'd had with the note she forgot to switch it on.

"He came out of his coma this morning, the signs are reasonably good." He smiled confidently.

Amanda felt as if she had scooped the whole lottery, Paul's eyes rolled towards her and he smiled, but they were still a little vacant.

"Oh this has got to be the best news I've had in a long time Doctor, Oh thank you so much."

He smiled warmly. "It's not me you have to thank Mrs Marriott, it's a higher being." He left the room quietly.

"Paul?" Amanda took his hand gently in hers.

Madeline watched, a huge lump of emotion had stuck in her throat her heart ached for Amanda, she loved him so *much* she was so very happy with him. And it was a match made in heaven so they say, Amanda had found her true soul mate and Madeline felt so sorry for him, he looked so helpless, so vulnerable a fragment of the Paul she met that first night in Stones nightclub. She took a chair from under the window and sat close to him.

"Hi Paul, how're you doing? Do you feel better?" she asked quietly.

She smiled but her eyes were filled with tears. Paul blinked with water-tinted eyes and she took his other hand and to her surprise his fingers curled securely around her.

"He knows who I am." She smiled at Amanda. "And that's got to be a good sign."

"It must be he is still a little confused it will take a bit of time."

Madeline almost cried as she stared into his eyes. "Paul?" She called softly and he turned his head and smiled.

"Oh Madeline look! He smiled at you that was such a great response he knows his name at least."

Amanda brought his hand to her lips and kissed his cool fingers.

"Paul, if you can understand what I'm saying squeeze my hand once for yes; and twice for no ok?" He squeezed her hand once.

It was gone seven pm by the time they left St Andrews, Amanda's mood had lightened considerably and at last she was able to smile. The drive back seemed longer than ever as they entered the Tynant highway; the mountainous road was bendy and windy with tricks waiting on every corner, namely the ones that sent you plunging front wheels down into the steepest ditch.

As they got nearer to the house, the tall familiar figure of Inspector Collins and Tom Page stood at her door, it seemed to Amanda that he was always the bearer of bad news; and for a moment her heart rolled over. She pulled up and they got out of the car.

"Oh please don't tell me you're here to give me bad news Inspector?"

He took a step towards her but smiled reassuringly.

"No Mrs Marriott, this time it is good news, the blood on the A4 paper was pure bees wax mixed with red food colouring, otherwise known as 'cochineal. It wasn't blood as we first thought, just simple furniture polish with a drop of food colouring added, that's what gave it a sticky substance."

Amanda relaxed. "Oh, I'm so pleased; at least it wasn't blood, that's something."

She headed towards the door, her red loose fitting jumper flapped in the wind shedding her long dark hair behind her. They followed her inside.

"Well at least we're not looking for another mutilated body" Collins said, rubbing his cold hands together.

"Yes, strange though." Amanda remarked. "Why on earth would he want to put food colouring on paper?"

"To scare you I expect, a nasty joke perhaps? This guys an expert on nasty surprises."

Madeline threw her shoes into the hall and headed for the kitchen.

"Well he succeeded on that one." She called.

Madeline was so relieved to know the blood wasn't human, but all the same she couldn't help feeling a little bit like a car that's petrol had been siphoned off, because right now she wanted to sleep for the rest of the week.

"I have a police patrol up here on the hour; also police dogs are combing the moors in case he's hiding out there somewhere."

"But they haven't found anything yet Inspector?"

"No not yet Mrs Marriott, but I promise you we will get him."

"Do you think he is a local man?"

"We don't know that's something we can't be sure of, personally myself I think he may well be, or was at one time because he knows the area so well."

"Mrs Marriott, did you know any of the victims?" Tom asked.

"No, I don't think so why?"

"I just wanted to see if there was a link somewhere, no doubt you will hear it on the news, there has been another girl murdered, a Melanie Thomas, did you know her?"

"No, never heard of her."

By the time they had left Amanda felt drained, after hearing about the recent murder it had jangled her nerves considerably.

"I wish he hadn't told me about the recent murder."

"He told you because you would have heard it on the news anyway." Madeline dropped her bag on the sofa and headed towards the kitchen.

"Poor kid, she was just a baby really." Amanda replied. "I feel so sorry for her parents."

"Yes, so do I, well I hope they catch him soon."

"Well, at least that blood wasn't human anyway."

"You know Madeline I couldn't stay in the house on my own if it wasn't for you."

"I told you I'll stay here for as long as you need me." She studied Amanda's tired pale features. "Hey," she said grasping her hand and giving her a warm hug.

"Don't let it get you down! They'll get him he can't get away for ever."

"I'm scared Madeline, I wonder what made him come all the way up here?"

"Oh, don't worry yourself so much, why did he go to other areas to kill innocent girls? Nothing can happen to us, there's police all over the mountain."

"I just hope you're right Madeline."

Madeline smiled. "Look, how do you fancy coming for a drink, we can drop Beth off at your mums, come on, it'll do you good I can take you to meet Evan?"

"At last I get to meet him"

The pub in town was packed with people to the brim. Madeline went to the bar, anxiously waiting for one of four people to serve her, her hair caught a flicker of yellow light turning it golden amber, a haze of cigarette smoke hung in the air and the atmosphere was relaxed. Outside the whole town hummed past her, everyone going about their business as Amanda gazed through the windows. She had started to think that perhaps she was overacting a bit, her mind had been crammed so full of worries about Paul that she really had no time or room in her head to think of anything else lately.

Madeline brought back the drinks. "Here you are." She smiled. "Hope you like Malibu."

"Malibu's fine." She took the drink from Madeline and took a long sip.

"Now relax." Madeline said, looking around her.

He had seen them come in, he stood by the bar one elbow resting on the counter the other holding a glass off whiskey. He saw Madeline look towards him, he put his glass on the bar nodded his head and gave her a smile.

"Oh, there's Evan." Madeline said.

He picked up his drink and walked towards them.

"I was waiting for you." He smiled, his hair hung over his eyes. He turned to Amanda and smiled. "You must be Amanda?"

"That's me, and you are Evan, am I right?"

Madeline grinned. "My elusive man"

"Let me get the drinks, Malibu is it?" He asked with a boyish grin.

"Please" she liked him right away.

"You sure you don't mind?" Madeline asked.

"I wouldn't have asked if I'd minded, anyway just got back from London this morning."

"How is your Mum?"

"Oh, she's a lot better, had a really bad bout of flu."

Amanda felt a little like an intruder, these two hit it off really well, she wondered if she should make an excuse and head on home. Evan studied her for a moment. "Madeline told me about your husband, how's he doing?"

"Um, better, a bit, I think, he's getting there." she lowered her gaze. "It's not easy living on a mountain, in such a big house."

"Oh, I know the house, used to be owned by a farmer, he had a couple of kids and loads of sheep, sold up in 1989 I think, and it's the only house for miles isn't it?" He looked at her with deep concern. "Bit of a lonely place?"

She looked at him and smiled, "Oh yes, it can be, but thank heaven I don't live on my own."

"Maybe I could give you a lift? Make sure you get home safely"

"That's very kind of you Evan, but we are staying at my mother's house, I don't drink and drive, I left my car there so we can go home in the morning."

"Well." He said getting to his feet. "It's been nice talking with you." He turned to Madeline and kissed her softly on the cheek. "I expect I'll see you Monday lunchtime then?"

Madeline nodded. "Same time as usual I expect." They watched as he walked to the door.

"What a nice guy!" Amanda laughed.

"Yes, he is." Madeline watched him through the window, he draped his coat over his shoulder and opened the car door.

By the time they got to the hospital Paul was lying in his bed propped up by three pillows. His eyes were heavy lidded and slightly cloudy from all the drugs he had been given.

"Paul." Amanda whispered she felt uneasy at the way he was propped up like a rag doll, his head lolled to the left. She ran a cool hand over his brow, and then straightened him, so he was in an upright position instead of him trying to see them from a strange angle. His eyes wouldn't focus on her properly, they looked different to what they were yesterday, and his personality had seemed to undergo a radical change, he was quiet, submissive and withdrawn. She wasn't sure she liked this change at all.

She turned to Madeline and whispered. "He looks worse than he did yesterday."

"It's probably the drugs they've been giving him, why don't you ask the doctor?"

Madeline looked around to see if there was a doctor nearby, but there were only the nurses busy at their stations, so anxiously she turned back to Amanda.

Madeline smiled and nodded her head. "Talk to him, perhaps he'll answer you."

Amanda leaned over Paul and kissed him on the forehead, and to her surprise his hand came up to caress her hair. "M..Manda?"

"Oh Paul!" she cried taking his hand and pressing it to her cheek. "Yes it's me, I'm here." she turned to Madeline. "He's remembering, he remembered my name."

"I told you it was probably the drugs, oh its great how he has improved in a day." Madeline smiled.

They were unaware of the door opening behind them. "It's a remarkable improvement isn't it Mrs Marriott?" Doctor Richards smiled as he suddenly appeared at her side. "I told you he would start to remember things in time."

"Its wonderful doctor, when did this happen?"

"He started to get part of his memory back this morning; he will still be groggy a lot of the time and still need pain relief for a while yet, his speech is still a little impaired but he will get that back in time too, he should recover full use of speech and movement in a few weeks."

It was all she could do to stop herself from throwing herself into the doctor's arms with gratitude.

Once again she thanked him. "Oh doctor thank you so much for the care you have given him, you got him back for me!"

"He's been so lucky, he's strong and otherwise healthy that's what really pulled him through."

He picked up Paul's chart and studied it for a moment, and then quietly left the room.

Amanda held his hand to her face once more, so afraid that if she let go she would lose him forever. His eyes rolled towards Madeline and he smiled, it was the smile of a child and it tore at Madeline's heart as she lifted his other hand and gave it a gentle squeeze.

"I'm so glad to see you back with us Paul, get better

soon my love I really miss not having you around, you are my sparring partner, and I miss that."

At this Paul's smile broadened, and she knew he had understood every word she had said, he remembered the little jostling play fights they used to have and her joy was apparent by the tear she had in the corner of her eye.

For tense seconds that seemed to stretch into minutes Madeline watched closely, her face was pinched, and her teeth clenched her lower lip anxiously, she turned her eyes towards the tumbler of water on the single locker by the bed and the jug beside it, her throat had suddenly felt like hot sand.

"Yes." Paul replied with the same childish smile. "Good to see you too."

He ran his fingers through Amanda's hair, but his eyes were still staring vacantly.

They were surprised to find the door unlocked when they got back. Amanda turned anxiously to Madeline.

"I'm sure I locked the door when we left, did you go back in the house for something?"

"No." Madeline frowned. "You did lock it, I saw you do it."

"Well, it's not locked now." Amanda said irritably.

"Don't worry so much, maybe we didn't lock it, Amanda

you have a lot on your mind right now maybe you forgot?"

"No, I wouldn't forget under the circumstances."

"Perhaps you thought you had locked it, sometimes the lock sticks, it's happened to me before." Madeline lifted Bethany and carried her into the hall.

"I did, I felt it engage as it locked." She shook her head as she followed Madeline, glancing behind her at the now closed door.

"Let's get Tubby here to bed and we can have a glass of wine, or watch T.V. or play monopoly or something, but let us just be happy that the day has turned out to be the best!" Madeline kissed Bethany and held her close.

There was no mistake! Amanda knew she had locked the door, when you live in such a remote place like this you get into the habit of locking and bolting things, especially after recent events. She walked into the kitchen to close the curtains and instantly knew there was something wrong; she looked around the kitchen anxiously, taking in every detail. Everything was as she had left it this morning, except, there was an unfamiliar aroma she couldn't identify, someone had been in here! She could smell them.

Madeline put Bethany to bed then went down to the kitchen. She looked at Amanda and knew something was troubling her. "What's wrong?" she asked.

"Someone has been in here, can't you smell the odour?"

"What odour? Like body odour or something?" she gazed at Amanda strangely.

"No, it's like a scent of some kind."

"I can't smell anything." Madeline frowned, her eyes shifted around the room, sniffing the air like a bloodhound.

"Someone's been in here." Amanda said.

"How could there be? No one has keys except us."

The phone rang suddenly; Amanda looked towards the hall extension then hurried to answer it.

She ran her hand through her tangled hair, lifted the receiver, "Hello?" she said.

"Hello to you, how did you find him?"

"Who…who is that?" At first she thought it was David because the voice sounded so familiar, but then she noticed he had a slight Irish accent, and then she knew who he was. Her hands began to shake.

"Is he still in the land of the living? Or has he become your favourite vegetable?" Maniacal laughter echoed down the line. "Get the joke? Huh, my favourite vegetable!"

"Why don't you just FUCK OFF!" Her heart beat so loud in her ears she could hardly breathe.

"OH, now that is not nice, not nice at all, and you know you really should lock up behind you when you go out you never know who might come in these days."

His words were shed through gritted teeth. Amanda felt physically sick, sick to think he had been in here while they were out, he had violated her home.

The phone suddenly went dead. She looked at the receiver as if she was afraid the man behind the voice would suddenly materialise in front of her.

"He has the keys to the door." Amanda gasped fear spread through her like an intercity train; her eyes grew as wide as saucers.

"I told you someone had been in here, where did he get my door keys from?"

Madeline paled. "Call the police, and after that get David to fix a deadbolt on the door."

The phone rang again and this time Madeline snatched it up.

"Oh, I forgot to tell you, have you heard about my latest flame? Poor little thing! She is almost as dead as a doornail. Or should I say soon! I have already chosen my next little playmate and what fun the chase will be; talk to you soon my dear, very soon."

"Who do you mean you bastard? And how did you get this number?"

Again the line went dead. Madeline looked into the receiver the way Amanda had just moments ago.

"My God, you are right, he has us marked next on his list, and he has you're keys alright! But how the hell did he get them?"

"I'm not missing any keys!" Amanda looked about her frantically, she had just used hers to get in, and Madeline had hers so… *That awful realisation hit her so quickly it sent shudders of fear through her.* "Oh Christ of course, he has Paul's keys he must have! The night of Paul's accident he must have took his keys."

"But how did Paul get in?" Madeline answered.

Amanda shook her spinning head. "I haven't got a clue."

"Okay, we know he has your door keys but who have you given the phone number to?"

"Only family, and the hospital, no one else has it, oh and the police have it also."

"You can count out any of those." Madeline said.

"It could be anyone, the phone was already here when we moved in, and it was already connected."

They stared at each other for long, long seconds; both of them were too frightened to voice their real thoughts.

Haldane stood inside the large hall, Tom Page stood next to him. Although the house was nice it was also creepy, too many ways in and too many place's to hide. The first time he met Amanda Marriott he thought she must be extremely wealthy to live in such a big house as this one, but as he stood in this vast hallway he realised she was not wealthy at all but a normal person leading a somewhat normal life, uncomplicated and straightforward, until Paul was struck down that night, and now as he looked at her she reminded him of a startled little deer caught by bright lights in the forest.

"Thanks for coming Inspector." She smiled at him warmly leading him through to the living room, where she motioned him to sit on the oatmeal armchair.

"Actually I'm detective Sergeant, haven't got to that stage yet." he gave her a warm smile. Can you tell me exactly what happened?" he asked her thoughtfully.

"He rang me twice, the second time Madeline answered, he has another victim and I think she is still alive."

"How do you know that?"

"That's what he said; she's almost dead, dead as a doornail."

"I think he was referring to Melanie Thomas. Did he have an accent at all?"

"I'm not too sure, in fact he sounded more like an Irishman, all I know is, he has made threats to me and my husband, he knew Paul was in hospital and he *knew* because it was him who put him there."

"How can you be sure?" Tom asked.

"I just know it! Call it instinct if you like."

Haldane looked worried. "I am familiar with your husband's accident Mrs Marriott, but up until now nothing has been proved."

"Oh I am aware of that, but I know what happened to him, I am sure he hit him from behind."

"And I believe you." Haldane smiled, and was grateful to see the relief on her face.

"You do?"

"It's not impossible, your husband hasn't been able to say how he sustained those head injuries, also it was dark, and he was riding his bike on a steep mountain road, it's not impossible for him to have hit something and gone head first and then hit his head on a rock either."

Amanda gazed down at her wedding ring, the wide band had become loose over the last few weeks where she had lost a lot of weight, and she twisted it around thoughtfully.

"I know it's also a possibility."

"The call was not local, it came from outside the district but he was clever enough to hang up before we could trace the call. For now Mrs Marriott, I suggest that you make sure everything is locked up and you use your mobile for any calls you need to make, I will double up on the police patrol but the most important thing to do is get yourself a good lock for the front door, that's essential and do it tomorrow! I have no idea how he got in here, but just make sure he doesn't get in again."

Tom page headed towards the door, he stopped and looked around at them "I'll take a look maybe search the cellar to make sure there is absolutely no way anyone could get in." He suggested.

"Thank you tom." Haldane replied, "But I'm absolutely certain beyond reason of a doubt that the cellar is secure."

"I'll check anyway, if there is we'll get it boarded up right away."

Amanda felt so much more at ease the last few days than she had in weeks now that Paul was making such a good recovery.

In the last week he had started to talk properly forming his words into coherent sentences; he still didn't remember anything of that night he went out to buy cigarettes, the night that had left him waiting on deaths dark doorstep, but Amanda knew that in time his memory of that evening would return.

She had slept so deeply that when the telephone did ring it was just a feint echo of her peaceful dreams, and the constant ringing awakened her, and brought her up from the depths of sleep. Her hand flew out from under the duvet in a desperate attempt to silence the ringing before the whole house was awake.

"Amanda?"

"Oh hi mum, everything okay with you?"

"Fine, I was just wondering if David and I could go visit Paul today?"

"Of course you can, that would be nice, and I'll probably see you there later."

His feelings had turned into a thunderous anger and he didn't know quite which way he was going to go, because now things had started to go wrong! Dreadfully wrong. The more he tried to control the rage the more the rage controlled him. He lay in the grass staring into nothing; an insect crawled onto his trouser leg, he flicked it off with the blunt edge of the machete and then gazed up at the sun, squinting and shading his eyes with one hand as he thought some more.

He heard noises to the right of him that sent him jumping to his feet with the fluid elegance of a cat into the bushes and out of sight, crouching and laying as still as a stone statue.

The young guy appeared first then the girl followed. They both stopped suddenly as if they had heard something, but of course they hadn't, they had stopped because they had found a quiet place; he pulled the girl close to him running his fingers through her short dark hair, he was at least a foot taller than her so he had to bend to reach her full perfectly pouting lips.

He studied her for a second and decided she was quite pretty with elfin-faced features and wide dark eyes. But, she hardly had any breasts at all; they looked so flat and insignificant, and wouldn't really turn any man's head for more than a fleeting glance, the nipples only just managed to poke through the plain white tee shirt she wore. He couldn't hear what he was saying to her, but he expected they were stupid words that meant absolutely nothing, stupid and mushy things! He moved carefully to lie flat on his stomach so he could watch what happens next.

The young guy pulled at the button at the back of her skirt; then pushed it down over her perfectly rounded thighs, revealing legs that were tanned, as if she had just come back from somewhere hot and sunny.

He tensed and every muscle was taut like elastic bands ready to snap. She laughed teasingly as she pulled at the zipper on his jeans, then slowly with nimble fingers she pulled it down. He grabbed her wrists and yanked her tee shirt over her head to reveal those insignificant breasts that were no more exciting than a couple of fried eggs.

He smirked. She could easily pass as a boy with her trim straight figure, he thought. Now the young guy hurried, he slipped off his jeans and kicked them to the side, and they both fell to the ground in a tangle of arms and legs. There was no excitement in this! The girl was too bony and thin to give any man a jolt; she was nothing like a female she was too much like a man! Except for that perfect mound of hair and soft cleft between her legs as they opened to receive him! He would hardly know the difference between the two!

He felt a stirring inside him of extreme anger and rage, and then his vision was obstructed as the tall young guy covered her with his body.

He felt sick as he heard her moans, he reminded her of the girl on the mountains she was pretty also, and much too pretty to waste her time on a big time loser like the one she was with! And his rage grew to gigantic proportions, perhaps he felt so angry because it was her he wanted? But never the mind, he needn't worry his head about that right now, because if she didn't want him, then he would just take her! Simple.

Every man needs a mate; and every mate needs a man! That is how it's supposed to be. A smile sneaked across his face, he was just plain him today, no mask, no make up, just him and himself.

This girl had become her! She had become the girl on the mountain, squirming under the body of this virile young man, giving him her love! His face contorted with rage! The girls face had become the face of the girl on the mountain and he crawled on his belly through the long grass towards them, the machete gripped so tight in his hand that his knuckles turned milk white. He crawled nearer, his face became a sheen of perspiration running down his pale greasy skin, skin that was almost as pale as death, and now he was at their feet watching the thrashing bodies in their last throes of passion.

He raised the machete….WHAM….The guy stiffened, a choked muffled scream erupted from his lips and then he was still. At first the girl thought it was just his climax until she saw the crimson fountain from his lower regions spilling onto her.

"GEOFF!" she screamed. "What's the matter? What's happened?" Furiously she pushed at him it was then she saw the machete embedded between his buttocks. She gasped and tried desperately to free herself from her dead lovers embrace, she sobbed uncontrollably. With lightening speed and all the strength she possessed she pushed herself free and staggered naked, covered in his blood to a tree fifty yards away.

"COME HERE!" He snarled lumbering towards her, he stooped and gripped the machete in one powerful blood soaked hand and tugged hard. It came free with a wet squelching bone-crunching sound. The girl glared in a fixed frozen horror at the machete, its edges covered in blood and bone. She hugged the tree, her elfin features almost white, and her eyes wide and glazed.

"Well now, that must have been some climax huh? Did you enjoy that? How about that last nerve tingling thrust eh?"

She shook her head dumbly her hand felt for the bark of the tree as if it would give her some kind of comfort and safety. His maniacal laughter echoed around the forest and then the girl made little whimpering noises as she clung tighter to the tree; urine ran down her legs. He lifted the machete one more time tilting it sideways as he approached the trembling girl; she shook her head, her eyes wide in terror.

"No, please, don't kill me…please…. I haven't done anything to yoo…" her words were cut short as her head flew from her body.

He walked calmly over to where the girl's head had come to rest and gazed down at it, the eyes were wide glassy and vacant, the lips parted in a soundless scream, and then he turned and walked back towards the highway.

Amanda hurried from the hospital to the car park as heavy droplets of rain had started to fall. Her visit with Paul had gone so well, he looked so much better day by day he was returning to himself, the way he used to be, his speech was more audible now than it had been a few days ago.

She had noticed that he had become a different person than the one he used to be, and Amanda wasn't sure if she preferred the old one to the new. The doctor had explained to her in some detail that people who suffered severe head trauma, usually reverted to the opposite person that they were before, so if someone was bad tempered before then after the head injury they became a much milder natured person, thus the reverse. It didn't matter that much to her in the first place because she loved him anyway, he had always been such a gentle person and the only thing that worried her at the moment was his submissive attitude, he seemed to agree with everything anybody said. His poor mind was still full of muddle and mayhem with still no recollection of going out that awful night to buy cigarettes, in fact he had not smoked one cigarette in the time he had been in the hospital since that night.

After picking Bethany up from Megan's she drove a little faster than she normally did, the dark threatening sky warned her there was another fierce storm heading their way very soon. By the time she got to the steep mountain road the rain had already started lashing at the windscreen making huge bubbles as if she had just been through the car wash without waiting for the rinse and dry.

Amanda peered through the rain and for a moment her foot came down on the brake. The gate was locked again. Maybe it had slammed shut in the wind? Pulling on the handbrake she got out of the car, rubbing her hand across her freezing nose, it felt like a stiff block of ice.

The latch had stuck and she cursed angrily, finally it snapped open and she jumped back in the car; she hated cold rain seeping down the back of her neck, so she fumbled about in her bag for a wad of tissues to wipe her face and the back of her neck. She glanced around; twilight became night, and she realised how vulnerable she was out here alone on the dark mountain road. The killer could be waiting anywhere, it was too dangerous to be jumping in and out of the car to open and lock the gates. There were no sheep or animals around anymore, so from now on she would make an aluminous sign and post it on the gates saying 'DO NOT LOCK GATES'.

The second gate was also securely locked. Furtively she glanced around her before she got out of the car, realising how easy it would be to stalk someone up here! Total silken darkness and that was what probably happened to Paul, he didn't see him coming! Her small space where she stood descended into a deathly hush and all she could hear was the purring of the engine as it hummed smoothly. Her hands froze painfully with the cold as she struggled with the stiff hinge, managing to free it after snagging a piece of skin from her finger, she swore, then stuck the sore finger into her mouth and jumped back into the car.

She had never been as happy as she was right now to see the big old house rear up in front of her. She felt a calming sense of relief as she saw Madeline standing at the door with an umbrella in her hands; that was one of the things she loved about Madeline, she was so thoughtful.

"I saw the cars headlights, here; let me take Bethany for you while you lock the car."

She held her arms out as Bethany gave her a sweet smile then holding Bethany close to her she dashed inside.

Amanda locked the car and followed. She could sense there was something wrong the minute she got inside.

"Is everything ok Madeline?"

Madeline put Bethany down and the child ran towards the living room. "It's my aunt; she has had a massive heart attack at work."

Amanda frowned. "I knew there was something wrong the minute I saw your face. Is it bad?"

"Bad enough, they had to resuscitate her, she's in St Vincent's; Amanda I need to go and see her, my mother called to tell me about half an hour ago."

"Oh Madeline I'm so sorry, do you want me to drive you?"

"No, no don't be silly, I'll call a cab, I shouldn't be long." She turned on her way to the stairs, and then looked back. "Will you be ok on your own?" she frowned.

"Of course I will." She smiled warmly.

"We could call David if you like; he could sit with you till I get back."

"No, don't be daft, I'll be okay, your not going to be gone all night are you?"

"No, I should be back before nine, if not I'll call you."

It was five by the time a disgruntled cab driver arrived, Madeline anxiously turned towards her as she put her coat on. "Are you sure you'll be alright?"

"Yes of course, now go or you won't get back at all."

Amanda watched as the cab headed towards the road, she closed the door and leaned against it for a moment. She was scared at being alone in the house, in fact she was more than scared; she was terrified, but she wasn't going to let Madeline know that, the last thing Madeline needed right now was being made to feel guilty, she had her own life to lead.

This was the first time she had been alone since the night of the intruder, she would have to get used to it when Paul returned from hospital, and he wouldn't be here all the time he had a job to go to, she couldn't expect people to baby-sit her every time Paul went to work.

Madeline was such a warm loving person and she really didn't want to burden her with her problems. She turned on the television and sat for a while watching programmes she had never been interested in before; but she found herself becoming entranced by them. The next time she looked at the clock it was already nine thirty, which made her wonder where seven and eight had gone.

Amanda rubbed her tired eyes and then went into the kitchen, completely unaware of the face that peered in from the darkness outside, the grotesque features that studied her every move.

CHAPTER EIGHT

Collins gazed at the telephone; its constant loud irritating buzz made sure he would answer it eventually. It always happened every time he was busy and short staffed someone always managed to choose their moments well! He dropped Melanie's autopsy report onto his desk as he snatched up the phone.

"Inspector, it's Tom, I've just picked up a suspect I caught him out on the Bridgend road, he told me he was poaching, but I just have a feeling he's not telling me the truth, I'm bringing him in."

Shaun sat on a chair with his arms folded across his broad chest and a confident grin on his face.

Collins watched him from the door. "Wonder what he finds so amusing?"

The smile vanished as they entered the room. Collins pulled out a chair and sat down, he studied Shaun intently for a few moments. Haldane took his chair to the other side of the room, placing his hands behind his head and stretching his legs out in front of him as if he was going to be there for quite some time.

Shaun Riordan was thirty years old; he was tall and broad,

his sharp chiselled features and stone blue eyes looked as if they had been allocated to a showroom dummy standing in the window of the local superstore

He had a list of violent criminal convictions dating back from 1993."

Finally Collins sat forward staring right into those stone cold eyes.

"You are Shaun Martin Riordan, is that right?"

Shaun let out a bored sigh. "Yes." He answered simply.

"Why did you have a shotgun?"

"I poach, as you already know."

"Guns are illegal or hadn't you noticed?"

Shaun looked down at his large calloused hands, without replying.

"Do you know where Tynant is?"

"Should I?"

"I'll ask the questions, you answer them."

"I have been there once or twice."

"Were you there last night?"

Shaun frowned. "No I wasn't, I went to visit friends."

"What friends were these?"

"Just friends."

"Oh." Inspector Collins said sarcastically. "So you actually have friends do you?" He smiled sarcastically.

"Look! What's the problem here? I know I'm getting nicked for poaching, and by the way I got a license for the gun, got it in County Cork."

The confidant grin was back; he pulled himself up in the chair folding his arms once more across his broad chest.

"What are the names and addresses of these 'friends'?" Collin's asked, he noticed the elbow of his jumper was torn and mud covered his boots.

"Look, my poaching has nothing to do with my friends, I don't want them involved."

"It's not the gun or the poaching we're interested in Mr Riordan." Collins frowned heavily.

"What do you mean?

It was Collins turn to grin. "Oh come now Mr Riordan surely you have heard about the murders recently?"

Collins got up and circled him; Shaun turned his head, watching him as he moved towards the back of his chair.

"Murders? Oh you can't be serious?"

The bravado of his past confidence was now quickly slipping away.

He circled around him and then stopped right in front of him examining his short clean fingernails.

"How long have you lived here?"

"Round about a year or so."

"Right at the time the murders started then?"

He looked down at him and smiled. Shaun paled and the unfeeling eyes now showed a hint of emotion, Collins was already reading as fear.

"Now wait a second here! You can't pin that on me I have nothing to do with murdering anyone."

Shaun got up and Collins placed his hand on his shoulder forcing him back down on the chair.

"But you kill animals?" He taunted, he liked animals; sometimes they were better than people.

"Yeah, but that's different!"

"Why?" he frowned.

"What are you, an animal conservationist or something?"

"Something like that."

Collins fixed him with a gaze like steel, Shaun felt himself shrinking from his deep penetrating eyes.

"Tell me Shaun, do you own a knife or a machete?"

"Both, I use a knife for skinning Rabbits, and by the way, the rabbit is dead before I skin it!" he said with sarcasm "And an axe for chopping wood."

Collins took out a packet of cigarettes, lit one and blew smoke into the air.

"Well, I hope you do kill the rabbit first. Why did you run when the officer stopped you?"

"Oh come on Inspector!" he said impatiently. "You done your homework, you know I have a criminal record."

"Yes we know, and it was armed robbery wasn't it? Assault with a deadly weapon; that was a machete wasn't it?"

"Yeah and it was also self defence, the other guy had a knife."

Collins looked down and opened the file he had in front of him.

"Show me the license for the gun."

Shaun reached into the inside pocket of his worn jacket and pulled out a mangy piece of paper he threw it down on the table.

Collins studied it for a few moments and then looked up. "I cannot for the life of me imagine how they gave someone like you a license for a gun?"

Shaun turned his head and pursed his lips together cursing silently under his breath.

"Until I am absolutely convinced that you had nothing to do with the deaths of these young woman, I'm holding you on suspicion of murder, I want the machete and the knife that are in your possession for further investigation…is that clear?" Collins got up and stubbed out his cigarette in the overflowing ashtray.

Amanda listened to the news, her mind wasn't really fixed on the television she was more worried about Madeline's aunt, but when she heard that there was a man in custody for the recent murders of three young woman her heart almost leaped out of her chest.

She rang the police station and asked to speak to Inspector Collins, or Haldane. Collins answered her.

"You have him?"

"Well, we have a man in custody Mrs Marriott, he was found near the scene and his actions were suspicious, but we have to question him further."

"Would you let me know Inspector?"

"Of course, but at this stage we can't be sure it is him, Miss Richards said he had an Irish accent, is that right?"

"Yes, he did."

She rang Madeline. "Madeline, I'm sorry to bother you I know you're busy but I thought you might like to know they have picked up a man for the murders and are holding him in custody."

"Oh, that's great news did they tell you his name?"

"No, it might not be him but I'm sure it is, it should be on the news later, listen, take care coming home, if you get a problem call me. How is your aunt?"

"She's stable at the moment anyway I shouldn't be much longer now."

"Okay, see you later."

Amanda had been clock watching for the last half hour wondering what was taking Madeline so long to get home; it had been three hours since she'd called her to tell her about the man in police custody. Perhaps she had found trouble getting a cab, it was difficult to get anyone to drive up the mountain, too many hidden pot holes. Her relief was short lived when the phone rang; anxiously, she reached forward to answer it.

"Hello darling, everything okay?"

She was pleased to hear Megan's voice yet disappointed it wasn't Madeline.

"Oh hello mum, yes everything is fine, the baby's alright we're all doing well at the moment."

She laughed so as not to give Megan a fragile illusion that everything was not really okay at all, she was beginning to get worried about Madeline walking up that dark mountain road on her own, even though she felt confident that the man in custody was the killer.

She glanced up at the clock once more it was going on for ten.

"What is the time Mum?"

"Isn't your clock working, it's almost ten, in fact it is nine fifty eight."

"Yes it's working, it's just that Madeline isn't home yet, she should have been here by now."

"Maybe she got held up at the hospital, or perhaps she can't get transport home?"

"Yes I expect your right." She replied, turning her head towards the window, expecting to see the headlights of a taxi as it dropped Madeline at the door.

"When is Paul getting out of hospital?"

"Uh, I'm not too sure, he still has some way to go yet, it's been a slow painful process, he still has some confusion and he can't remember what happened to him that night."

"He still doesn't remember how it happened?"

"No, it's just like his mind has become like a blackboard

wiped clean of all his memory, it worries me sometimes, I wonder if perhaps he will forget the past life we had together."

"Oh Amanda, don't worry about that, he'll remember eventually, the brain is a strange thing, yet brilliantly unique."

"Yeah I know, but the good thing is he hasn't even had one cigarette since it happened, he has even forgotten that he ever smoked in his life, and he doesn't remember why he went out that night."

"Well, that's one good thing at least; he was so lucky to survive."

"And they have a man in custody for the murders of those girls."

"Yes, I know I heard it on the news, he hasn't been charged yet though?"

"No, but I'm sure it is him."

"Are you sure you're alright up there on your own?"

"Yes, I'm fine; Madeline will be home soon, anyway, I'll clear the line in case she's trying to get through."

"Ok darling, goodnight."

"Goodnight mum."

She put the phone down, and paced the room a half

dozen times, studying her fingernails that were chewed and cracked where hours of anxiety had given her something to do. She walked over to the window and looked out at the blackened twig like fingers of the trees almost in front of the big bay window, and the creepiness made her feel all the more uneasy as she worried about Madeline.

Madeline stood at the bottom of the hill to Tynant .She had tried desperately to get a cab but, as usual no one wanted to drive over the rocky mountain and risk damaging their exhausts or their suspension. It was one of the things she hated about living on the mountain, it was a steep and rocky walk to the house and it usually took her over forty five minutes. She should have brought Paul's bike down with her and chained it to the gate and then all she had to do was ride it back up again.

It had suddenly turned colder; the night air was accompanied by strange smells, smoke, tar, and an earthy musky aroma that drifted down off the mountains. Recently she had been thinking of moving, starting somewhere new, not in North Wales, or the UK for that matter, but abroad, Spain, Italy, maybe even the States, she was only twenty four she had loads of time left to start a new life somewhere else. She had become bored with life in general, it was the same old thing day in and day out, North Wales was a beautiful place there was no doubt about that but for a young vivacious woman like herself it didn't hold a lot of interest, it was a small village that was more suited for the older generation. The only thing holding her here at the moment was Amanda and Bethany, oh God she would miss the baby so much. It would be out of the question to leave Amanda now, even though she had her own family she just couldn't do that! When Paul got out of hospital and recovered, maybe then she could start thinking of emigrating, maybe Evan would go with her, things were going so well for her at the moment, he had already suggested going out more together.

She looked ahead and the road looked bigger and wider, and steeper, she sighed and walked on.

She felt relieved the police had a man in custody for the murders at least she could walk home without jumping out of her skin at every shadow. Suddenly she heard a noise, footsteps walking closely behind her.

"Who's there?" she called, when no reply came she started sprinting along the road. The main reason she sprinted like an Olympic gold medallist was because this stretch of road was desolate, no one used it; and for someone other than herself and Amanda to use the road would mean only one thing; they were out for trouble!

"HEY!" came the voice. "Slow down, why are you running?"

Madeline stopped sharply and almost fell into Haldane's arms.

"OH! You gave me a scare Sergeant Haldane."

"Why on earth were you running? I was just checking the area surrounding the house when I saw you, I was going to offer you a lift but you took off like a bat out of hell."

Madeline felt stupid; she looked down at her feet and noticed her shoes were covered in mud where her panic had sent her trudging through the wet sludgy ground.

"I'm sorry Sergeant I don't know what came over me."

"It's alright miss Richards I'll get the car and give you a lift the rest of the way."

At last Amanda felt a heavy burden lifted from her shoulders as she saw the lights of Haldane's car flood her drive.

Madeline hurried inside with Haldane following. "Amanda, I'm sorry I'm so late, I missed the last bus."

"Why didn't you phone me?"

"Because I was too busy making a fool of myself in front of D.S. Haldane here." She gave him a weak embarrassed grin.

"Oh, it's okay." He turned to Amanda and smiled. "I gave her a bit of a fright I came up behind her suddenly."

"Well, I am just so glad to see you safe and sound."

"I was just looking around the grounds, as you know we have a man in custody at the moment."

"Is he the killer?" Amanda asked.

"I can't give you his name or give you any information about him until he is formally charged, I'm sorry it would be like giving myself the sack."

"That's okay, but you will let us know Sergeant won't you?"

"Yes, of course. By the way how is Mr Marriott?"

"Well, he's getting there he is improving day by day."

"That's good news I hope he continues to improve as I'm sure he will, well, I won't take up anymore of your time."

He had watched the house for ages, thought's came back of his childhood, he could almost see the crates of beer in the larder, the cans strewn across the floor, the broken mirror in the scullery, the blood on the floor from his mothers cut and bruised body. The voice that echoed across the mountains that voice had belonged to his father on drunken bouts of brutish behaviour.

But the house belonged to him now! Mother was gone and no brutish pig of a father to tell him what to do anymore, he did what he pleased, and to whom he pleased. He shifted position, his binoculars came out of his rucksack and he looked through them intently at the girl in the house, if he was going to get back inside, he needed cunning, it was no good charging in with military precision and taking back his property, the police would get him. So, he would just have to be patient.

He slipped his hand into his pocket and pulled out the key, he smiled, he still had his door key and while he had possession of the key; the house would always belong to him, he held it in his hand it seemed to come alive, it felt comfortable, the cool steel heated up from the heat of his palms, and his hand closed tightly around it.

He jumped to his feet placing the binoculars back in the rucksack and he made his way down towards the road.

Collins stared at the report he held in his hand. "There is nothing to connect him to the three victims, no skin, blood or fucking bone!" Collin's threw the forensic report on the items they had taken away from Shaun onto his desk.

"We have to let him go." Haldane replied. "Maybe it isn't him?"

"Can't think of a better candidate, he's got a criminal record up to his armpits, and he has an Irish accent."

Collin's wasn't in the least surprised by the sudden dread he felt, the killer was still on the loose.

"Put out a news report, make the public aware that the man in custody has been released, I don't want this slapping us back in the face."

Amanda fastened little Bethany into her car seat while Madeline loaded shopping into the boot. They had been to see Paul and both of them felt happy at the progress he was making, he even held Bethany on the bed beside him. The phone rang Amanda fumbled in her pocket for her mobile. "Hello." She said.

"Mrs Marriott, it's D.S. Haldane, I'm just calling to let you know that the man we had in custody has been released."

"Released?" she asked, a shadow of despair creeping over her face. "Why?"

"I'm afraid we had nothing to hold him for, all the tests came back negative, there was no evidence to charge him, but I am sending a patrol up to the house tonight."

"So, he's still out there?"

"I'm afraid so."

Amanda looked shaken as she put her phone back into her pocket.

"They had to let him go."

"They had the wrong man then?" Madeline frowned.

"Looks like it, the killer is still out there, and it's going to start all over again. Madeline do you mind if we call in at Mum's?"

"No, of course not, we're not in any hurry."

Amanda had never before felt such an overwhelming sense of fear and danger, and she had no idea why she was so scared? It could have been because of the pure evil nature of the killings that frightened her she certainly didn't want to end up like those poor girls. By the time they had arrived at Megan's the sun had set and a finger of twilight pointed to the mountain peaks to unveil a mist across the moors.

David opened the door with a look of expectation on his face; he had already heard the six o'clock news on the release of the man held in custody.

They sat down while David made coffee and Bethany played with her toy box in the corner.

"Why don't you put the house on the market, it's so remote up there, sometimes Amanda, I feel as if you're a sitting target." He looked worried.

"That is what I intend to do once Paul gets out of hospital."

Amanda leaned towards the coffee table and placed the cup back on the saucer.

"Why not now, why wait until Paul comes home, he could be in rehab for a long, long time?"

"I know that David, but I'd rather wait."

"Why don't you stay here?"

"Because the house is so small, Bethany is a handful, sometimes she's pretty restless at night, it wouldn't be fair to you and Dad, besides you both get up early in the morning for work, I'm pretty safe and Madeline is with me, it would be different if I was there on my own."

David argued. "But it's better than staying in that Mausoleum of a house! Do you want to go back there?"

Amanda glanced at Madeline as if the question had been directly aimed at her.

She shrugged her shoulders and said. "It's entirely up to you, if you want to go back there, then I'll stay with you, we have police protection now, and as you said there are two of us, he's hardly likely to break into the house with the two of us there."

Amanda frowned questioningly. "Do you think it's fair of me to ask you? You could be putting yourself in danger."

"Look." Madeline replied. "As long as we have a police presence and we stay together then it is okay by me, the only thing I wouldn't want is for either of us to be left alone at night."

"Neither of us will be left alone at night, if you're happy with the situation and don't mind staying with me, then I'll stay, after all why should I be chased out of the home Paul made for me and Bethany?"

"Because there is a serial killer out there Amanda, that's why, I think you're crazy."

David replied shaking his head.

"Squatters could get in, and then it would be my responsibility to get them out."

"What about Madeline? No buses go up that far it means she has to walk! Have you thought about that?"

Madeline looked from David to Amanda. "I could use Paul's bike? It would be so helpful, besides I would be a lot safer riding the bike home than I would be walking up that road, I could ride across the grassy banks, and there are no stones or bricks there."

"No Madeline I could pick you up at the bottom of the Tynant road, I have done it before, the only time it would be difficult is when I go shopping. But, that would be a good idea in emergencies I never thought of the bike."

"No!" David said. "That's just the trouble with you two, you never think of anything, I'll come back with you and fix deadbolts on the doors."

Reece suddenly appeared from upstairs, he gave David a warning glance, he could see a row brewing.

"Let me come back with you, what she needs is an alarm, I think I have one in the shed, wait, I'll go and have a look."

Amanda looked surprised to see her father. "I didn't know you were here Daddy, did you hear the news?"

"Yes, they let him go; he obviously isn't the man they're looking for then is he?"

He sighed, Reece knew the argument could go on forever between Amanda and her brother, he knew how stubborn both of them could be at times, and he'd had the experience with both of them before. "Well as long as you have company you should both be okay. I would have preferred it if you stayed here with us."

He replied disappearing out the door to the Garden shed where he kept his tools.

Reece stopped outside. They sat for a few moments while Amanda gazed intently at the dark sombre house. She had never really liked the outside from the very first time she had seen it, and David was perfectly right it did remind her of the house on haunted hill. It was dark, dreary and too big for just three of them. Paul had worked so hard to buy this house a place he thought would be ideal for them, and it would have been; had it been built in a different location! She remembered every detail of the day Paul had brought her here. She lowered her head and stuck her fist in her mouth while she pondered over what she really wanted to do. Now the suspect had been released she knew the nightmare could start all over again. Overhead seagulls cried and their haunting calls echoed over the hills while they swooped above.

Madeline studied her closely, she knew her well enough to know there were cracks forming already in her decision to move back into the house. She draped her arm over the back of the seat.

"Don't feel pressured to go back if you really don't want to, I told you it would be alright by me whatever you decided to do."

Amanda took her hand and gave it a gentle squeeze. "You're a good friend Madeline; I don't know what I would do without you."

Madeline sighed. "Okay then, what do you want to do go inside?"

Amanda nodded. Madeline got out of the car and a shudder raced up her back, she looked up at that piece of guttering that Paul never got round to fixing and suddenly wanted to say. 'No! Don't go in, let's just get the hell out of here and pretend the damn place never existed.' But she didn't.

It was after ten when the phone rang for the first time since they had been back, she hesitated before she lifted the receiver.

"Mrs Marriott?" Collins asked. He was relieved she had got home safely.

"Yes."

"Oh you decided to go back then, are you both alright?"

"We're fine, I thought it would be better to come home than put everyone to so much trouble, maybe he won't come back?"

"As I said this morning I will be sending a patrol up there tonight."

"Thank you."

"Make sure you lock all the windows and doors."

"Yes Inspector I'll make sure I lock all windows and doors, in fact my father is here putting new locks on everything." She smiled; her shoulders slumped in relief. "Thanks for calling."

"The patrol should be with you soon, and they will be around all night so you have nothing to worry about. Tom page will be popping in also, if there is anything you need tell Tom."

"Oh that's great Inspector, Paul should get out of hospital in a few weeks but it makes me feel so much better to know there is someone looking out for us."

"That's good news, how is he?"

"Getting there, he seems better day by day."

"I'm glad to hear that, anyway goodnight and make sure you lock up ok?"

"Ok, and thank you once again Inspector, Oh, and by the way, I'm sorry for my rudeness the other day, I was so scared."

"I understand, sometimes it looks like we're just sitting on the fence, but I am as frantic to get him as you are."

As she finished her conversation she smiled, at last she felt so much safer than she had done in the last few months.

Snow had fallen thickly during the night as Amanda looked out of her bedroom window. They had been back a month now and she was relieved they came back when they did otherwise the heavy snowfalls would have prevented them reaching the dirt road. This was something that always worried her, there would be no way to get off the mountain until the snow had been cleared by the snow ploughs, at least they had prepared for the heavy snow season and had plenty of groceries because the road would be blocked by now. But at least there were no more night prowlers, and with two foot of snow she doubted anyone would be able to haunt them up here! She found herself in an almost trance like state as she watched the picturesque sight before her, the trees covered in a white coat. She gazed at the big snowflakes as they came down thickly, accumulating on the window ledge. She let out a small breath that misted the pane then cleared it with her hand. It was cold and frosty. She reached for her robe and tightened it around her. It certainly was a beautiful place to live.

It was six thirty and grey clouds had just become visible as the night slipped quietly over the horizon. Madeline sat up rubbing the last depth of sleep from her eyes. Looking towards the window, her mood was one of despondency. With legs that felt like granite rocks, she knew that moving them was going to prove quite a task as she threw back the bedclothes and tumbled from the bed. Perhaps Paul's homecoming was bothering her? She just hoped he would continue to improve the way that he had done so far. Madeline was happy that Paul would be coming home in the next day or two, he was extremely well apart from the occasional headaches he was having, and the doctors said they would lessen in time.

She shuffled towards the window, smiling warmly at the picture postcard view that greeted her. "So this was where photographers came to air their lenses?" She said aloud throwing open the window and then closing it quickly as an icy wind whipped her face and soughed through her hair. The trees ducked and bowed as a wind tore through them shaking snow from their branches.

CHAPTER NINE

Madeline was shovelling snow from the drive when she heard the telephone ring, dropping the shovel she ran back inside to answer it.

"Hello?" she answered breathlessly.

"Hi! Miss Richards?"

"Yes, hello Inspector what can I do for you?"

"Is Mrs Marriott there?"

"She is in the bath I think, hang on I'll call her."

He heard her lay the phone on its side while she went to call Amanda and in the background he could hear buzzing noises and the low rumble of a radio. He gazed out the window at the high peaks of snow that covered the mountains. It was a lovely place to come to if you were into photography. Ducking down slightly he looked at the sky, a heavy dirty dishwater colour told him that more heavy bursts of snow were a little more than likely, this worried him because he couldn't get up to Tynant, the roads were completely blocked at the moment, that was the next thing on his list, get the plough's out to clear a path.

"Hello Inspector."

"Mrs Marriott, I have had to call the patrol away, the area is just too hazardous for the vehicles to get up to you, and you think you will be alright up there?"

She frowned. "Oh, of course, I'm sure we will, there has not been any more murders have there?"

"No, but our investigation is still going on."

"Oh, that's okay Inspector."

"I called in to the hospital to see how your husband was doing, he's getting on well he should be coming home soon?"

"Yes, but there is a slight problem; the doctors are quite pleased with him, except the cut he received to his ear needs to be corrected properly. They may do a skin graft? It means a delay of a day or two that's all really."

"That's not too bad." Collins replied. "At least it is better to get it done while he's in there than have to go back at a later date."

"Inspector?" Amanda said.

"Yes?"

"Look, thank you for your concern, I appreciate it very much."

"Oh." He smiled. "You're very welcome."

By February the snow had started to melt, snow ploughs had cleared most of it. It had been a really hard winter, but there had been no more incidents and they were so much more relaxed. At last Amanda felt she was going to have some peace, and Paul was coming home the same as he was when he left a year ago after that terrible night, and for that she was eternally grateful.

Madeline tossed her long auburn hair from her eyes as she scattered salt all over the drive, now the snow had melted it would soon freeze over and make walking a slippery nightmare. She threw more salt and scrubbed with the broom, her thoughts had turned to the last remaining winter nights, there was still some nasty weather to come, but then the nights would become lighter and the weather would turn milder, and summer would soon be here!

Looking up quickly she heard the crunch of boots walking towards her, hardly daring to believe who she saw walking towards her with a suitcase in his hand.

"PAUL!" she gasped dropping the broom and hurrying to meet him. "Oh you look so well! How did you get here, don't tell me you walked?"

Paul gave her a warm broad smile.

"I did, but I'm okay, needed the fresh air, I wanted to get all those hospital smells out of my lungs."

She turned suddenly and yelled. "AMANDA! IT'S PAUL!"

Amanda lifted her hands from the soapy dishwater, with a look of startled surprise on her face she turned towards the door, drying her hands on the tea towel. Madeline must be getting short sighted or something Paul was not due home for another day. She ran up the hall towards the front door. For a moment she stood erect and squinted, her eyes misted they were bathed in shadow from the opaque sun; and then she was in his arms.

"Why didn't you ring me? Oh God you should never have walked all that way you look exhausted."

"Madeline told me how well I looked, and now you say I look tired?" he laughed as he hugged her tightly.

"Come into the house." She said slipping her arm around his waist.

For a long time they just held each other, both of them remembering the year they had missed and how lucky Paul was to be here at all.

Madeline smiled and took his hand. "You look good Paul." She said, she also lied he looked terrible.

"I had almost forgotten what the world looked like, where's Beth?" he asked looking around.

"She's at mums today; I'll go and get her soon."

As they entered the house Amanda put his case down by the door, he seemed to be so weak, half a shadow of the man he used to be and his weight had dropped drastically, she had a good mind to call the hospital and ask them why they allowed him to come out on his own. He was out of breath and his face was as white as a sheet.

Paul looked around at the vast living room as if he had never been there before. Amanda took his hand and led him to the sofa. "Come on sweetheart, you'll be okay." She said softly, reassuringly. Paul sat down weakly.

Madeline came back carrying a tray of hot coffee and biscuits.

"Drink this it'll warm you up, you know you should have rang one of us we could have picked you up." Madeline studied him closely, "You are okay though aren't you?"

Paul nodded his head and smiled.

"Yes Madeline, I'm fine, really I am it's just that I don't remember much of the house though."

Madeline spooned two sugars into his cup, she wasn't sure if he even took sugar, but at least it would boost his energy levels a bit.

"It is bound to take some time Paul; it will all come back to you soon."

The fire burned in the grate and Paul seemed transfixed by its glow, although a chill seemed to invade the air.

"Wasn't I going to install central heating?"

A worm of confusion invaded his poor mind, he vaguely remembered shivering and getting up to put coal on the fire, but there the memory faded, and for a second he gazed into the fire.

"Is there something wrong love?" Amanda asked suddenly worried by the strange vacant look in his eyes.

He turned to her and smiled. "Oh no, nothing at all, it's just that I get flashbacks sometimes, I remember things but then it's gone, I'm sure it'll return in time."

"Of course it will Paul." Madeline said handing him the cup.

"It'll feel strange for a while; after all you didn't just have a bump on the head it was a little more serious than that."

She steadied his hand as he drank his coffee then he put the cup on the table. He stared at Madeline as she was about to sit down and he grabbed her hand.

She looked at him with surprise. "Madeline I want to thank you for staying with Amanda, you are a good friend and for that I will be eternally grateful to you."

She looked into his eyes and relaxed, he'd given her quite a scare, and instead of finding a cold look of despair, she found warmth and compassion in his eyes. She gripped his hand and leaned forward to plant a warm kiss on his cold cheek.

"Oh Paul! You are so welcome. I would never have left

her here alone." Madeline cleared her cup put it on the saucer then got up to leave.

"Where are you going?" Paul asked.

"To pack."

"What on earth for?" he frowned.

"Well now your here Paul you won't be needing me anymore, you need your privacy, get back to normal."

"No!" Paul sounded abrupt. "Stay please! That is unless you want to go, we would be happy to have you stay as long as you want to, the house is big enough."

His eyes smiled, his face softened, Madeline had never seen him like this before. She sat back down and nodded.

"Okay, if it's alright with you then its okay with me, I can help around the house while Amanda looks after you."

"Then it's a done deal."

Tears filled Madeline's eyes.

Paul seemed to settle as if he had never been gone. He took a biscuit and finished his coffee, and then he asked. "How has everything been while I've been gone?"

Amanda almost choked on her biscuit. "Fine." She answered. "Everything has been as rosy as an apple tree."

Amanda had noticed such a change in Paul since he had

come home, he was so gentle and caring, sometimes she wondered if perhaps he thought she was made of china and would break if he held her too tightly, and with each passing day so her love for him expanded, at last her life with him was coming into fruition. Selling the house had become a forgotten conclusion, as riches in the house grew, it became home, a warm loving place full of security and comfort like it was before his accident, she could never leave this house now because Paul was here and together their memories faded of the past rocky months. Bethany was growing up to be a beautiful little girl just like her mother, but her hair colour and eyes were so much like her father, in fact she was a clone of him. Every week Megan, Reece, and David would come for dinner and she would make that day special. Christmas came and went and it had been the best Christmas they'd had in years, and before she knew it Bethany was celebrating her fourth birthday. Paul never regained his memory of what happened that night, and the murders had stopped so they forgot about it altogether, the main thing was, he was alive, and since that night he had never lit another cigarette.

It had been so long since Collins and Haldane had seen Amanda or Madeline, but they were both pleased that they were getting on with their lives, they still had no luck in finding the killer, and the Shaun Riordan lead had gone stone cold, but investigations were still going on. Haldane and Collins decided to drive up the mountain and update them on the Shaun Riordan case, and just to check all was well in the Marriott household. They walked up the gravel drive, Collins rang the bell.

Amanda opened the door, she was so much more relaxed than the last time he saw her. She smiled as her eyes lit up.

"Oh Inspector, come in how lovely to see you."

"We were on the Tynant highway and thought we'd pop in to inform you of the current situation?"

"Listen Inspector, Paul doesn't know anything about the killer; please don't mention it in front of him." Collins smiled and nodded his head.

"Of course not, I wouldn't say a word."

"By the way, what was the man's name you had in custody?"

"Mrs Marriott, I wouldn't be at liberty to tell you, as the man was released without charge, I'm sorry."

"It's okay, I understand, I just wondered if he was local."

He felt a little nervous as she led him into the living room. He was quite unprepared to see the tall good-looking guy that confronted him. The last time he had seen him was lying in a hospital bed on a ventilator so near to death.

"Paul, this is inspector Collins, and D.S Haldane, they looked after us while you were in hospital."

Paul got up and smiled warmly, he held out his hand.

"Oh I'm very pleased to meet you sir, thanks so much for all you did for my wife."

Collin's took his hand he was surprised at the warm feel of his hand.

"Oh, it was nothing, they were on their own up here and it is so desolate for two young woman; I just made sure there was a patrol up here every night just to make sure they were safe." He waved his hand dismissing it as if it was of no importance.

"All the same it was good of you." Paul said. "Mind you," he laughed, "What could happen to them on a mountain?"

Collin's shifted uncomfortably. "Oh well, you never know." He grinned.

CHAPTER TEN

Verna Jeffries didn't get to sit down and drink her tea so she drank it while she worked, with three kids and a severely disabled husband to look after time seemed to move on like an intercity express train. Verna glanced quickly at her watch it was already five p.m. she had to be in work for seven.

Puffing up pillows for Billy so he could sit comfortably in his wheelchair, she fussed around him. "Is that better?" she asked him. Billy's head waved defectively from side to side and then he nodded and she smiled.

"Good." She said, then she carried on with the daily duties she needed to do for him, he nodded again and she noticed how his movements had deteriorated. Over the last couple of months he had got worse. Billy had been a builder until he contracted Multiple Sclerosis at the age of thirty-five, and until then he had never had a days illness in his life he had been a strong healthy man.

Billy first noticed there was something wrong at his brothers wedding two years ago. Verna had teased him about drinking too much because he was so unsteady on his feet; at times he found it difficult to coordinate his movements and Verna often accused him of drinking in his lunch hour. But Bill knew that was not the case, there was something much more serious than drinking, in fact he hardly ever drank much more than a pint in the local pub, and that was only twice a week. The first symptoms came not long after; pins and needles in his legs and arms, about a month later he found he couldn't walk in a straight line he was all over the place, people used to laugh when they saw him. "Hey Bill! Had a few too many?" They were well meaning of course and Bill just used to wave his hand in gesture instead of having to answer them. At first he wondered if he had something wrong with his inner ear. That caused the symptoms he had experienced, the unsteadiness maybe, and the inability to walk straight, but not the pins and needles! And then one terrible morning he couldn't lift a boiling kettle and almost spilled water over two year old little Janie. So he went to the doctor. And after waiting agonizing weeks for the results of the tests he was told. "I'm so sorry Mr Jeffries but you have M.S." And that was the first time he knew what the meaning M.S was.

"It is far advanced Mr Jeffries; you must have had it for a long time?"

Bill was devastated even if he had gone to the doctor sooner there was nothing they could do for him. The news was cataclysmic! He was due to spend the rest of his remaining years in a wheelchair, with nothing to look forward to but an awful death. Bill felt his world collapse around him, it was even worse to watch Verna hold down two jobs to keep the family going; and that hurt him more than his illness did! He was forced to sit in a wheelchair all day watching the woman he loved more than life, slave all day in a hot café and then in a crowded pub until eleven at night to pay the mortgage on the house. He felt so angry, he was angry at God, at the doctors for not finding a cure, and at the thought of dying and leaving his beautiful Verna to face life alone, he would sit for hours and cry, cry because he would miss her so much! That was why he never complained, he never ever wanted her to feel that he was ungrateful and drive her away. Verna wiped her hands dry on the towel and reached up on the shelf for hand-cream.

"Now you tidy up after yourself Sophie, there's a good girl, please don't worry daddy will you? If you want anything wait until I get home okay sweetheart?"

"Okay mummy, I'll put Janie and Tommy to bed for you, and give daddy his dinner." Sophie said.

Sophie was the eldest of Billy and Verna's three children and was fast becoming a little mother to her younger siblings. Verna ruffled her long blond hair as she passed.

"You are so precious darling, and I love you so much."

The little girl tilted her head to the side and gave Verna a cheeky grin. "Do you mum?"

"Yes I do."

Sophie crinkled up her nose. "What time will you be home mum?"

"Same time, I get a lift usually so I may be earlier. I want you in bed Sophie, school tomorrow."

She turned to Bill, his eyes were glazed he was almost asleep, her heart melted and she ached for him, she had watched the slow deterioration over the last few months. Suddenly his eyes opened and he focused on her.

"Ver…Vern…Verna?"

"Yes my darling, what is it?" She knelt by his side, her eyes full of concern she brushed her hand against his cheek.

"T…T…bacca?"

"Mild tobacco, okay sweetheart I'll get it on my way to work, do you have enough for now?" He nodded awkwardly.

His eyes glistened as she kissed his forehead. She had been married to Bill for fifteen glorious years, those fifteen years had been the happiest of her whole entire life, and she had certainly found her soul mate. He had been a good provider, a wonderful husband and father, she could never have wanted better, that was until the miserable illness struck him down so suddenly and changed their life so tragically. They were like two pieces of a jigsaw that fit so perfectly together, he was still a good looking man with thick blond hair and warm blue eyes that were once so full of life but now they had been reduced to orbs of sadness and unable to focus anymore. But her love would never die, even death would not part them and often Verna wondered how she would go on without him, but she knew she had no choice for the sake of the children. She had already decided that she would struggle on in a cold and lonely world because the children were a part of Bill as much as they were a part of her. At night she would lay in bed beside him praying that the Angels wouldn't come in the night to take him to his final resting place. Not just yet! Please God, just let me have a few more years with him...Please!

June popped her head around the door as she did every night before Verna left for work; she was a good neighbour even before Billy's illness, she was so lucky to have someone like June.

"Everything okay Verna?" she asked.

"Oh yes June, thank you, I've given Bill a wash and shave, and you know the number in the pub if you should need me urgently."

The last three words seemed to freeze on her tongue she lived in constant fear of something happening to Billy while she wasn't there.

"You worry too much Verna, I pop in at least twice to check on Billy and the kids, they are such good children."

She smiled warmly at Sophie who sat at the table with a pen in her hand studying her homework book. Verna had given June a spare key and that had lifted a great strain from her shoulders knowing June could get in anytime.

Verna grabbed her coat, walked to the door and hesitated. "You will ring if you need me?"

June grinned at her and shook her head. "Of course worry wart, now go on before you're late."

The usual Saturday night crowd pushed into the bar, loud music blared with buzzing voices that were undetermined in their chorus chatter. Cigarette smoke cloyed the air as Verna blinked; her eyes were beginning to smart.

Verna was pretty, not attractive but beautiful, her hair was naturally blond she had never once in her life used any kind of colour on it, her eyes were large and soft with the pupils a shade lighter than emerald green with tiny grey flecks. Her skin despite having three kids was smooth and supple, and she moved with the gracefulness of a Swan. Bill had always told her how lucky he was to have such a beautiful wife. Her beauty had not got her anywhere though, she wished she had got herself a better education and gone to university, life would have been so much easier for them both, especially now, but she was damned if she was going to live on state benefits, whatever time Billy had left on this planet, then she was going to make sure that time would be spent making sure he had everything he needed to make his life a little more comfortable.

Verna cleared the glasses taking six at a time in both hands dodging out of the way of drunks as they swayed towards her, spilling the last remains of their dregs over the floor.

"How's Bill?" People asked.

"Fine thanks." She replied hurrying towards the bar.

It was around eight o'clock when the stranger came in, Verna caught his eye as he lounged across the bar propping up his chin on a curled fist. She looked directly at him and found herself shaking there was something in his eyes that frightened her. Taking a cloth she wiped the bar counter and emptied ashtrays overflowing with dirty cigarette butts and stale ash trying to ignore his penetrating gaze. But his eyes stayed on her, a cold malevolent glare that made the hair on the back of her neck stand up. It was not the usual friendly eye contact that always resulted in a warm smile, but a dark soulless gaze that sent shivers up her spine. Who the hell was he? She wondered, she hadn't seen him in here before, and he wasn't local either, Verna knew all the local men in the village. She wanted to get away from him, to another part of the bar but here was where she was needed tonight.

"Hey!" he called. "Pint of lager." His voice had no feeling, a dull nebulous sound that could have been barked from a computer. Verna felt frozen to the spot, but she moved toward the pump and reached for a pint glass. She placed the pint in front of him, without warning he grabbed her arm, Verna shot him a startled glare and pulled away with a gasp.

His lips drew back in a snarl "You gave me a short measure!" he snarled.

"No I didn't sir, it's filled to the top." She indicated with her finger to the top of the glass. She didn't like the way he looked at her it was a glance of pure hatred, and she found herself wondering why he had taken such a dislike to her for no apparent reason. She went to walk away as he grabbed her again but this time she pulled away sharply. This guy was beginning to piss her off!

His fist thundered down on the bar sending glasses flying, Verna stepped back, then pointed a finger at him.

"Don't grab at me like that again!" she warned him.

Now she met his glare with an angry one of her own, she didn't care what his problem was but he wasn't taking it out on her!

"What did you say?" he asked her.

Verna pulled another pint from the pump and a half pint to follow, she slammed it down on the bar smiled and said, "Here Sir, have this on me."

And then she hurried away from him. Her heart was pumping madly, this was the first time she had ever had trouble before.

The stranger never took his eyes off her all evening she wished he would just finish his drink and go, if he caused any more problems she was going to have him thrown out.

Every time Verna looked up to see if he had gone his eyes were on her, still with the same angry glare as before, she felt unnerved by him, this guy had a serious problem it was so evident in his eyes. She could no longer look at him, he terrified her but he seemed to be drawing her like a moth to a fiery flame.

Dennis, the bar manager appeared from the other side of the bar she wondered if she should tell him about the angry customer but decided to leave it for now.

"Dennis, don't look now, but have you seen the guy standing at the end of the bar before?" "You mean the one in the blue V neck jumper."

Dennis threw the tea towel over his shoulder and bent down as if he was reaching for something under the counter flicking his eyes towards the man at the end of the bar.

"No, can't say I've ever seen him in here before, why?"

"Nothing, I just wondered."

"Looks a bit of a strange one though?" He turned and took a bottle of lager from the shelf flipped open the top and then hurried back to the other side of the bar.

Verna was rushed off her feet for the rest of the night but she still felt his eyes on her. Her blouse popped open revealing her cleavage and the top of her black lacy bra, pulling it together she buttoned it quickly. A rush of blood flowed to her face as she saw the strangers eyes travel slowly towards her soft pale flesh. He never smiled, not once; maybe if he had at least it would have shown he was human, but he made her feel as if she was a bug who had crawled out of the woodwork and trudged through shit! Anger flushed through her so suddenly she felt like going over to him and asking him what his problem was. How dare he make her feel like that! Even if he had a low opinion of barmaids he had no right to act like a complete moron!

The rest of the evening passed uneventfully, it was half an hour later that she realised something was missing. There was still a lot of noise from the regulars who were as good as gold, she thought of them as a smiley happy little bunch of rowdies. The music had stopped and Verna looked at the clock on the wall it was already five past eleven, she heaved a sigh of relief because it was soon time to go home. As she looked down towards the end of the bar she noticed the stranger had gone. The two empty glasses stood side by side on the bar. Verna ran her hand through her hair and smiled to herself. She was so relieved to see the miserable bastard had gone; he had made the whole evening so tense. It all seemed so silly now, all she really had to do was tell the landlord and he would have asked him to leave long ago.

Outside the night yielded to a crisp sharp frost, a wind gathered momentum to announce the arrival of another bad night. Verna cleared the rest of the glasses and glanced towards the latticed windows where she could see the dark shadows of passing cars. Suddenly she realised that she hadn't seen Mary all evening, they lived five minutes away so Mary would give her a lift home every night, and Verna crossed the bar to look for her.

"Dennis?" she called, he appeared once more from the other side of the bar with the same tea towel draped over his shoulder. "Have you seen Mary tonight?"

"Oh she called in sick, I'm sorry Vern I meant to tell you, how are you going to get home?"

"Oh don't worry about me, I'll call a cab."

She took her purse from her pocket and looked for change. Saturday nights were not the best nights to try and get a ca, and a sinking feeling hit her almost immediately. She walked over to the phone booth she would need to call Billy first to let him know she would be late. Lifting the receiver she hesitated, she couldn't really call Billy and tell him she would be home soon because she didn't know what time her cab would get here, it would only cause him to panic, it would be better to call the cab office first. She dialled the number and hung on for ages then a voice answered. "Eddie's cabs." And her spirits lifted.

"Can you send a cab to the 'Woodman's' arms?"

"You have to wait about an hour and a half lady, I'm sorry but all my cabs are out and there are four people waiting already."

"Oh no! I can't wait that long, isn't there anything sooner?"

"Sorry Miss, Saturday nights are the busiest, and due to the weather conditions half my cabbies haven't turned in."

"Ok, thank you anyway." She put the phone down wondering how she was going to get home. All the staff she worked with lived within walking distance from the pub, except Mary.

Verna had always kept the phone beside Bill's chair so he wouldn't have to struggle to answer it; she was going to have to call him he would worry if she was late.

The phone rang half a dozen times as a vivid picture formed in her mind of poor Billy trying to coordinate his hands, manoeuvring them into picking up the phone and then she heard his voice.

"H..He..lo."

She sighed gratefully; she hated to put him through the agony of trying to pick up the phone before it stopped ringing.

"Bill darling, it's me, look, I can't get a cab and Mary isn't in tonight, so I'm going to have to walk so expect me in an hour, are you okay?"

"N..N..Wait for a cab!"

Bill stammered badly as his frustration grew in anguish, he had read the papers, the murderer still hadn't been caught, he felt totally helpless.

Verna tried to soothe him. "Bill, listen once I'm across the wasteland I'll be home in no time, I'll be fine, it's better to walk than stay here all night waiting for a cab, besides I'd have to wait outside, they are locking up now."

Before he had time to struggle out any more words of protest she blew him a kiss. "I love you." She whispered then she put the phone down.

Verna picked up her coat from the back of the pub and slipped her hands into her woolly gloves, making sure Bill's tobacco was tucked securely into the pocket, and started the lonely walk home.

The night was a freezing mass of sleet and rain, she hurried over the bridge down the hill towards the wasteland; visibility was bad and she strained her eyes to look ahead. A man passed with his dog but she paid him no attention, it was too cold to be hanging about.

Verna pulled up the collar of her coat, and quickened her pace. It was dark by the old railway bridge and now the last street light was behind her, she was almost near the road that would lead her down a steep hill, that curved sharply to the left and then it was straight on from there.

A shadow caught her eye to her left and she turned quickly. There was no time to run the tall figure was almost in front of her. Verna gasped spinning to her left and running straight ahead, and she found herself in a field of overgrown weeds and grass that was littered with tin cans and discarded food containers. Desperately she looked behind her hoping that man with his dog might come back but there was no sign of a man or dog, or anyone else in fact. Fear passed through her like vibrations through a wire. In her panic she realised how stupid she had been to run into a field instead of racing down the hill to the main road! He stood there, his hands at his sides a cruel smirk sneaked across his lips. Verna recognised him immediately as the hostile man who had stood at the end of the bar all evening glaring at her.

"What do you want?" She challenged.

"You gave me a short measure, do you remember?"

Verna remembered all too well and her heart thudded dully.

"And I gave you a free pint and a half as a gesture of apology."

She looked to her left and saw an opening that could bring her back onto the hill, Verna chewed her lip anxiously if she was going to make a break for it then it was going to have to be now! She turned suddenly, the blow to the back of her head sent her sprawling face down into the ground, sharp stems of grass seeds cut into her face. Rolling quickly onto her back she found her hand plunging into her pocket to clutch at Billy's tobacco pouch as if it held some form of comfort. Nothing had happened! Nothing at all, okay, he got his revenge and now he had run away. As her eyes adjusted to the dark and her senses returned she was relieved to find he had really gone. He had hit her and then run off like a frightened animal. Verna pulled herself up, she was shaking so badly it was difficult to gain her balance and walk straight, the shock of the attack had made her feel sick, both her hands were in her pocket as she headed quickly back towards the hill. The first chance she had she was going to find a phone box and call the police, *he shouldn't be out on the streets, the guy had a serious problem.* Her hand explored the back of her head feeling the bump that had already started to swell and tears flooded from her eyes. He had hit her with something other than his hand she was sure of that by the force of the blow, and on closer inspection she saw the dark stain on her fingers. Anger had replaced her fear because she had put herself at risk! Billy needed her, and her kids needed her. How could she be so stupid? It was too late now, but if she had called the landlord when he grabbed her arm he would have called the police and maybe this would never have happened!

Verna hurried, there was still no one about and it was going to take her another ten minutes to get to the main road. And then she heard his voice.

"You're not a bad looking woman, come here Bitch!"

He stood with folded arms ahead of her leaning against the brick wall, Verna screamed. "YOU BASTARD, LEAVE ME ALONE!"

He seemed to move at the speed of sound and grabbed both her wrists in his strong powerful hands they locked around her small wrists hurting her painfully as if they were clamps.

"No…PLEASE, please, don't do this I have a very sick husband and three kids at home, please don't hurt me!" her fear raised a whimper. "Look! If it's money you want then take every penny, but please, please don't hurt me!"

He laughed at her terror, his eyes narrowing in a malevolent expression of cruelty that clouded them into shallow hollows of nothing except pain and the will to inflict suffering. Verna stiffened, pulling back as his hands tightened and sharp nails dug into her soft flesh, then a bone cracked in her wrist and the agony almost made her vomit.

"GET OFF! STOP IT!" Now she was aware of only one thing. If she wanted to see Billy and the children again she was going to have to fight! Fight for her life. One strong hand covered her mouth, the other tangled in her hair as he dragged her kicking and screaming into the field she had just escaped from.

He threw her down onto the rough sodden ground tearing at her clothes like a hungry animal devouring its prey. Verna felt a terrible anger inside him, nails tearing into her flesh and then his lips mashed down on hers and she felt blood trickle from the corner of her mouth, his tongue forced her lips apart probing obscenely inside, to bite him now would have signed her death warrant, her clothes were shredded on the ground beside her and she felt the terrible cold tighten her flesh. Verna struggled, she bucked and she fought but weakness and exhaustion soon took their toll as her screams became feebler and her struggles became weaker. She desperately wanted to live and so a strange new strategy took the place of her terror. She knew he would kill her, so she lay still with a certain amount of equanimity as her frosted breath plumed the air and her breathing became more controlled.

"Ok, but don't hurt me." She pleaded as tears ran from her eyes, but as long as he stopped hitting her, hurting her she didn't care, she would blank it out of her mind; think of Billy and how much she loved him.

But he didn't stop hurting her! Instead he rammed into her tearing at her insides, she gritted her teeth as the pain became almost unbearable, his fist crashed into her face and she felt her eye socket burst and then she began to struggle once more as panic and terror washed over her like the worlds biggest tidal wave. Verna knew that no matter how submissive she was…He wanted to hurt her! And maim her and this was his game, this was how he got his kicks, this was the creature everyone was looking for, this was every females worst nightmare! This was one hell of an unlucky night for her!

She felt something wet and warm trickle between her open legs, she knew it wasn't semen he hadn't got that far yet! She drew a breath and screamed until she thought her lungs would burst, but she didn't care anymore because she knew she was going to die.

He pinned both arms above her head and with one powerful-balled fist he punched Verna into total submission. All the fight had gone, there was no use in fighting anymore, and then blackness claimed her and she sunk into blissful oblivion.

Bill was frightened and sick with fear. He looked at the clock again it was four a.m. it wouldn't take Verna that long to get home, there was something wrong! Bill felt utterly helpless, useless and angry! He had thought of calling Sophie, but if anything had happened to her mother then he'd rather she didn't know until he was absolutely sure. Tears splashed helplessly down his face and he couldn't even wipe them away. He tried for the phone again to call the police; but his hands shook so violently it slipped from his grasp and went crashing to the floor. Frustrated he uttered a curse, balled his fists and then he gazed at the walking frame he was using less and less now. He struggled to his feet, one hand reaching out for the frame as the other clung on desperately to the arm of the wheelchair and he pulled himself up gasping each breath as he did so. Billy knew his lungs were finished, he'd known that for some time but his shear determination for Verna drove him on.

He dragged himself to the door, closing his eyes and gritting his teeth for a moment, and then with one hand he let go of the wheelchair while clinging onto the frame with the other, slowly, uncertainly he reached out for the handle and the frame tipped sideways, sending him crashing to the floor. His hands waved about in a defective way as he tried to coordinate with the rest of his body, he had landed with his hip facing the door. He reached up for the handle and missed every time. Finally through exhaustion he sat with his back resting against the door. It was another task he would have to perform by trying to turn around to face the right way. He cursed, his anger was almost at boiling point and all the time his frustration grew, If Verna needed help she needed it now! Once his breathing had settled and he wasn't gasping anymore he started to manoeuvre his body by rocking on his haunches until he was facing the door. He reached up, grabbed the handle and turned. Now he had the door open he could swing sideways and tackle the walking frame, once he had done that he could get outside and call June. Bill studied the frame for a few moments; he knew it was no use trying to pull himself up on the walking frame the effort would be too much.

He almost screamed in euphoria as he managed to pull the door wider and drag himself out to the garden patio, the freezing night air soaked through his pyjamas and into his bones, he crawled along now down the step through puddles and muddy grass into Junes garden. There he lay exhausted, and with one weak arm he grabbed hold of a stone and banged on the window.

June woke from a fitful sleep, she sat up and listened, there was someone banging on the window downstairs. She listened intently and there was no mistake she had heard it again, June shook her husband as she slipped out of bed.

"RON! WAKE UP! There's someone banging on the window downstairs!" June grabbed her robe and headed for the bedroom door.

"WAIT, WAIT June, don't go down on your own!"

Ron nearly tripped over his jeans in his haste to dress. They found Bill soaking wet and lying in mud on the patio in a near state of collapse.

"OH BILL! BILL what's happened love?"

June cradled him in her arms; his face was covered in tiny drops of rain.

"Ver…Vern…Somethin, happened, not come home!"

"Okay love, don't worry, we'll find out."

"Call the police Ron!"

"Ok Billy old man, let's get you inside." Ron lifted him and carried him inside.

"June I've got an old pair of trackies in the airing cupboard and a jumper, put them on him and get a blanket to keep him warm, I'll call the police."

Once she had got Bill dry and put warm clothes on him he sat in the chair wrapped in a blanket, his hands disorientating in desperate explanation.

Verna was found on that Sunday morning naked and barely alive, she was lying in a ditch by an old hedge as if she had been an old piece of garbage!

Billy sat passively as June broke the news to him, he had expected the worse anyway, and then tears splashed down his face, they were tears of anger and frustration, and sadness, and maybe there was a little bit of humiliation mixed up with those feelings, because he felt he had failed Verna so much.

"Bill, at least she is alive! That's the most important

thing, she's alive Bill!" she took his cold hands in hers and held them tightly. "I'm going to be here for you Bill, don't worry I'll be here for you."

But June knew it was borderline for Verna, if she survived her working days would be over, and her heart ached for Billy and the kids.

"Paul, I'm going to the shops is there anything you need?" Amanda pulled on her coat and gloves.

"No, I'm okay." He replied weakly.

Amanda noticed the change in him and hurried towards the kitchen. Paul sat at the table with his head in his hands, she gazed at him for a while then concern spread across her face.

"Are you okay?" she rested a hand on his shoulder. "You look kind of pale."

Paul looked up at her and smiled, although she easily read the pain in his eyes.

"Yeah, I'm okay, it's just one of the head bangers the doctors said I would get from time to time, don't worry, I'll be alright."

His face looked pinched and his eyes seemed to retract back into his sockets.

"Paul, are you sure, you're as white as a ghost! Do you want me to call the doctor?"

She laid a cool hand on his forehead.

"No, no really it will go away in a while. I've taken some painkillers they gave me at the hospital." He took her hand reassuringly.

"Okay then, but if you're still the same when I get back I'm calling the doctor."

She touched his forehead again; it felt cold and clammy as if he was coming down with a fever. "I hope you're not getting the flu."

"Honey don't worry, I get these headaches a lot, the hospital said I would, it's an after effect of head injury and surgery, now stop worrying and get to the shops or you'll never get back." He smiled, but his smile was not the usual warm sunny one, it was cloudy and dull.

"I'll try not to be too long, go and lie down for a while."

"That's a good idea, are you taking the baby?"

She was about to say, 'I'll leave her with you' When Bethany appeared at the kitchen door with her hat and coat in her little hands. "Do I have a choice?" Amanda laughed.

The road ahead was quiet; it was unusual for this time of the day. Amanda glanced at Bethany sleeping peacefully in her car seat, her thumb tucked securely in her mouth. It was unrealistically silent for this time of the early evening so she put the radio on. She hated driving in silence. The news came on reporting the savage rape and serious assault of a local woman Amanda found self clutching the steering wheel tightly, wondering if it was starting all over again? In the report it said she had been brutally raped and battered, not mutilated like the rest of the victims but lucky to be alive! So, possibly this could be a whole new crime and perhaps the killer had after all moved on, maybe it was getting too difficult for him to carry on with the murders in such a small village.

Her eyes fell on the tiny clock on the dashboard, it was already three thirty, and the afternoon was quickly relinquishing into the early throes of twilight. She hadn't been gone more than two hours but she had an overwhelming urge to put her foot down on the gas and speed up the Tynant road, she was well aware of the fact that if she did she would probably end up in a ditch, so she took it steady all the way.

Amanda pulled into the drive and banged twice on the horn expecting Paul to come out and help her as he always did. She gazed through the windscreen but the house was quiet, she guessed he was either in bed or in the bath trying to ease his headache. As she looked up she saw a light on in the upstairs hall.

She got out of the car and opened the boot, piling the shopping bags in a row beside the car, leaving Bethany asleep while she took the bags inside. She lined them up in the hall, looking briefly around to see if Paul was there, then hurried back to the car to fetch Beth. Amanda lifted the sleeping child carefully from her seat and carried her into the living room placing her on the sofa still asleep, thumb in mouth while she went to put away the shopping.

"Paul?" she called standing at the bottom of the stairs, he didn't answer. She rested her hand on the banister and took one step up. "Paul, where are you?" Fear and dread washed over her suddenly as a little voice inside her head warned her not to panic, but she did! There was something very wrong. Amanda hurried up the stairs and by the time she had got to the bathroom her heart was pumping wildly. He had been in the bath, the water was still in the tub with towels everywhere, water covered the floor and she knew he had got out in a hurry. Amanda ran along the landing to the bedroom, it seemed to take forever until her hand finally curled around the handle and she opened the door.

Paul was slumped on the bed his legs hung over the edge as if he had been struggling to get up from his intolerable situation to get to the telephone! The left side of his face drooped grotesquely to one side and his skin was a sickly grey colour, mouth and nostrils tinged with blue, his beautiful blue eyes were wide and staring straight ahead with no recognition in them at all, they were so cloudy and dull like glass eyes with no sparkle, the soul had gone out of them, and in that moment it dawned on her that he was dead!

"PAUL! OH, NO, NO, NO!" Tears shed from her eyes, grief grabbed hold of her tightly as she thought about what life was going to be without him, terror washed over her like a deep wave. She darted forward forgetting everything; even Bethany for that terrible moment and dragged him onto the bed. "Oh No, God, Please!" She fumbled with the phone, and later in the nightmare hours that followed she couldn't even remember calling an ambulance, or even Madeline and Evan who had raced in behind her trying to breath back what little life Paul had left in him, she didn't even remember the drive to the hospital as Paul clung pitifully to life, or her mother who arrived to take care of little Bethany.

The hospital room was oppressively hot with a hint of antiseptic cloying the air. She remembered what Paul had said about hospital smells the day he came home. A melamine coffee table was in the centre of the room with old magazines and cigarette burns on the centre of its grubby surface. Over by the door stood an overflowing rubbish bin; and scattered around its base were the remains of cellophane wrappings; and empty cigarette packets that anxious people had discarded.

Madeline stood in front of her holding a styrene cup of syrupy coffee. "Drink this it'll make you feel better."

Evan gently took her hand. "It'll be okay Amanda, we're all here for you, and if there's anything you need?"

"Thanks Evan." She smiled. Then looked up at Madeline; silently thinking nothing would make her feel better, not any more! She looked milk white yet her face was shadowed with grief, and Madeline almost cried for her.

"What happened to him?" Amanda mumbled; everything was looking more like a dream than reality.

Madeline placed the cup on the chair next to her. "He's, he's had a very bad stroke."

"He's going to die?" Amanda asked fearfully.

Madeline struggled with the question wondering how she was going to answer. "I, I don't know, the doctors are fighting for him now, he has stopped breathing twice, so Amanda you must accept the worse possible scenario."

"He can't die!" she cried, "He's been through too much to die now!" She entwined her fingers together in an anxious knot.

"Amanda! Paul's a fighter, we know that, but you must accept that this time the fight may just be a little too tough for him, you have got to accept that." She rubbed Amanda's hands to warm them they had suddenly turned ice cold.

Madeline was sobbing inwardly, she still held Amanda's ice-cold hand firmly, as her head rested on her shoulder she stroked her long dark hair.

A nurse entered, smiled and asked if they wanted to see Paul, Amanda got to her feet on trembling legs and together they followed the nurse to the intensive care unit.

Paul lay naked and covered by a single sheet on a life support system, Amanda gazed at the pump as it inhaled and exhaled and realised with a sudden frightening clarity that this machine was the only thing keeping

Paul alive for the second time in only a few years. His damaged brain had severed all links with the outside world, his bloodless lips were still, and the greyness of his face told her all she really needed to know. Amanda stood there, her hand resting on the doorframe while Madeline's arm draped her waist. Her tearful eyes were riveted on the still form of her husband and her mind turned back to the first time they met, and in that instant she willed him to live. Evan looked silently on from the doorway.

A tall grey haired man waited silently behind her. "Mrs Marriott?" His kind grey eyes creased into a smile.

"Yes." She murmured.

"Can we go into my office?" Amanda nodded. He led them down a hall to a room on the right. It was a bright office a far cry from the gloom of the intensive care unit. The walls were light beige with a soft pastel blue blind at the window. He pulled out two chairs and gestured for them to sit.

"I am Mr Simpson the senior registrar in charge of stroke patients." He laced his hands in front of him on the large mahogany desk. He regarded the two women for a moment and his expression changed.

"There is no easy way to say this but your husband has suffered a massive stroke, this was due to an embolism, no one could have foreseen this unfortunately, but I'm afraid the outlook is very grim."

"But he will recover?" Amanda asked hopefully.

Mr Simpson looked down and unlaced his hands. "No, I'm afraid he won't, he has suffered severe brain damage and his left side is completely paralysed, he will never walk again even after therapy the damage is permanent. It is not a short term condition even though he is a relevantly a young man, the situation has not been helped by the earlier accident a couple of years back."

Amanda gazed intently at the registrar unable to take in what he was telling her.

"So he's going to die?" Her hand went to her throat as if to ease the terrible constriction that was hindering her breathing.

Mr Simpson looked at her with sympathy in his eyes. He picked up his pen and tapped it on the ink blotter in front of him. "No one can tell you that dear, but if he survives he will need constant care, bathing, feeding, he will be in a wheelchair for the rest of his life he will not be able to converse with you on an intelligent level it will be like looking after a baby twenty four hours a day."

"OH NO!" Amanda sobbed; Madeline reached out and clasped her trembling hand.

"We can arrange care for him; that is if he survives this stroke." Amanda said grasping at as many straws as she possibly could.

Mr Simpson frowned slightly. "Look, I know this is all negative answers, but I am trying to be realistic, the last thing I want to give you is false hope, the outlook as I said before is extremely grim."

Evan looked shocked to see them as they came back to the intensive care unit, Madeline shook her head at him, and he knew instantly what she was going to tell him. He took Amanda's hand. "Come on love; let's get you home, you can come back later."

Shaun threw his bag down on the old sofa and then hurried into the kitchen that also served as a bathroom. The bath was hidden under an old piece of hinged block board that was attached to a rotting waste pipe.

Peeling off his old sweatshirt he wiped his face with it then threw it in the corner with the rest of his dirty washing, those things he would deal with later.

Turning the tap on full, the water coughed, gurgled and then spurted from the rusty tap as it splattered into the bath. He was worried, his eyes fell on the bloodied shirt he had left overnight to soak in the small sink; snatching it up he wrung it out effortlessly while he gazed at the big ugly stain to see if it had vanished but It was still there despite scrubbing and washing and soaking in cold water, even vinegar wouldn't get it out. He muttered a curse and started scrubbing it again with a bar of soap, he had tried bleach but that had made it worse. He held it up and studied the stain; it had turned orange now from the bleach. He would have to burn it otherwise he would find himself going back to his youth, more time spent in police custody than at home enjoying his freedom!

He left the water running while he went back to the living room to look for the matches he had put down somewhere earlier on this morning. Where was he going to burn the shirt? He looked around and scratched his head. Somewhere in the woods would be a good place, and no one would find it there if he buried it underground! Running his hands through his greasy hair, he remembered the water and ran back to the bathroom.

Lowering himself into the water he was still worrying about the shirt and what to do with it. How could he have been so stupid to get blood on his shirt! He was angry with the police, they now knew about his past record? Perhaps it was time to move on? It was no use staying around here anymore it was just too dangerous. He closed his eyes and tried to relax, but he couldn't, so he opened them again staring up at the ceiling where a huge spider hung precariously from a web, he watched as it curled its spindly legs around the silken sheen and hauled itself up to the ceiling.

He had to hurry now, must get rid of the incriminating evidence. Dressing quickly he shaved cutting himself on the chin and nipping his upper lip, he cursed and blotted the tiny cuts with pieces of toilet paper, then he grabbed his watch from the edge of the sink, took a plastic bag and stuffed the wet shirt inside.

Tom had seen Shaun jump into his car with a bag and decided to follow him, he had a hunch about Shaun Riordan, it was too coincidental that he owned so many weapons and he was a likely candidate for violent crime, so he decided to follow him, see just where he was going in such a hurry. Night was closing in fast, if he had anything to hide now was the time to do it, and it looked as if they were heading towards the forest. Tom hung back as he saw Shaun turn off the road into a small clearing, he saw him take a shovel and an axe from the boot of his car. Tom parked on the tiny slip road and followed him deep into the forest.

Shaun turned, picked up the axe and dug a hole about three feet deep, next he picked up the plastic bag the shirt was in and tipped it into the hole; he took out a box of matches and lit one, it promptly went out the minute it touched the wet shirt, muttering a curse he tried again. The same thing happened. He sat back for a moment and studied the situation, wondering how he was going to burn a shirt still damp with water. He took the material in his strong hands and tried wringing out the last remaining drops of water and then he shoved it into the hole. "There! That's the best thing to do, bury the fucking thing so no one will ever find it!" He got to his feet brushing his hands over his jeans to get rid of the damp mouldy earth that stuck to them. He picked up the axe and shoved it into the bag.

Tom watched; a smile sneaked across his face. "Only an asshole like him could try and burn a wet shirt!"

Shaun took the stairs two at a time, his heart beat at an alarming rate, how he wished he had never gone near the place, he should have got rid of the shirt in the confines of his own room. He pulled off his sweatshirt and threw it into a corner and then collapsed in the armchair gasping for breath as sweat trickled down his brow like tiny rivers. The pounding in his head wouldn't stop and now he heard another sound, the running of feet, several feet! Nervously he glanced towards the door and then got up to look out of the window, he knew what was about to happen, his worst nightmare was going to unfold in less than a minute. Shaun studied the drop from the window, it was at least forty feet; from a height like that he would just end up either dead or seriously hurt!

The pounding on the door reverberated off the walls. Slowly he walked to the door.

"Police! Open the door!" Shaun paled and ran his fingers through his sweat-streaked hair.

"Good evening sir, may we come in?" Collins pushed past him without waiting for a reply.

"Where were you between eight and nine this evening?"

"Uh," Shaun thought quickly. "With a friend."

"Oh," Collins laughed, "Can't you be a little more original than that? Everyone has that alibi." He looked at him with amusement.

Shaun ran his fingers through his hair once more. "I was with a friend."

"Not in woods on the south side of town then?"

What was the point in lying? Someone had seen him

bury the shirt. He sat down defeated. "Okay, I went to burn some clothes, that's why you're here isn't it?"

"Only you didn't succeed, the ground was too damp and only you could try and burn a wet shirt, after all you're not the sharpest tool in the box are you Shaun?"

He hung his head. "So now you know what I was doing in the woods." He said quietly.

"Are you confessing to murder?"

Now he looked up angrily. "Murder? If I was confessing I wouldn't be telling you for a start, you're a fucking head case! I'll tell you the truth seeing as you asked so nicely. I was out poaching a few weeks back and I sat on the grass, I noticed a small medallion lying on the ground and I leaned forward to pick it up, I didn't notice there was blood there and my shirt sleeve rubbed in it, I hadn't noticed it until you pulled me in, I thought it was best to get rid of it I just knew I would be the prime suspect with my criminal record, that's why I wanted to burn the shirt."

"And you expect us to believe that?"

"It's true, I swear to God."

"Haldane, could you show him what you have in the bag?"

D.S. Haldane held a plastic forensic sealed top bag and held it up to Shaun. "An officer saw you in the woods; this is what you were trying to burn."

Shaun frowned he studied the shirt for a moment, and for a fleeting second an immense wave of relief flooded through him. "That is not my shirt! That is not the shirt I was trying to burn."

"No? This was the shirt you dropped, only you weren't clever enough to realise it was gone in your panic to get rid of all the evidence." Haldane said still holding the plastic bag in front of him. "I saw you wearing it the night you were at the police station."

"Not that one! It is not the same shirt, take it out of the bag I'll see for myself, I have one similar, but that is not mine, it has a bright orange stain on the front, its blood I admit but this shirt is red with blood!"

"I can't take it out of the bag it's for forensic evidence." Haldane replied. "You dropped it Shaun, you must have; it was lying on the floor after you passed."

"You mentioned a medallion, where is it now?" Collins asked him.

"Over there on the television…I am telling you the truth, that shirt is not mine, I buried the one I tried to burn." His face had gone the colour of grainy marble.

"I know." Haldane told him. "We recovered it I wonder which of the victim's blood will be on that one?"

Collins walked over to the television that was perched on top of a small table. As he picked up the tiny medallion his heart raced, he turned it over and on the back were the words. 'To Mel with love from Nana' He turned it over again and gazed at the praying hands, what a lovely present to give a grandchild. Here was little Melanie's medallion covered in her killers fingerprints, he couldn't have wished for a stronger, better conviction, Shaun Riordan had sealed his own fate.

He turned to Shaun. "This used to belong to a little girl of sixteen who was hacked to death on her way home from a party on a lonely road, and this my friend, is as good a confession to murder as we'll ever get." He lifted the medallion with the tip of his ballpoint pen and placed it in a sealed forensic bag.

Shaun stepped towards him. "WAIT! I didn't kill anyone...I swear to God!"

Collins looked at him sourly. "What a bloody hypocrite! How on earth can you use the lord's name in vain after what you did?"

"I never killed anyone, I didn't do it! I swear I didn't, and that shirt isn't mine!" He looked at Haldane who met his gaze with accusation. "You don't believe me do you? None of you do."

Haldane ignored him, turning to Collins he said. "If you look in the kitchen Inspector I'm sure you will find other items of clothing and an axe which could be the murder weapon."

Collins nodded his head. "Well, if any of the clothing apart from the shirt matches blood from the DNA samples from Melanie then you are in big shit mate, real big time!"

"He could pull through!" Madeline mumbled to herself, but she knew that it was just hope that made her voice her thoughts.

Amanda turned around in her chair. "Do you really feel he will?" She was hoping that Madeline's was right. Amanda crossed the room quickly, desperately, she gripped Madeline's arm. "If we pray together, our prayers will be answered, he has fought so hard to live Madeline" Her eyes searched her face pleadingly.

"Ok," Madeline whispered and took Amanda's hands in her own and together they prayed. Madeline could feel every hurt that Amanda was feeling, it was like a knife going through her own heart and it was breaking, it was as much as she could do to hold back her own wracking sobs.

They sat for hours watching Paul, stroking his brow, whispering to him, willing him to live when Madeline took his cold hand in hers she suddenly noticed his eyes.

"HIS EYES!" She said. "Their open!"

Paul's eyes looked so dull and lifeless as if his soul had departed his body and left an empty shell.

"Paul?" Amanda called softly, her heart thudding in her chest. "Paul can you hear me?" She studied his prince like features they were still the same as before.

The Doctor arrived so suddenly he startled her and she moved away from Paul's side as the doctor shone a torch directly into Paul's eyes, he blinked and Amanda took this as a positive sign.

"Is he getting better?" she asked hopefully.

"He is still critical, not much change I'm afraid."

Collins was reading over Shaun's statement as Haldane walked in. "By the way more bad news, have you heard about Mr Marriott?"

Haldane turned sharply, dropping his gloves onto his desk. "No, I haven't, why what's happened to him?"

"He's had a massive stroke, could have been caused from the head injury."

"That was ages ago." Haldane replied. "He was doing so well."

"Sometimes things take time to come out."

"Is he going to be alright?"

"No, I'm afraid not this time, it doesn't look good, he's still critical."

"Well, that means we could charge Shaun with grievous bodily harm with intent, I don't think he should get away with the injuries caused to Mr Marriott."

"He's not going to get away with anything. " Collins went hurriedly towards the door.

"Oh, by the way, the forensic reports are back, the blood was a match, you can charge Shaun Riordan with the murder of Melanie."

Amanda tried lighting the fire and each time she struck a match a wind gusted down from the chimney and blew it out. She lit the match a third time burning her finger as she watched the glowing ember and carefully pointed it towards the paper. "Oh FUCK IT!" she yelled dropping the match, it flickered and then went out once more.

She slammed herself down in the chair holding her head in her hands as if it was about to drop from her shoulders. The news had been bad from the hospital; just before they had left Paul had developed breathing problems again and had to be put back on the ventilator, and by the time they had got back home Madeline developed a sickening migraine.

Wiping a tear with the back of her hand she was beginning to feel as if she had taken too many sleeping pills and given herself a hangover, she felt sick, weak and drained of her energy. She stared angrily at the unlit fire; she knew she needed to buy some firelighters the next time she was in town, if she had to do things on her own then it was better to be prepared. She opened the box of matches, lit one carefully and finally it caught the paper. At last she felt as if she had achieved something, she walked over towards the bay window and pulled back the curtains. The grey lumpy clouds greeted her with conviction and added to her already dismal mood. She wanted to cry; in fact she knew if she didn't stop crying now she never would.

She had decided to leave Madeline sleep this morning; after all, she had put her own life on hold for her and Bethany, and she hardly saw Evan; he only managed to get up here once a week and she was more than aware that their relationship was getting stronger by the day, he had been such a rock to them both.

She staggered towards the kitchen to make coffee, filling the kettle and plugging in the socket, she felt like a robot, just doing things on command. The sudden tap on the window almost made her collapse with shock, she spun around and her hand flew to her chest. Tom Page's face appeared at the window. Amanda gasped as she headed towards the back door to let him in.

"I wasn't aware the front door had vanished overnight! You almost gave me a heart attack! What are you doing here?"

"Oh I'm sorry, I'm really sorry, I came up to tell you how sorry I was to hear about your husband, is there anything I can do?"

"No, there's nothing anyone can do at the moment, anyway. Are you looking for Madeline?"

"No, not in particular, I just came to say how sorry I was to hear about your husband."

Amanda smiled, she felt sorry she had been so sharp towards him besides it was kind of him to come all this way.

"Would you like to come in for a coffee?"

"That would be nice, thank you."

By the time Madeline had roused herself from sleep, Amanda had been talking easily with Tom.

CHAPTER ELEVEN

Jay Greenford was an American lawyer; he had come to England to gain some insight into the British Justice system, and his experience of the American criminals and the law courts in the USA gave him enough bite to send any decent criminal to hell and back with hair triggering nerve tingling justice, because Jay was a good lawyer, one of the best. He wasn't 'handsome' but 'cute' as the Americans would say he liked to think of himself as a 'serious minded intellectual sort of guy' His sharp cute features paled almost to insignificance by prominently large hazel eyes that peered like two orbs from light tortoise shell glasses. As he entered Shaun's cell his eyes travelled slowly over his client.

"Good morning Mr Riordan, my names Jay Greenford I'm going to be representing your case. He walked over to the desk, took out a notepad and a pen from his briefcase and then placed it on the floor beside him. "Okay if I sit down?" without waiting for a reply he sat on the high-backed chair facing Shaun.

Shaun studied him closely, there was no hint of a smile on his face, just silence for what seemed to be an age and then he said. "What's a Yank doing here?"

"I'm here to help you Shaun…May I call you Shaun?" he asked. Shaun nodded.

Shaun sat forward lacing his calloused hands in front of him. "Oh well, what the hell! Maybe you could get me a treble life sentence or even the electric chair." He said without humour.

"Mr Riordan, if you had been living in the United States you would have been found guilty of first degree homicide and that is exactly what you would have got!" Jay smiled to make him feel at ease, at ease enough that he wasn't living in the United States.

"I'm not here to convict you I'm here to help so let's get that straight from the beginning, I'm not on their side, I'm on yours, and I'm your defence Lawyer."

Shaun looked at him, the corner of his mouth curled into what could be taken as a kind of smile.

"So, getting back to the night of the murders? Well, let's just concentrate on the Melanie Thomas case first. That is the only murder you have been charged with isn't it?" Frowning as he turned over the notes he had made on his notepad.

"Yeah, I've never even met the girl, I don't know her, never even seen her!"

"Okay, did anyone see you that night, talk to you?"

"No Sir."

"Can you prove where you were that night?"

"No Sir."

"Is there anything you can think of that could prove where you were that night? Or a neighbour you might have seen or talked to, it could be possible that you might have forgot? Did you go to a pub; or a restaurant that night?"

"No Sir, I don't have the money for all those stylish places, don't even have any friends really, I'm a bit of a loner."

Jay leaned back on the chair, his notebook empty his pen laid at the side of the pad. He ran his hands through his hair and looked at Shaun.

"Mr Riordan, I don't think you realise the seriousness of the situation we have here! There is blood all over your clothing that matches the blood taken from Melanie, they have the axe! Now you're in deep trouble pal, if you can't find anything of real help and try to cooperate with me, then our case is out the window before we even get into the goddamned court!"

Shaun looked mortified, it was now dawning on him that the situation he found himself in was serious, extremely serious if he couldn't prove where he was that night or who he was with then his liberty was in dire jeopardy!

"I'm trying to cooperate; I don't know anyone around

here! I can't even remember where I was that night it's all a blur! I know I'm fucked."

Jay leaned forward he looked concerned and anxious all in one go. "Shaun," he said picking up the notepad again. "There must be someone who saw you that night, *think!* Did you go to a local pub? Did you see the girl? Try and remember were you in that area?"

"I can't remember because it never happened! I swear to you Mr Greenford I never killed anyone, I didn't see the girl, even if I had I would never have known who she was! Why won't anyone believe me?"

"With your history of assault, armed robbery you're expecting people to believe you! Oh get real Shaun, I don't think a grand jury would believe you for a minute, you were seen trying to burn the evidence, I've never worked on such a cut and dried case such as this one!"

"Look, I poach, right or wrong that's what I do, I sat on the grass and noticed the small medallion lying on the grass about a foot or two away from me, I leant over to pick it up and noticed a lot of blood around the area, before I knew it the blood had got on the cuff of my shirt, and then as I picked it up blood was all over my fingers so I wiped it on my jeans, I admitted trying to burn the shirt because a week before the police had picked me up regarding these murders, I panicked! The reason I panicked was because of my previous record, also there was a second white shirt they claimed was mine, it wasn't, I have never seen it before in my life! And it was not there before so where did the second shirt come from? It certainly wasn't there when I went to burn the shirt that belonged to me".

"So are you saying there was another white shirt identical to the one you were trying to get rid of buried in the same place?"

"No, I'm saying it wasn't there before I dug the hole, someone else put it there."

Jay shook his head. "I'll look into that."

He knew this was going to be a very difficult case to prove unless something came up.

"Tell me Mr Greenford, what is the least that could happen to me?"

Jay clasped his hands together and frowned.

"I'm not going to kid you Shaun, there is nothing to prove you were never at the scene of the crime, all the evidence points to you, there are all the forensic material that says you are the killer, it is going to be the devil of a job to convince a jury otherwise." He looked at Shaun doubtfully.

"So, what does that actually mean?"

"It means Shaun that you are looking at being institutionalised without limit of time."

"Institutionalised? What does that mean?"

"It means Shaun that you don't get out until they find the cheapest ply shaped in the form of a long wooden box."

Collins waited while Amanda unlocked the door. She looked shockingly pale as she saw him standing there with his police hat in his hand.

"Is my husband alright?" She asked, her face paling even more as panic built up inside and almost made her slam the door on them.

Inspector Collins smiled to calm her obvious fear. "I haven't come about your husband; I have some positive news for you both." He noticed her looking down at his hat. "Oh the hat!" he grinned. "I always carry it when I visit somewhere, its called manners."

"That's what made me think bad, police officers always take off their hats when they arrive on the doorstep to give you terrible news."

Haldane stood beside him his eyes fixed anxiously on Amanda.

Inspector Collin's smiled at her broadly.

"I called to see if Miss Richards is in also?"

She was about to say that Madeline was in the bath when she heard her voice from behind. "I'm here Sergeant."

Madeline stood at the foot of the stairs with a green

ribbon tying back her hair. The green jumper she wore made her eyes stand out in stark contrast; the sapphire blue visibly clear. She walked towards them.

"Ah, Miss Richards, we have charged a man with the murder of Melanie Thomas, and obviously the other deaths too; although he can only be charged with one murder, we are almost certain that he is the same man we arrested before."

"Are you sure it is the same man Inspector?"

"Absolutely, he has been found with all the evidence on him, and we are going to see if we can get him on assaulting your husband, but we need evidence of that, and it is going to be difficult to prove."

"I'd say it is virtually impossible after so long." Amanda said. "You'd never prove it now."

"You're probably right Mrs Marriott, the only trouble is there is no one to identify him because the only survivor is Mrs Jeffries and she is unable to give a description at the moment, the only other person to see him that night was the bar manager, we showed him snapshots of the suspect but he couldn't be sure it was the same guy that night in the pub."

"Did he attack her?"

"He gave her grief, but he may not have been the same man that attacked her, but we have concrete evidence that fits Melanie's DNA it was found on his clothes."

"I am so glad Inspector; at last he's been caught after all this time! What will happen to him?"

"Well, no doubt he will be incarcerated for the rest of his life, probably in a hospital for the criminally insane."

"What happens if he gets off?" Madeline asked frowning.

"Oh he won't, not a chance, the evidence on him is too strong, we have him sewn up so tightly the case could never fall apart, even without an identity parade he's stitched so secure he will never ever get out of prison; or hospital, and I can give you my word on that Mrs Marriott."

"So at least I can take comfort in the knowledge that he is going to pay for wrecking mine and my daughter's life? Can you tell us his name?"

"Yes, it will be released on the news later today, his names Shaun Riordan."

Amanda frowned and looked at Madeline, she shook her head.

"I've never heard of him." Madeline replied shaking her head.

Madeline walked across the road to meet Amanda for lunch in the café, Amanda didn't have much to say either they were both stunned by the recent news of Shaun's arrest. After all this time she could hardly believe that her nightmare was finally coming to an end, this man had stalked her for almost two years and now he was going to be safely locked away for the rest of his natural life. All there was to worry about now was Paul, she was so bitter Shaun was the main cause for all this. He had robbed her of everything, her life was over with Paul as a man and wife, Bethany would never have a brother or sister, the killer had made sure of that! It was thanks to him that Paul laid in a hospital bed a helpless invalid, his life destroyed along with his soul, she would never have anymore children with Paul, he was incapable of that now, her sex life was finished, her child production was finished and she hated him more than anything in the world for that! How she wished the death sentence were still law, she would just love to witness his execution! But her love for Paul remained intact she would care for him until the end if that is what it took, for as long as he lived.

Amanda looked up as Madeline came into the café, she had lost all track of time, she could have been sitting there for ten minutes or two hours, a depression had hit her so bad this morning. She briefly gave Evan a wave, he was busy serving two customers, but as soon as he saw her his eyes lit up.

She put her bag on the floor and pulled out the chair. "How are you feeling Amanda?" she knew how badly Amanda had taken the news of the killers arrest, it was a finality to a heartbreak Amanda had lived with for a long time and would continue to live with until Paul's death.

"How do I feel?" she replied still looking into her coffee

cup that had now gone cold on the table in front of her. "I feel…Angry, devastated. I want him dead for what he's put me and other woman through."

"So," Madeline said. "What happens now?"

Amanda seemed to lift from her deep seated depression. "We go to the trial, he has been charged with one count of murder, unless he admits to the others which I'm sure he will; let us hope that he will be sent to hell and back twice."

Madeline lowered her eyes to the ground. "Well, I'd better hurry; I might get home a little earlier if I shorten my lunch hour."

"I'll go on to mum's then." Amanda said. "I'll pick you up at five."

"Ok, I'll wait outside the firm for you." Amanda watched as Madeline left the café, she could see her crossing the road towards her firm.

"Amanda, what would you like to drink?" Evan asked.

"Oh, I'll have coffee please"

He took her empty cup as she watched him walk to the counter, in some ways he reminded her of Paul except he was dark opposed to Paul's blond hair. This started a deep painful gnawing deep inside her of things that would never be now, no more romantic dinners; no more evenings alone together, no more lovemaking and this sent her world crashing through her! How on this Gods earth was she going to get through without his love? Never again would she feel his arms around her, his lips brushing hers. His words of love, his body pressed so closely to hers. He would never be capable of lingering moments of tenderness. His life had been so awful; maybe not to him it didn't, but she thought his life had been so lonely, no family, no mother or father. He had spent most of his childhood in care with people that didn't really worry about him they were paid for doing a job! There were so many kids they cared for how could they possibly care about one solitary child? Tears began to fall and she grabbed a tissue from her bag and quickly dried them away before Evan came back!

He returned with the coffees. "Thanks." she said taking the mug from his hand.

"I'm glad they've got him." he said.

"No more than I am."

"Have you seen him? "

"No, the police wouldn't let me see him, as far as they are concerned, there is no proof he attacked Paul."

"I know." he said quietly." Doesn't help you though does it?"

"If he just gets a life term in prison at least I know he can never hurt anyone again."

"Let's just hope so, everyone can relax now."

Amanda looked away from him turning her attention to an old couple sitting together two tables away, they must have been married for years they looked so comfortable with each other.

"I'll be able to relax when Paul gets better and comes home... In one piece." she replied with a faint hint of a smile.

"I know love, God willing, Anyway Amanda, better get on or I'll be getting the sack. Anything you want don't hesitate to call me, I'll always be here."

Amanda smiled and nodded her head. "Thank you Evan."

She pulled the car out of the car park. The muscles tightened around her shoulders and a headache had started thrumming at the back of her eyes.

Megan glanced at the kitchen clock, rubbing her wet hands down her apron front. "He's late again!" She snapped heading towards the stairs, "David!" She called, resting her hands on her hips. "David Williams, you're late for work!"

She hurried up the stairs angry with him because he'd made her climb the flight of stairs with a painful hip that had been playing her up all morning, she had just been diagnosed with an arthritic hip, and now she was on the list for a hip replacement. Megan looked surprised as she opened the bedroom door and found his bed empty. He hadn't come home last night! She shook her head anxiously he never stayed out when he knew he had to get up for work in the morning.

Limping along the landing she went back downstairs. It had hit her a long time ago that David was no longer a little boy, she couldn't run his life for him and of course, she had no intention of doing so, but she wasn't going to have him disappear without telling her when he was coming back! "He's so selfish." She mumbled.

She was halfway down when the door opened.

"Where the hell have you been?" For a moment she stared at his white shirt, it was covered in blood and a few of the buttons were missing, her eyes travelled towards his hand where the left one supported the right. Blood seeped from the injured hand, and his face was covered in mud.

"What The hell happened to you!!" She gasped, heading towards him.

David threw his car keys down on the table. "Oh I just killed a woman, chopped her up and buried her in the woods, she put up quite a fight!" he laughed.

"David! That isn't funny!"

"Oh lighten up mother! It's just a joke, bad taste though I must admit, I had an accident on my way home, and I went to see some mates over at Black rock and got a bloody puncture." He headed for the kitchen grabbing a wet cloth on his way.

"David!" Megan called; she was already reaching for the first aid box.

"It's okay Mum, it looks far worse than it is."

"Why didn't you phone?"

"Oh I left my phone here; I forgot about it, I'd left it on charge."

"Well, you could have found a coin box?"

Megan had David's hand flat out on the kitchen table examining it like a true professional.

"What was the point in that?" David replied irritably. "I left the guys at two thirty this morning, what was the use in ringing you at that time, to give you a stroke or something?"

"Well how did you hurt yourself so badly?"

"The Jack slipped and cut my hand it's not that bad."

"I think you should go to the hospital with this." Megan frowned deeply at the wide gash in his palm."

"Stop fussing mum, it'll be fine once I get it dressed properly."

"Oh have it your way; you usually do." She put the lid back on the first aid box and screwed the top back on the T.C.P. bottle.

"Mum?"

"What now?"

"Will you call work for me, tell them I've cut myself badly and I need to go to the hospital."

"Huh." She shrugged. "I thought you said it was okay?"

"No, perhaps I should get it looked at, it may need stitches."

"Trust you always Boy, Just when I need some wood chopped something like this happens. By the way, where is the axe? I always keep it in the shed hanging on a hook."

"Oh, the axe, I've got it in the boot of my car, I'll get it for you later."

"If you give me the keys to the car I'll fetch it myself."

"No! I'll get it later, I don't want you disturbing everything in the boot, it's somewhere among the rubbish."

She gave him a strange look and then went out to the kitchen.

The girl had never felt alone so much as she did right now, sitting in this man's car, he frightened her and she guessed that she would not be getting the deal she hoped for. She had been drifting for days, she was homeless, another government statistic that had forgot how to use soap and water, or what to do with the taps on a bathtub. A musky odour seemed to seep from her pores; her hands and face were ingrained with filth. She looked at him helplessly.

"Why did you pick me up?" she murmured. "I only want a couple of pound for a drink and a bed for the night. She was young, he reckoned her age to be twenty, to twenty five.

"Well don't think it's sex I'm after, I wouldn't touch you with a twenty foot barge pole."

"So, what do you want then?"

The girl had been a drug addict from the age of twelve, an unwanted child from an uncaring mother, pretty much the same as him.

"A bit of fun you sad bitch."

She sat in silence, used to being abused, it was nothing new to her, but the thing that worried her now was; what form of abuse was she going to take. He looked a cruel man, a strong spiteful man that she was not going to be able to stop should he wish to really hurt her! But if he was going to give her money for her next fix then the risk was worth taking.

"Does anyone know where you are?" he snapped.

She looked towards him quickly. "No, I don't have anyone, no family, nothing, why?"

"Where do you live then?"

"Streets, shop doorways, hostels if I can get one."

"You took a risk in the dark you don't know who I am."

"Look Mister, I need cash real quick, and I'm willing to do whatever to get it, take me to a hotel. I can have a shower and you can do whatever you like…But I need money." She begged.

"Oh, really, you think I want to screw your ass off? You know what? You're just like my mother, out for what is best for HER."

"Ok, don't get out of your pram, I only made a suggestion." Fear was slowly uncurling inside her.

He reached over and grabbed her throat. She gasped, terror lit up her eyes.

He opened the door and dragged her out of the car.

"Are you scared? I can even see what you're thinking! Yes, it was me who killed those entire woman, me!! And do you know why I did it? Would you like me to tell you? Huh? I did it for the hell of it! I just can't help it you see. Always had this urge to kill since I was ten! Not animals though, I love them, they are the only loyal creature's left on this planet my dear. And you are just another piece of shit!"

He dragged her down the rocks; there was no use

fighting anymore her resistance was unyielding. Her head fell forward, her hair hung over her face and she whimpered.

"You see." He snatched her hair from her face and lifted her head. "At times life can be a BITCH! Like now!" he raised his hand and pulled back his arm, the iron fist rammed into her face knocking out three teeth and splitting her lip, the second shattered her cheekbone splintering her eye, and her whole face seemed to explode. And then he pulled the axe from his rucksack.

Amanda took up her usual position beside Paul's bed, staring at the ventilator, each day watching him deteriorate even more than the day before. Sometimes he would open his eyes only for a second, but they looked the same, there was no change. She took his hand and leaned close to him.

"Paul, come back darling, we need you so much." Then cradling his hand she gazed down on his still grey features. His left eye was not as cloudy as his right one, but she knew he had completely lost the sight of that eye permanently.

"Oh God!" she sobbed. "How I wish things were the same as they had been before this nightmare happened, we had each other, and things were normal. Paul, I love you so very much."

She couldn't stop the tears; they flooded down her face like a fast flowing river. Just then Paul opened his eyes, he seemed to be staring at her as if he was trying so hard to remember who she was and he was frowning, and then he gave her hand a gentle squeeze in a gesture that was so weak it was hardly noticeable, but she knew the significance of it. As she looked at him she noticed a tear roll from the corner of his eye.

"Oh Paul! I love you so very, very much, I always will, forever."

Madeline had been cooking by the time Amanda had got back; she dried her hands on the tea towel and went to meet her at the front door. "How is he?" She asked, but she knew the answer was going to be the same as it always was.

Amanda shook her head. "He squeezed my hand." She said.

"Wasn't that a good sign?"

"It was more like a goodbye." She replied almost choking on a sob.

"Come into the kitchen." Madeline replied. She had watched Amanda's mood drop to its lowest ebb the last couple of days.

They sat down to eat, Amanda's appetite was low she picked at her food shoving it carefully around the plate. Her nerves were like raw ends, she had made sure to tell people not to call her at home due to the gravity of Paul's illness so her evenings were taken up calling people to give them the rundown on the days events, so when the phone did ring for a few minutes they both sat gazing at each other as they had done a few hours ago, neither of them wanting to answer it. It was Madeline who got up wearily to answer it, trying to lighten her mood by saying. "It's probably your mother."

With legs like leaden weights she walked slowly towards the telephone. A dread washed over her like none she had ever experienced before, she knew who it was before her hand reached out for the receiver.

"Mrs Marriott?" A cultured voice asked.

"Uh, she's right here, who's calling?"

"St Andrews hospital."

She turned and handed the phone to Amanda who had followed her down the hall.

"It's St Andrews." Madeline already knew why they were calling, she knew and she was ready.

To Amanda it all seemed like a dream, it was as if she was floating towards the telephone, her hand outstretched but not really wanting to take it as a sudden coldness engulfed her and she knew what they were going to tell her.

"Mrs Marriott?"

"Yes." A sudden pause, her heart was thudding so loudly that for a moment she thought she would never hear the other person's voice on the end of the line.

"I am afraid I have some very bad news." Another pause. "Your husband passed away at five fifteen this afternoon, I'm afraid it was so quick we didn't have time to contact you, he suffered another severe stroke and it caused a cardiac arrest, we did try to resuscitate him but I'm afraid there was nothing more we could do. I'm so sorry for your loss, you may see him if you wish."

The phone fell from her hands; she dropped to her knees and her face crumbled. Madeline took the phone, mumbled her thanks and then cradled Amanda in her arms.

"OH No! Paul, Paul, he's gone Madeline!! He's gone."

Madeline tried to calm her, to shoulder some of the pain but it was no good. "At least he's not suffering now; try to think of it in that way Amanda, he's out of his pain."

But Amanda's pain was only just beginning, and her grief was almost consuming her.

The first person Madeline rang was Megan, and within a half an hour Megan, Reece, and David were at the house. It was not really a shock to Megan as she had always expected it. Amanda lay wrapped in a blanket, with her head on David's lap, she had felt so cold, it got into her bones and made her feel as if her blood had turned from fluid to ice. David stroked her hair in an attempt to calm her between sobs while Megan gazed out of the window at the bleak evening, although the sun had appeared in the sky like a bright orange duster the day had been so grim it had hardly been noticed at all. Reece sat in the armchair sombrely smoking his pipe and gazing into space, he had never really been very good at offering words of comfort, so he chose to say nothing. The air was charged with emotion.

The telephone rang, it had been put on low but Madeline heard it. "Just a minute, I'll see who it is." She left the room quietly and lifted the receiver in the hall.

"Miss Richards?"

"Oh Chief Inspector, I'm afraid now is not a good time."

"Yes, I had heard, I am just calling to offer mine and D.S. Haldane's deepest sympathy to Mrs Marriott, it's dreadful news, I'm so sorry. When did he die?"

"This evening, he had another stroke and that was the end unfortunately, he was very ill for weeks."

"Oh, dear, we all thought he might make an improvement, but obviously it was not meant to be. Would it be alright if we came to see her? Not today of course, but maybe later in the week."

"Yes of course, that is so kind of you, I'm sure she will be pleased to see you." Madeline replied quietly.

Ray Collin's put the phone down the sadness of Paul Marriott's death had somehow shocked him. He looked out of the window in his office and watched the sun slip off the edge of a streaked dark purple horizon, and he began to wonder how quickly things can change in one afternoon. Although he didn't know Paul very well he liked him, he had touched everyone's life even though it was only briefly, he could still hear Madeline's voice sounding like a feathery echo drifting breathlessly across the airwaves and softly diminishing into a silent wave of grief.

Megan handed two painkillers to Amanda; she held out her hand then cupped them tightly in her palm. Her grief had reached the anger stage; her face was white as chalk and her eyes became as dark as a threatening thunderstorm. She pulled herself up to a firmer sitting position and pushed away the blanket. David took it and laid it on the side of the sofa.

"I can't believe I'll never see him again!" she whimpered. "Of course, inevitably we were doomed from the moment we set foot in this damned house!"

She turned to Madeline who sat beside her on the floor with her knees bent up to her chest and both arms wrapped around her legs, her chin propped miserably on her knees.

"I feel so cheated! My little girl has been robbed of her father, and all this is due to Shaun Fucking Riordan! I hope to God he rots in hell, and they pick the hottest spot for him!"

Megan walked towards her she held a tissue in her hands that was damp from her tears she sat on the edge of the sofa and draped her arm around Amanda's crumbling shoulders.

"Darling, look, it is no use accusing anyone now, it's happened; you have no proof of anything."

Amanda looked up at her. "Oh yes I have, I know in my heart." She replied bitterly. "That is what led to his death."

"Let's just see what the inquest brings, its no use punishing yourself my darling." It was Reece who spoke now and it was the first words he had echoed since his arrival. He tapped his pipe on the ashtray, and grey ash fell into the ashtray perched on the edge of the armchair.

"Punish myself! I'm going to live in purgatory for the rest of my life!" her voice cracked to a mere croak; her eyes were red and puffy, her face stained with pale lines that looked like welts. "Paul was too young to die in the way he did, old people die from strokes, not thirty nine year old men!"

"Amanda." Madeline said. "I know Paul was young, that is what the Autopsy is for! Because he died so young from an illness usually associated with age, but young people do have strokes too, even small children sometimes, not often thank God but it does happen!"

Megan had made her some hot chocolate to chase the painkillers down; Amanda took the mug from her mother's hands and nodded blankly, then swallowed them. She had a sensation that she was in a dream world where reality was so far away and it made her feel as if she wasn't really here at all! The pain she had in her head had become a real cracker, thumping away at the back of her eyes, it didn't take her long to realise that it was the same kind of pain she got the night Paul was attacked!

CHAPTER TWELVE

Amanda went to the undertakers on that Sunday morning; she had to see him one last time

She wore a simple black dress with no lace or frills, it emphasised her shockingly pale features. She wasn't in control anymore, her world had been broken; her grief was swallowing her up so fast that she wondered how the hell was she going to get through the ordeal of seeing her dead husband lying in a white satin coffin! It just wasn't real.

Right now she couldn't see any future, her days had no endings, her nights were full of desolation, and in the morning when she finally woke up she knew she had to face another day with no visits to the hospital to see Paul! At least when he was in the hospital unit she could see him, she could feel him, touch him, and at least that was something even if he didn't wake up! He was there, he was alive and she had something! But now she had nothing.

David locked the car and followed her inside. Madeline slipped an arm around her waist as they opened the door to the undertakers. The red carpet seemed to go on forever as they walked along the hall towards the chapel of rest. Soft music was playing 'Ave Maria' in the background. The undertaker showed them the chapel where Paul lay. "Take as long as you like my dear." He nodded his head slightly and then left them quietly alone with their thoughts. Candle bulbs lit the tiny chapel giving it a depressing sombre appearance. The lights were low and softly glowing, 'the twilight effect again' she murmured softly.

Paul lie in a light Oak coffin his face was so pale and wax like in appearance against the pure white silk pillow that rested beneath his head. Despite his rapid death he looked so young, Amanda knew he had gone back twenty years, there was no laughter lines around his mouth that she had once found so attractive, there was not one line on his face, his mouth didn't droop anymore, in fact there wasn't any sign that he had died from a massive stroke! His lips were firm. She looked on him brokenly and for one moment she wondered if he wasn't really dead at all, that this had all been a terrible mistake and he was just sleeping! She expected him to open his eyes and smile at her. But she knew that was not going to happen. She reached out and touched his face and a chill shot up her arm as if she had touched something cased in ice. She watched his chest, it was still and the little pulse in his neck that she had gazed at so often in the hospital was no longer beating. It was final! He was dead. Her eyes moved over him in total disbelief, this body now a shell that had cast out a beautiful spirit in the form of a handsome young man!

Hopelessness washed over her then. She leaned forward with her head resting against his chest and Madeline bit her lip in despair.

"Paul, I don't think I can live in this world without you!"

Madeline stepped toward her. "It's Okay, it'll be okay."

"No it will never be alright ever again Madeline, how can I go on without him in my life?"

"For Bethany you must." She soothed.

The lights had gone out in her world, and they would never come on again.

David stood at the door waiting for the hearse to arrive; watching his sister with quiet concern. He had always seen himself as the man of steel with a heart as soft as marshmallow, but now his hard steel like image started to melt faster than warmed up butter; he felt himself fighting back the tears.

With his hands held together in front of him he stood there, silently like a sentinel. Amanda sat as tensely as a man in the death chamber awaiting that final jolt of electricity to surge through his body, two arms resting stiffly with white knuckles gripping the arms of the chair. A black veil hid her shockingly pale features as they waited silently for the hearse to arrive. Megan, Madeline, Evan and Reece watched from the window for the hearse while David went over to sit on the sofa next to Amanda.

Quietly the undertaker arrived removing his hat as he entered the room. "We're ready Miss Richards." He said bowing his head respectfully.

Frost lay on the ground as an imitation of snow in its sharp and silvery whiteness that was mirrored by a ray of sun that hit the ground. It seemed like forever the drive to the cemetery, no one spoke, no one moved, their heads turned towards the windows. In everyone's hand was a Kleenex as the limousines rolled over the gravel. This was the resting place of the dead, and she could hardly bring herself to believe that this was where she would be burying her husband in his final resting place

Amanda kept her eyes on the Oak coffin as it was lowered into the grave. In her hand she held a single red rose with which she hesitated before she threw it down on top of the coffin.

A chasm! Oh God Paul that's where you ended up! And her tears came, they flowed once again like a river, she wondered if they would ever stop until the last ounce of fluid had left her body. She was so cold now despite the frost of the early morning, it was turning out to be a reasonably bright day. The sun warmed the earth a little, but it did not warm her soul. She felt so cold her brain was numb she couldn't think, besides, she had nothing worthwhile to think about right now. She wrapped her arms around herself until Madeline moved closer slipping a warm comforting arm around her small waist.

How cold Paul must be, she thought and she shivered. "You okay?" Madeline asked with concern. Amanda nodded. She could barely hear the words as the priest read from his prayer book, except "Ashes to ashes, dust to dust." and she watched his cassock as it whipped about in the wind.

"Goodbye my darling." she whispered as David and Madeline led her away from the grave.

Jay Greenford had waited in reception for half an hour for Dan Haldane, he closed the file on Shaun Riordan and put it in his case, they were still waiting for a court date for the trial, but he had been remanded in custody until that time. He got up as he saw Haldane enter through the main door.

"Ah, I've been waiting to see you D.S Haldane. I thought you had forgotten me."

"I'm sorry for the delay Mr Greenford, come into my office."

"What can I do for you? I take it you have come here regarding Shaun Riordan?" He gestured to the chair in front of his desk.

"Yes, look, I have been to several places since we last met, I have talked to people that knew Shaun and no one is convinced he killed Melanie Thomas, D.S. Haldane I have serious reservations about this case."

"Have you?" Haldane leaned forward and opened his own police file on Riordan. "He was convicted of serious assault in 2001, in 1993 he was convicted of armed robbery, he served seven years in prison, uh, Belmarsh in London?"

"I know that, but if you look at his history, none of his crimes were against woman?"

"Yes, I know that too Mr Greenford, but there is always a first time for everything, he is a very angry young man."

Haldane studied him for a moment thoughtfully, now he was putting doubts in his mind.

"The shirt we found, apart from the one he tried to burn, it was on the killer the night he killed Melanie, and it has her blood all over it."

"He says that shirt did not belong to him."

"I know, but it was found near the place where he dug the hole to burn the evidence, he must have dropped it without realising."

"Look, you're going to get a conviction, we all know that including him; he hasn't got an alibi and no one saw him that night, either that or they didn't recognise him, I am combing all areas on this one, Detective. I just have a feeling that he's telling the truth"

"Mr Greenford, I disagree with you, we have all the forensic evidence, the medallion Melanie wore the night she died, and his blood stained clothes, it's a tighter fit than a glove."

Madeline put away the iron and folded up the ironing board. Amanda sat patiently watching her pale tired face.

"Madeline, you look very pale are you feeling okay?"

"Yes," she smiled, "Just a little tired, I didn't sleep very well last night, once I get out into the fresh mountain air I'll look more like a tomato just cleaved from the vine."

She hoped her little joke would cheer Amanda up, it didn't, and she pursed her lips thoughtfully.

"I need to go into town to get some things then I'll be back before you know I've gone."

She hated the thought of leaving her on her own she was still so very depressed.

"I'll meet you then?" Amanda asked.

"No, no don't worry because I'm not sure what time I'll be back, it won't be late though, I can get a cab." She smiled as she headed for the stairs, her white blouse hung over one arm Bethany's pinafore dress over the other. She paused for a moment and then turned to Amanda. "Will you be okay for an hour or two? Or would you like to come with me?"

"No, I'll be fine, I'll be okay I promise, I have some things to do later." Amanda grinned. "I have Bethany here with me and later on I'll take her to see my mother."

"I'll definitely be home before you and Beth."

"Are you sure you don't want me to meet you somewhere?"

"No, honestly I'll be all right; I'll probably meet up with Evan."

Amanda walked over to the big window and looked out at the warm June morning, the daffodils swayed ever so slightly from the fresh warm breeze and the crocuses stood like tiny erect soldiers with purple hats on. It lightened her mood and lifted her spirit just a little, but enough to get through another day. Paul had never seen the joy of summer on the mountain his time had been spent in a hospital bed; he would have loved the sight from this window it looked like a fairy tale she thought miserably. Another thought had been playing on her mind over the last few weeks, and now she was going to have to tell Madeline. Her fingers tapped gently on the glass.

"Madeline?"

Madeline halted halfway up the stairs. "Yes?"

"I've been meaning to talk to you about something."

"Have you? What about?" she came back down and laid the clothes over the arm of the chair.

"This house Madeline…I'm thinking of selling up, finding something smaller, more central."

Amanda's eyes wondered around the room taking in every detail, her mind going back to the day Paul brought her here, how excited she had been! She couldn't believe he had bought her such a lovely house, a house that turned out to bring her such misery.

"There are too many memories here, painful ones opposed to good ones, I see Paul everywhere. you know

Madeline, I can even smell his after shave everywhere and it hurts so bad!"

Her eyes brimmed with tears, Madeline could feel her pain, her suffering, and she could understand why she wanted to sell.

"I need to put everything behind me, start again fresh, and I have the money to do it."

Madeline crossed the room and took her in her arms she knew they were in for another crying session.

"Okay sweetheart, it's perfectly alright! I understand Amanda, you do what's best, and I knew all along you would want to sell after Paul's death that's only natural love! You would be better off to find something more local, near your mother, start again Amanda."

She smiled through her tears, pulled a tissue from her sleeve to blow her nose.

"I want you to live with me, we could buy a place together, and anyway I have more than enough money."

"Now, you know how I feel about that, if I can't buy, I pay rent to you okay? That's the deal?"

"Okay, madam, you win." Amanda smiled, she knew how fiercely independent Madeline was, she would never take anything from her.

"I was thinking of putting it on the market this morning, is that ok with you?"

"Of course, maybe a large family would be interested in buying?" Madeline suggested.

"Or we could sell it to Hammer Horror films incorporated." Amanda laughed; it was the first time in a long while Madeline had seen her laugh.

"Only they aren't in business now, didn't they go out of circulation in the 1980's?"

Madeline smiled, now her own spirits were lifting, she was happy that the thought of getting rid of this big house was making Amanda think more positively, giving her a way forward, and starting her on a new path, but she knew for now at least, her plans to leave the UK were going to be on permanent hold.

"You know something Madeline?" she said gazing up at the ceiling. "Paul has given me two wonderful things to remember him by, the two most precious things I could ever possess, and he never failed me, not once."

"I guess I know what you're going to say." she grinned.

"This house, I'll never have to worry about renting an expensive accommodation, but the most precious thing he could ever give me was Life! He left me a part of himself that I will always have close to me."

They both looked at little Bethany playing quietly on the floor with her dolls, such a sweet little girl a mirror image of her wonderful father, such a good child, she never cried or moaned she was like an angel. Madeline had no need to reply, she just smiled sadly a tear rolled from the corner of her eye.

She said, "Well, hadn't we better be going? Or we won't get back." Madeline picked up the clothes and headed once more for the stairs.

By the time Madeline was ready it was almost midday. She picked up Bethany and hugged her close. Amanda appeared from the kitchen dangling her car keys in front of her.

"Ready?" she said reaching for her coat.

"Ready." Madeline replied. As they left the house she looked back over her shoulder, a terrible sadness almost choked her as she closed the door.

It was twenty past three by the time she had started to make her way home. She was happy that she had got everything done that she needed to and was able to get home before four o'clock it gave her plenty of time to get the bus and be home well before Amanda and Bethany, after trying to persevere with Paul's bike she had decided it was safer to walk now that Shaun Riordan was safely behind bars until his trial. She could hardly believe someone could be capable of such horrific crimes! Madeline shuddered visibly. She saw the bus coming and hurried towards the bus stop it would take her right to the bottom of the mountain road. It was such a lovely evening the sun was still warm and the walk would do her good. She didn't mind walking in fine weather the evenings were lighter now and she felt more secure. Her thoughts turned to Amanda, this year would be her first Christmas without Paul, but at least by the time December came round hopefully they would have moved out of the house. She remembered the first time Amanda had met him, he was a charmer right from the word go! Those lovely blue eyes that had an air of mischief about them and his kind thoughtful, unselfish ways, he would certainly be someone not easily forgotten.

Sadness had taken a toll on her more than she had realised because she missed him too. She got on the bus and sat at the back, there were only three other people, a middle aged woman sitting a row in front with a blue headscarf and a jean jacket on, what a strange attire Madeline thought, what was she doing wearing a headscarf in the middle of summer? On the other side to her right, three rows in front was a young man in a dark blue uniform he was obviously a security guard. Directly opposite her was a young woman in her early twenties who nervously worried at her wedding ring. Madeline glanced briefly trying not to draw too much attention to the fact that she was watching her, *she has marital problems I'll bet,* she thought, looking at the woman's eyes that were darting about furtively.

She started to think about Amanda and little Bethany they were starting a new life without Paul, and tears stung her eyes. She felt a lump in her throat and swallowed it absently. She turned to look out of the window at the mountains and wide-open spaces and her tears fell silently. 'What the hell is the matter with me?' she wondered. 'God I'm getting as depressed as

Amanda, get over it!' She pulled a tissue from her bag glancing around quickly to see if anyone was watching her. No one took any notice.

It was probably her own grief pulling her down, over the last few years she had become very fond of Paul, he was such a nice guy, he had impact, after being so unsure of him in the first place, just goes to show, first appearances don't always give a true account of what that person is really like! They had all come through such a lot together.

Sudden she had the urge to jump up stab her finger on the bell and get off the bus! This was what she thought were 'panic attacks' they had only just started about a month ago, it was obviously due to what they had experienced with the murders, and the death of Amanda's husband. It has got to be nerves, or maybe they call it Agoraphobia, Claustrophobia, or some other phobia! She now used the tissue to wipe sheen of perspiration from her brow. Madeline gazed ahead, sucked in a couple of deep breaths and then she saw the mountain road, heading towards them she jumped up and rang the bell.

The sun had started to fade as a cloud lazily rolled across the sky, grey shadows formed as a light mist started to come down from the mountains. At last her 'panic attack' had passed and she felt much better. The last time she walked up this road alone she nearly met her maker! Or so she had thought at the time, it was Haldane creeping about the mountain. No fear of that happening again. But even so psychologically it made her nervous.

It had turned chilly now a wind had accompanied the mist and started to form a North Easterly mini gale. She jogged towards the first gate; stopped to catch her breath cupping her palms to her face and exhaled warm air into her nostrils. By the time she had reached the second gate exhaustion had got the better of her. "Wow, really out of condition recently." She mumbled as she fumbled in her bag for her door key.

She slipped the little key ring with the furry Koala over her middle finger and walked the rest of the way instead of running she needed to save her energy; but that didn't help much because by the time she got to the third gate, she was almost dragging her feet. She fumbled with the lock until its stiffened hinges came free. Who had shut them? Amanda didn't bother anymore, there was no need really, no one ever came up the mountain road and cabs certainly wouldn't be bothered to lock or unlock them so who had? Oh, she would be so pleased once they moved! How simple to just go out and come home without all this effort!!

At least when Amanda arrived she would be able to drive straight through. She was wondering what kind of house they were going to buy, obviously it wasn't going to be small, Bethany needed space to play, it was a shame Tynant was so far away, the house was ideal for a family, there was plenty of room to play, and Bethany would be safe from passing traffic. Madeline trudged on and suddenly the house reared up in front of her it had never been a welcoming sight to either of them, but tonight as the shadows of early evening closed in and the house looked more than positively unwelcome.

Just fifty yards from the house she stopped to catch her breath, a stitch caught her left side so she bent over with her hands on her knees to ease the pain; and then a familiar voice called to her.

"Hi Madeline, I've been waiting for you."

"Oh I didn't expect to see you tonight, come inside I'll make you a drink, I'm glad to see you I wish you had come earlier, and you could have given me a lift."

"Oh Madeline, you know what? I always knew you were an angel."

Madeline laughed. "Oh I know I am have you only just realised that?"

It was almost seven by the time Amanda reached the mountain road. She had been sitting for over an hour in a traffic jam that seemed to stretch for miles in front of her, but she didn't mind too much, nothing could darken her happy mood right now, the thought of moving out of the big house gave her a look into the future, at least they could start again with fresh memories, even though nothing could ever be remotely the same without Paul in her life, but leaving behind her the sad memories was definitely the way forward.

Everyone had told her she was doing the right thing selling the big house, it was too big for her anyway and too remote, there were loads of three bed-roomed houses in Bedgellert and one was for sale just yards from Megan and that was exactly what she needed, besides she could go back to University and Megan could look after Bethany for a few hours. Amanda decided they could look at it tomorrow. At last she had mapped out a life for her self and Bethany, in fact she had not been as happy as this for a long time, she started to sing as the car headed up the mountain road.

She stopped at the first gate obviously the wind had blown it shut, she was sure she had wedged a stone against it the other day. She hopped from the car to throw it open when her foot slipped on mud and she swayed to keep her balance. Once the gate was open she was quickly on her way. Her mind was still on her new future when she felt the front wheels slope downwards veering towards the right; she struggled to keep from skidding into a ditch. Frantically she tapped on the brake, gently at first then shoved her foot down hard; it was too late, the front wheels dropped right into a muddy ditch. She got out of the car as the wind whipped her hair into her eyes, and stood there angrily looking at the wheels in the ditch.

"Oh Fuck no matter how warm it is, or how fucking cold it is, there is always a muddy sludgy part of the ground that collates into the ditch!"

This brought sudden tears into her eyes as she remembered Paul's words it was as if she could actually hear him saying. *"You have to watch out for ditches, if you get caught in one you'll need a crane to get you out!"* She searched around in the twilight for a stone or a large rock that she could put under the wheels and then drive the car up over the rock and she'd be free! To her left there was a large stick covered in mud, they had a lot of rain over the past couple of days which hadn't helped to clear the muddy ground, and then on the right hand side of her she saw a fairly large brick, all she needed now was something strong enough to dig them out with, she grinned as she remembered the spanner she had kept in the boot of the car. With spanner in hand she dug out both objects, she placed the brick under the wheel and used the stick for support wedging it tightly behind the brick. Her luck was in, she reversed the car over the brick and she was free!

Suddenly it had got dark she switched on her little overhead light and glanced at her watch, it was almost nine fifteen! She could hardly believe it. It had taken her almost two hours to get home. She put her headlights on full beam as she neared the house; it appeared in front of her so suddenly she was shocked to see there were no lights on, *where was Madeline?* She wondered. Grinding the car to a halt at the driveway she lifted Bethany from her car seat and hurried up the drive; one hand fumbling in her bag for her door keys.

She snapped on all the lights and called "Madeline! Are you home?" With no reply she hung up her coat and took Bethany upstairs to get her ready for bed.

The house was cold and quiet, she put on her white Nike Track suit then hurried down to light the fire; that was the trouble with such a big place she thought, you have to heat it all the year round. After putting the kettle on to boil she peered out at the unyielding darkness, night had arrived so quickly. She had always disliked the darkness because both sides of the house looked out onto the fields that stretched for miles across the moors, it was so open; closing the kitchen curtains tightly she reached into the drawer and took out an elastic band to tie her hair back from her face. It had been so unmanageable lately; lank and greasy. She wondered if it had anything to do with the shock of Paul's death, she knew that shock sometimes causes hair problems.

It was not until the ten o'clock news came on that she really began to worry, she had called Madeline's mobile several times but it went straight on to the answer messaging. She looked at the clock again Madeline should have been home hours ago! She rang Madeline's mothers phone but it kept ringing so she guessed they were both out somewhere and forgotten the time. It was so unusual for Madeline! She was always so precise with everything, when she said she wouldn't be long, then that was exactly what she meant

The sound was quite identifiable the floorboards above her were creaking as if someone was walking about upstairs. She knew by the sound that it couldn't be Bethany walking across the floor to get into her bed? Her little footfalls were too small to hear anyway. It was someone with a heavy tread! She crossed the room quickly and went into the hallway. Her eyes fixed on the stairs as if she expected Madeline to pop her head around the corner. She heard a 'tap'tap'tap and her blood froze in her veins; her eyes darted about as she mounted the stairs one at a time. She checked every room carefully and then quietly opened Bethany's door, the little girl was fast asleep in her bed with her thumb tucked securely in her mouth Amanda smiled and closed the door behind her.

She sat in the big armchair, Madeline would be home very soon now, her eyes fell on the phone, reaching out she lifted it to her ear and dialled the number carefully. She waited and waited while the constant ringing echoed inside her head. They were still not at home, at least Madeline's mother wasn't!

She wondered if she should ring her brother, maybe he would come up and sit with her? She picked up the telephone again deciding should she call him or not? And then replaced it back in its cradle; she was angry with herself for being so stupid! He's probably out with his friends she thought. *Why are you bothering him? Why are you panicking? The killer is caged, everything is cool, and so what is wrong with you? Just because Madeline has got held up? Perhaps her mobile is off? Then if that is the case why hasn't she come home?* A delicate frown lined her brow and she rested her head against the back of the chair and tried to relax. Maybe I'll just give him a call anyway, she thought. She sat forward again and picked up the phone in her slightly trembling hands. There was no dialling tone, anxiously she tapped the plunger, then listened again the only sound she heard was the distant echo that filled her head. "Oh No!" she breathed as fear took her in its grip she was completely cut off from the world now!! A hot flush spread through her at an alarming rate. As she fumbled about in her bag for her mobile, the clear picture image of leaving it on the arm of the chair in Megan's sent shock waves coursing through her because this was the second time she had done this! Now I can't contact anyone! She must have forgotten to pick it up in her rush to get home before the heavy traffic started. Her anxiety was growing, she became agitated. *Where was Madeline?*

The bottle of Brandy stood on the table invitingly she needed a shot to calm her unhinged nerves, after all who could blame her after what she'd been through the last two years? She got up and poured a small measure sipping it slowly while she gathered her thoughts. In the stillness she waited, the only sound was the ticking of the clock in the hall…tick, tick, tick. And then the footsteps thundered above her. She jumped spilling some of the amber liquid into her lap staining the white tracksuit, *'come on!* She told herself, *'Steady yourself it's just the movements of the house, there isn't anyone up there! You've already been up to look'* She looked up at the ceiling and then placed her glass on the table. She got up slowly moving stiffly towards the front door maybe it's the wind outside causing the noise? Or was this all in her mind? She opened the door expecting to see Madeline standing there with her door keys in her hand and breathless from the rush to get home. *"Oh I'm sorry Amanda, didn't mean to scare you, got held up and my mobile wasn't working."* She could even hear her voice so clearly. But Madeline wasn't there!

"Madeline?" She called as the wind snatched her voice and tore at her sweater. She watched the trees duck and bow then closed the door quickly.

She heard it again, heavy footsteps coming from the main bedroom. Seconds passed that seemed more like hours and now her heart hammered painfully against her ribs. Her eyes were pinned on the top landing once more expecting a dark shadow to lumber towards her and for a moment her legs refused to move, and then she thought about Bethany alone upstairs! And her instincts took over. Once again, hugging the wall she mounted the stairs one step at a time. Something was wrong! Her mouth began to feel like sawdust, it was so dry not even saliva would pass her larynx. Stupid thoughts passed through her mind that Madeline was probably asleep in her room, she'll wake up and smile and then say that she had been so tired that she went to lie down for a while and hadn't heard them come in! Of course! Amanda thought. That's it! She's sleeping and she hadn't noticed her before that's all! She'll wake up and her blue eyes will sparkle and she will say *'Where the hell did you think I'd gone? You know I'll always be here for you Amanda'*

Amanda checked all the rooms again; Bethany was still sleeping as she was before with the same thumb tucked in her mouth…so still, very, very still and not moving. She walked shakily a little way down the hall and opened Madeline's door, her bed was as empty as it was before. *Did you think she was going to sneak in like a naughty teenager who had broken curfew?* She thought to herself. And now despondency crept up on her, she knew Madeline was not coming home now…or ever!

She closed the door like an epitaph and a sob escaped her. She knew she had to do something, get Bethany out of bed and go down to the village to get help! Her thoughts were no longer rational and she groaned inwardly. Panic had replaced all her rational thoughts and things were getting way out of hand. "Obviously, I'm not over Paul's death yet! And I am beginning to imagine all kinds of things!" she said aloud. She slowed her pace a little and slowly walked towards the top of the stairs. *'Now what could have happened to Madeline? Nothing! That's what. She is late getting home, who said she had to live in my pocket anyway? Just calm down!'* she reasoned with herself. She knew she wasn't getting anywhere running around in a panic. She closed her eyes and took a few deep breaths. She would go back downstairs and make herself a strong black coffee and then try the telephone again if it was working she would call David, Collins or Haldane, and the problem would be solved in no time!

She sat at the kitchen table with a steaming cup of hot coffee in front of her, she took the elastic band out of her hair and combed her hands through the dark tangle then slipped the elastic band back on. She glanced at the clock on the kitchen wall and was startled to see it was almost a quarter to twelve! She knew something was wrong, something had happened to prevent Madeline from returning home, but what? She couldn't imagine.

She looked over at the phone again then slowly walked towards it, lifting the receiver listening to a humming that told her it had gone out of service. She wondered how long it had been out. Madeline must have called earlier and got no reply, and then when she tried again she found it out of order!

At last she felt she had put some kind of reason to

this madness. She smiled to herself, and began to think rationally, thinking clearly, she would sit and wait for Madeline to return home, after all Saturday nights were not the easiest of nights to get a cab, especially when you lived on a mountain! But, she grinned to herself it won't be for long now, a few more weeks and they would be out of here, living a normal life in a small house surrounded by friends and family. And she sighed.

Amanda looked at the clock again stretching to ease her tense muscles. She got up and put her coffee cup in the sink. For a moment she stood staring out at the black beyond thinking about the new move and then she froze, something was wrong? What was it? Here in the kitchen? Her eyes swept the room and then she saw it, she had been looking at it for the last few moments….The curtains were wide open.

Her breath caught in her throat. "I closed them! I know I did." Her hands went to her head to calm the pressure building there. "Is this some kind of a joke?" But she knew Madeline would never play such a trick like that on her, she didn't have a sense of humour as wicked as that. She turned quickly and ran down the hall stopping outside the reception room.

Something drew her in; she hesitated then entered with her heart almost bursting in her ears. The room was dark, the curtains were open, and the moons glow cast an eerie light of drifting shadows but enough to be able to distinguish objects. Everything was the same as it had been before, the bureau was exactly in the same place by the right hand wall, the old grey armchair behind the door, Aunty Mabel's dining chair still tucked in the corner where it normally lived. And at the very end of the room against the very last wall to the back the old ancient armchair sat.

Amanda strained her eyes she had never bothered to put a bulb in the ceiling light, as they never used this room. A figure sat in the chair!

"OH." She breathed, standing there smiling, a great sense of relief flooded through her as she realised that Madeline had fallen asleep waiting for her to come home! But why choose this room? Why had she chosen to take a nap in here? She had never used this room before, only to get something she had stored in here that maybe she had forgotten about. Amanda crossed the room quickly; couldn't she have heard her call her name? She might have taken a sleeping pill? Madeline never took sleeping pills!

The figure sat so still in the chair. And then Amanda switched on the table lamp.

"Madeline! I've been home for hours worried sick! Didn't you hear me call you?"

For a moment, even seconds she stared, her brain refused to register what she was seeing, and then she gasped, her breath caught in her throat as shock waves passed through her like live electric wire through water. Amanda staggered backwards as her hands flew to her mouth defying what she was seeing. The small candlelight did nothing to disguise the abhorrent mutilation of her friend.

For seconds Amanda stared uncomprehendingly; her mouth open, eyes wide in terror. The white blouse Madeline had so carefully ironed this morning was now drenched in her blood. A gaping neck wound had almost severed her head that had been so perfectly positioned to rest against the back of the chair, her windpipe exposed; muscle and bone clearly visible. Amanda's eyes widened even more as they travelled down towards Madeline's hands that hung limply over the arms of the chair. Four fingers lay on the carpet; blood drenched the cuffs of the blouse where her wrists had been cut leaving a thick dark puddle dripping onto the carpet. Madeline's ponytail hung in untidy strands the rustic hair caked in blood. Her eyes fixed on Madeline's face, even in the opaque light she could see how deathly white she was, her eyes half open yet dull and empty, her spirit had gone! Madeline's warm wonderful spirit had gone! She gazed at Madeline's mouth it was open in surprise, now her heart beat so furiously that she was so sure it would stop suddenly, as suddenly as Madeline's life had ended. Then her words blasted from her own strangled voice.

"MADELINE! Oh Madeline, oh no, no, no, why? She wanted to hold her, sooth her, try to revive her; oh she wanted so desperately to bring her back! But she knew it was far too late, no one could survive such hideous injuries, and Madeline had been dead some hours. She was filled with revulsion and terror like none she had ever known before as she backed out of the room. Her hand clamped tightly over her mouth to stifle the scream she knew would be never ending. She slammed herself against the wall in the entrance hall gagging, holding her hand to her mouth so tightly she could feel her lips pressed painfully against her teeth, she blinked, then blinked again as if to clear the vision of her friend ripped apart like a rag doll by an angry child! This is Madness, it isn't happening!

Tears flooded her eyes and panic shadowed her as she thought about Bethany, she had been so still! So quiet! What if…the thought was almost too terrible to comprehend? She had to get help! She must try the phone again! Call the police. She stumbled blindly towards the living room, her fingers felt like stiffened door bolts as she tried to dial, she tapped the cradle praying for a dialling tone, and then placed it to her ear…and then she froze!

The heavy breathing followed by a chuckle sent the phone crashing to the floor. She groaned softly. He was in the house! On the upstairs extension! He got Madeline's door keys! That's how he got in! Her painful breaths came in short bursts as she looked around for something to defend herself with. And then she saw the heavy brass poker. Although she moved with lightening speed, sinuously, towards the living room it seemed to take forever until her sweaty palms closed around the poker. A moist sheen of perspiration ran down her brow stinging her eyes painfully; she hit the switch plunging the room into darkness and crouched behind the sofa listening intently, but the house was as quiet as a graveyard at midnight. Brushing the cuff of her sleeve across her brow she rammed her free fist into her mouth as she thought about Madeline, the shock was too great to really take in, she still hoped help would come and they could save her! They had to! How could she go on without her?

Her only instinct now was to get Bethany out of the house, *(If she was still alive)* she shuddered with terror at the thought, there was no way they would get out together, he was too fast! Why didn't she see him? She went up there twice! Where was he hiding? Suddenly along with her fear came anger, an explosive rage! They let him go! They must have, Madeline was so afraid of that and now she's dead! Collins promised that wouldn't happen! He was so fucking sure! Well how wrong he was!

Hardly able to breath and almost certain that the drum beat inside her chest would make it possible for him to hear her she cupped her hand to her chest. The metallic taste in her mouth almost made her vomit, was it the taste of blood? They say it tastes metallic! She knew she was never going to get out of the house alive, but she was determined to go down fighting, she had to! There was no choice.

And now she waited, her instincts became savage, her hearing acute, she would shed the last drop of blood for Bethany, he was not going to harm one hair on her head. She could hear him moving around upstairs, She looked up towards the ceiling he was on the landing now, the floorboards creaked heavily under his weight, he moved along to the top of the stairs.

With footfalls sounding like thunder he made his way down. Then she heard him laugh, a heinous sound that made her tremble. She stayed where she was, counting each step that he took until he was at the bottom, her hand gripping the poker so tight her knuckles shone white in the glow of the moonlight.

The shadow appeared at the bottom of the stairs; the grotesque head turned to the left and then seemed to swivel to the right. He stopped briefly and then entered the living room she could see his thick black Wellington boots that made a squelching sound on the carpet. He walked towards her with the machete raised in front of him. Now Amanda could see him clearly, her terror knew no bounds as she looked up into the grotesque mask, the ugly hooked nose made more prominent by his sideway stance, he was dressed all in black and it looked like he wore a black track suit with a hood on the back, she realised with a mounting horror that this was the man she had seen on the bridge on the night she walked home in the sleet! If he had looked to his right he would have seen her.

He acted like a legion with a multitude of forces behind him, and bellowed.

"COME OUT, COME OUT WHEREVER YOU ARE!"

Amanda jumped to her feet, making a conscious gesture in a split second as she drew in a jagged breath, the poker almost slipped from her sweaty palms. Now as she confronted him she thought about Madeline and what her life had meant to her, she thought about Paul, her love for him that would always be with her.

"HERE I AM FUCKER! COME AND GET ME, I WON'T BE AS EASY AS MADELINE WAS."

His laugh was low and guttural.

"YOU BASTARD, WHY DID YOU KILL MADELINE? She never did you any harm."

"She did plenty of harm she would have put me away for the rest of my life!"

"GOOD ON HER!" Amanda yelled. "You killed my husband didn't you?" She needed to know and now was as good a time as any to ask, she could feel her hands shaking and all of a sudden the poker seemed to come alive.

"How clever of you to guess that one! But of course you knew that all along didn't you?"

"Call it instinct." She said, her voice quavering to almost a squeak.

"Whatever." He mocked.

"But why?"

"It's a little hobby of mine, don't know really, I enjoy the thrill of the hunt, well at least I did until you came along."

"What do you mean?" She frowned.

"I liked you…Perhaps you could have helped me, put

me back on an even keel so to speak, I wanted the house back! It was mine."

He looked down as if he was about to cry, in a strange way he reminded her of a mime artist.

"Liked me? You don't even know me! How can you like someone you hardly know?"

"Well, that's where you are very misguided Amanda."

It was all becoming clear to her now. She racked her brains she never knew Shaun Riordan before he was arrested! So what the hell did he mean? This monster was standing here telling her he had killed her husband and murdered her friend just to get this house? None of this made any sense how could it?

"You're fucking crazy! You need to be put away for life; No, let me retract that, the death sentence would be a much better option for you!"

He laughed, he threw his head back the masked face looked even more grotesque in the half shadows, and his voice seemed to bounce so loudly off the walls.

She bit down on her lip to stop from screaming. Her legs felt so weak but she knew she was going to have to fight as best as she could for her child's sake. He moved a step closer, she hung on tightly to the poker it was the only lifeline she had right now.

"I'm going to kill you Amanda, I have no choice, you are my only witness, and you are never going to stay with me are you?" He said questioningly. His grotesque head swung slightly to the right.

"STAY WITH YOU? YOU THINKYOU THINK I'M AS FUCKING NUTS AS YOU?" she screamed. "I'M READY FOR YOU."

The softness of his voice hardened as he turned his head toward her. "You think so? I could crush you like a bug in one foul swoop, so don't kid yourself Amanda."

She almost collapsed right then, her heart pounded, her head spun, and her eyes blurred with tears; one false move and that was it! She along with Bethany would become past tense.

"No Amanda, you must die along with the child."

She gave no thought to what or *if* anymore, Bethany's survival was the utmost priority. She leaped forward launching all her weight towards him, the poker held so tightly in her hands that it startled him making him drop the machete in surprise, this he had never expected! She dived for it but he was too quick, he kicked her in the side sending her hurtling across the room knocking wind from her lungs. She cursed her clumsiness as he lifted her by the hair, the elastic band snapped and snagged in her hair as it was forced free. She aimed for his head the poker swung above him but he grasped her wrist and twisted painfully until it was forced from her grasp.

"DON'T! DON'T do this…PLEASE!" she screamed,

but he had already swooped down and retrieved the machete. He lifted her by the hair like a rag doll.

The machete was levitated above her head and she closed her eyes waiting for that fateful blow. Suddenly, rage released adrenaline and sent it coursing through her body. She was not going to die and leave Bethany at his mercy, a soulless beast that had no pity or mercy for anyone! He had her facing him; dangling her like an old piece of cloth even the amount of pain she felt from her tearing scalp couldn't diminish her outrage. She brought her knee up into his groin hard, struggling furiously until she slipped from his grasp, he went down fast and Amanda swooped down and snatched the poker from the floor; she wasted no time racing for the stairs to Bethany's room.

By the rime she reached the fourth step his hand grabbed her ankle closing around it like a sash clamp, Amanda felt herself being dragged down she kicked out at him but her bare feet had no impact at all, his nails dug into her flesh as he pulled her down the stairs ripping the leg of her tracksuit.

This is as bad as it could ever get! She thought as he clamped his hand over her mouth, he had her in a firm grip now and she was finding it difficult to draw in breath! She kicked and struggled her rage heightening as she felt her teeth split her lower lip and blood swamped her mouth. She felt sick as she tasted his salty flesh so she bit down on his hand and tore at it until with disgust she felt flesh ripping away, her tongue tasted a lumpy piece of it in her mouth.

"YOU FUCKING BITCH!" He screamed, his voice sounded high pitched more like a squeal than a scream. He pulled his hand away from her mouth staring at her, under the mask his eyes were wide in shock as if he couldn't believe what he saw as blood flowed from the open wound. Amanda fought down the urge to vomit as she spat out the piece of flesh; she felt a sickening disgust as bile rose in her throat.

She gagged as he grabbed her and lifted her; his hands gripped her so violently that he tore the top of her track suit ripping it right down the front as he slammed her onto the step. She groaned at the sharp pain in her shoulder, her eyes pinched shut her face contorted with pain, she was sure he had broken her shoulder!

He raised his fist, his eyes were mad, staring, a rage burning in them so fiercely as if all his innermost anger had come to boiling point. For one second only; she thought of bargaining power; offer herself to him! But this was no normal person! He would do whatever he wanted anyway, and the thought of that could never describe the revulsion she felt. Amanda screamed as his fist rammed into her jaw, she felt hot searing pain, bone splinter and she moaned helplessly. She wondered how on earth she could think for one moment she could fight this maniac! She had made the situation far worse by angering him! She thought about little Bethany asleep upstairs and prayed to God she wouldn't die and leave her to his mercy! She couldn't fail her little girl. What if she was already dead? Maybe he killed her earlier? But he's said she would die with me! Was he bluffing?

Amanda could taste the sourness of his blood, or was it her own? He slammed her against the step once more the pain was unbearable. Her shoulder cracked as he tore away the sleeve. The strength was ebbing away from her now, black tides of unconsciousness began to wash over her; and she knew at that moment she was finished, there was no more fight left in her.

At first she thought it was her imagination, the frantic crying, and then through a blurry haze of pain she saw Bethany standing on the top landing rubbing her eyes, her hair tousled from sleep.

"MUMMY!" she screamed.

"RUN BETHANY RUN!" The grotesque head swirled towards the child; he left Amanda to crawl up the stairs to snatch at her tiny pink pyjamas.

Amanda froze for seconds as she realised he was about to grab Bethany and pull her headlong down the stairs. It was as if something superhuman had pulled her to her feet, she lunged forward and sunk her teeth into his right thigh.

"NO YOU BASTARD! YOU'RE NOT HAVING MY BABY!"

He grunted in surprise as he saw the blood oozing from his thigh. Startled he lost his balance and toppled down the stairs on top of her, she was trapped!

"OH RUN BABY, PLEASE RUN!" She couldn't see the child now; his bulk hid her from view.

Bethany stood on the third step from the bottom, hugged close to her little body was her pink teddy bear Madeline had bought her. "DON'T HURT MUMMY!" she screamed. "DON'T!" Her little shoulders heaved from her terrified sobs. Amanda's eyes went from Bethany to the machete lying at the bottom of the stairs, it was just three feet away but easily out of her reach, she wanted to tell Bethany to get it for her but she was too small for her reactions to be quick.

"You Bitch!" he snarled in her ear. "Now it's time to die, you and the kid!"

Arching her back she reached for his face trying to pull the mask off, she wriggled, struggled and then shifted herself around in a circle ignoring the pain in her shoulder, right now survival was of the utmost priority in her mind, she was going to fight until the last drop of blood had been spilt! She managed to curl her fingers around the machete and brought it up for all she was worth; she hit him on the left side of his head with the blunt end! For a second he seemed disorientated, she scrambled sideways and was free. Now she snatched up the machete once more slicing it through the air she heard the gut wrenching sound as it glanced off the back of his head, pulling her arm back again she brought the machete down once more blood burst from his skull and then she dropped it in disgust.

Snatching Bethany roughly in her arms she searched for the car keys. "WHERE DID I PUT THE FUCKING KEYS?" Then she remembered leaving them on Bethany's bedside table.

With Bethany on her good shoulder she limped towards the cellar, she opened the door and threw the child inside slamming both bolts top and bottom in place. Amanda almost screamed with the pain in her shoulder from the effort, it felt like her arm had been wrenched from her socket. Her broken ribs constricted her breathing, and hot tears of pain spilled from her eyes as she clung on to Bethany, to stop her falling headlong down the darkened cellar steps.

The smell of damp and decay hung in the air filling her head with another smell she could not identify, it was a smell she had never been familiar with before but it was putrid and foul! Bethany lay on her shoulder her cries had now turned into terrified sobs.

"Okay darling, it's going to be okay." Amanda soothed. She felt her way down in the darkness wondering how they would escape from the cellar. Unless Paul had been wrong and they were lucky enough to find a small window to crawl through, but if he'd been right then they were going to be here for some time.

She felt something warm scupper across her bare foot, cringing as her body stiffened in shock she glimpsed the small body of a furry rat that was more frightened by the warmth of her foot than the intruders into their dark abysmal world. If there was anything in this world that scared the shit out of her, it was rats, mice and spiders! But right now she knew there was worse to come. They reached the bottom and Amanda's eyes had acclimatised to the dark, there was a tea chest over by the far wall so she placed Bethany on it while she searched for a possible escape route.

"Don't move darling ok? Even if you can't see mummy, stay where you are, do you understand Bethany?" The child sniffed loudly and nodded her head.

The cellar was low, there were tea chests everywhere but definitely no windows, Paul had been right, the only openings in the cellar were air vents slatted and about four inches in width. Not even a mouse could squeeze through there. There was only one small advantage to those air vents! The house was situated so high up in the mountains that they allowed a small filter of light to pour through from the moon.

She fell to her knees and looked up at the darkened staircase, any moment now he would smash his way through! No sooner the thought had popped into her mind she heard the first crash as he hit the door. "COME OUT OF THERE YOU BITCH!"

Bethany started crying again, terrified sobs wracked her tiny body. Amanda looked around frantically; she lifted Bethany off the tea chest and carried her over to a heap of dirty rags laying in the corner stinking of badness and mildew; and then a thought hit her, most of the floorboards were rotting away. Glancing at the stairway and back to the boards she said to Bethany. "Listen sweetheart, I'm going to hide you under here and you must not come out until mummy calls you okay?" She looked into her tearful eyes as she cupped her hand under the child's chin. "And be quieter than a mouse, even much quieter than a mouse." She smiled warmly trying to give Bethany some confidence, but by the look on Bethany's face it was clear she wasn't wearing any fairy stories tonight!

It was only a vague idea, but it may buy them some time. She saw the damaged floorboard sticking up about four inches, if she could wedge it up, she could pull it free and place it on the stairs and if her luck was really in he would trip, fall, and break his fucking neck! She knew it was a fruitless thought but it may give them time to race up the stairs and escape, she would have to be quick though, because once he had smashed down the door she couldn't lock him in the cellar! Silently she cursed herself for not getting another set of car keys cut for emergencies she would have to get them from Bethany's bedside table before they could escape.

She was beginning to feel claustrophobic, unable to breathe freely and panic was closing in on her fast. She got to her knees and wedged her fingers under the damaged floorboard, hair hung in her eyes in damp strands almost hindering what little vision she had, her face was streaked with dirt, her shoulder hurt like hell, but she put enough strength behind her and pulled, the pain in her body felt as if she had been set on fire, it almost cut her in half to breath, but she held onto enough strength to complete her task, but it was strength that was quickly diminishing. Each time she pulled at the plank pain tore through her shoulder like red hot needles until she was afraid that she was going to pass out, but she gritted her teeth and pulled and pulled until with a loud crack it came loose, tearing away from its mooring almost hitting her in the face. Amanda fell backwards with the impact; the broken board still clutched in her hand, but she quickly caught her balance and sighed with relief. As she got to her feet to pull the whole board free something stared up at her through the dirty musty hole.

It was the decomposing body of a little girl, she couldn't have been no more than five or six; a spike about three feet long was embedded in her tiny pitiful body. Amanda dropped the board as her hand flew to her mouth to stifle the scream that almost choked her.

"OH! OH GOD!" she gasped, realising that was the awful stench she had noticed earlier.

For long moments she stared, the once pretty pink Disney nightdress was now stained a darker red, she could only just make out the Pluto designs in the material on the little nightdress from the dim glow, and her heart ached.

Another loud crack splintered the door and she knew that in another few minutes he would be in. She looked at the spike, "Call it poetic justice my friend!" Then clamped her hand around the spike and pulled. It came out with a heart-sickening squelch; she threw it down beside her; grabbed the damaged floorboard and ran back to the stairs. She placed it carefully on the fourth step from the top, and then ran back for the spike.

"Okay Bethany, I want you to stay hidden under those blankets, I don't want you to move, and you stay there until mummy comes back for you okay?"

"Okay mummy, but they smell!" She pinched her nose with her index finger and thumb.

"I know they do, but you must not move!" And then she said something she would never have allowed anyone to say to Bethany. "If you move, the bogeyman will get you!" She hated herself! But this was the only way she could protect Bethany as she shivered at the thought of that tiny child's body, he had no morals, or principles, he was mad! Insane, and thought nothing of killing a child, he was every mothers nightmare! She could see the light bounce of Bethany's huge eyes that were wide open with fright. The little girl shuddered and pulled the blankets up over her head. Amanda took up her position under the stairs.

"HEY YOU BITCH, I'M GONNA CUT OFF YOUR HEAD WHEN I CATCH YOU!"

Amanda trembled, her throat constricted and she found it difficult to breathe as she glanced around at the pile of blankets where Bethany lay. He hit the door again, the sound was thunderous, a roar that shook the house on its foundations, she was terrified the ceiling would come crashing down on their heads and they'd be buried forever. She gritted her teeth as sweat poured freely down her face. He hit the door again with such force it was as if all his rage had been buried inside a volcano and now it was allowed to erupt! This time splinters flew in all directions, then again shaking the door as the hinges creaked ready to give way to their cruel pounding. The door came crashing in slamming down the stairs and splitting in two sections, Amanda closed her eyes to avoid splinters as bits of wood hit the walls, and then it came to rest at the bottom of the stairs, luckily missing the plank of wood she had put there.

And then she saw him! He took the first step down, she could see his squelchy Wellington boots; he was so close she could almost touch him, she prayed that he wouldn't look down because he could see her through the gaps in the stairs from the hall light that now flooded the dark cellar. Amanda glanced slowly to her right at the pile of rags where Bethany was and she could see her tiny body shaking under the heap. Please dear God don't let her move!!

She held the spike in sweating palms willing her hands to stop shaking! A Rat scuttled by, its tail resting on her bare foot while it stopped to wash its whiskers with tiny paws. She gritted her teeth, sweat poured from her brow, the muscles in her jaw tightened, she wanted to scream and vomit at the same time! Scream her head off at the small creature she was so terrified of, her skin prickled with revulsion. It seemed like ages that it sat there on her foot taking its time washing, she felt the warm course fur against her skin, and to Amanda it was no more than her worst nightmare, and then with a warm damp tickling sensation the rat moved, its leathery tail slid over her foot and it was gone. Tears flowed silently down her face at the relief!

Another step, the stairs were now creaking under his weight, another, and then another.

"YOU CAN'T RUN AWAY AMANDA!"

She glanced at Bethany once more, she was terrified that the slightest movement would alert him to her position; and then it would be certain death for them both!

She looked up again, *'One more step you bastard....Come*

on! Just one more step.' But he stayed where he was, one foot on the third step from the top. It was then he looked down and for one paralysing moment she thought he had seen her, or the loose board! But he just gazed around the cellar looking for them.

He suddenly hit the stair rail, sending bits of wood flying, Amanda jumped and bit down on her lip, she felt her mouth fill up with blood again. Now he moved, one foot and then the other, the floorboards creaked again. She closed her eyes then opened them quickly as he took a tentative step down. It was her last and only shot. Leaping from her hiding place she grasped the spike tightly, she wasn't about to let it slip from her grasp as she had the poker.

"HERE I AM FUCKER! COME AND GET ME!"

"YOU BRAZEN BITCH...YOU HAVE TH..." And then he tripped, Amanda saw the damaged floorboard topple under his weight; she stood there in apoplexy her eyes wide and staring. He pitched forward, his arms waving about as if he was about to take flight. She held the spike in front of her, and just as she had hoped and wished and prayed for, in slow motion as it appeared to her then, she watched him fall towards her, she pushed her weight against the spike and watched as he landed on it, impaled, bursting through him piercing his internal organs. Amanda screamed in delight and disgust as blood burst from his stomach like a million lanced boils all at once, a crimson spray splattered her face and drenched her already bloody tracksuit.

She pushed all her weight against the spike until she could no longer hold onto it and then fell sideways, the weight of the of the blow punched air from her lungs, and then she lay there sobbing hysterically.

She sat there for ages watching his body twitch convulsively. There were no thoughts in her head except the one that told her she was finally free now, there was no more fear but she didn't feel happy how she had gained that freedom, freedom of fear. She had paid a terrible price for it. A dark pool of blood spread across the floor and with a cry of disgust she wiped blood from her hands, rubbing them down the tracksuit that had once cost her over eighty pound but was now only fit for the garbage.

"Bethany!" she cried. The child shook off the blankets and ran to her.

"Who is he mummy?"

"The bogeyman, just call him the bogeyman." She brushed hair from the little child's damp forehead, and soothed her. "And he's dead now; he will never hurt us again." Bethany laid her head on Amanda's chest and cuddled in tightly wrapping her small arms around her neck. Finally she pulled herself to her feet her arm hanging limply at her side.

"Come on honey, let's go home."

"We are home mummy?"

"No we're not sweetheart this was never our home."

She held Bethany in one arm and limped towards the cellar steps.

His hand snaked out and grabbed her ankle. "H...E...L...P MEEEEE."

Amanda screamed "NOOO! JUST DIE YOU BASTARD!" She kicked at him until he was still.

It was several seconds before she heard what she thought were shots being fired from upstairs and the pounding of feet above her. Clutching Bethany tightly her eyes fixed on the top of the stairs.

Pete Haldane stood there peering down into the darkness; next to him was Tom Page, and Ray Collins was behind him with armed police in riot gear. A light shone directly into her eyes. "AMANDA?"

She slumped to the floor still clutching Bethany to her breast. Haldane reached down and lifted the child in his arms handing her gently to a policewoman, and then he covered her nakedness with his jacket.

She looked up at him; her eyes were dead defeated eyes, full to the brim with grief, shock, terror and anything else you could name. For one moment Haldane wondered if they would ever regain that beautiful glow, that rich dark alertness with a tingling sense of humour.

"Madeline's dead! She's in the study, I can hardly believe it!" she started to cry now.

"I know." Haldane murmured.

Collins stood gazing at the carnage and he shook his head.

"She's dead! I can't believe it, she was so afraid this could happen…you promised her! You said he would be locked up for life, but instead he got out…Free, to murder Madeline who never hurt anyone in her life!! Why didn't you tell us he was out Inspector? At least we could have been prepared; he came after me and Bethany." Haldane held her tighter; her anger was aimed at Collins as senior officer.

"I came home and wondered where she was! She was never late back no matter where she went! I was *HERE* All evening wondering where she was! And all the time she was here dead in the reception room."

"Amanda…we didn't let Shaun go…Shaun Riordan was not our killer…Haldane, please could you show her." Collins almost choked on his words; yes he did feel guilty, if only he had known earlier.

Haldane gently laid Amanda against the wall; he went over to the dead man and pulled off the mask.

"Evan!" Amanda gasped. "BUT WHY?"

"We found his diary." Collins explained. "Amazingly, he had made every entry of every murder he had committed, and Amanda, you were right, he was stalking you, he had somehow or other become obsessed by you, he had pictures on his walls of you that he must have taken without your knowledge, he even killed the owners of this house. You see, his parents lived here in the early sixties, he was born here, the family were what you'd call 'Dysfunctional' His father was the product of an incestuous relationship between brother and sister, he was severely disturbed. His mother never really wanted him, she was a pretty peculiar woman, she had no feelings for the boy at all, his father beat him senseless, and then she left him. He stayed in the house for a while but then he left and went to London in the early seventies where he became completely obsessed with murder and mutilation of woman. I think he saw young girls as easy targets, he didn't kill anyone at that time but he attacked a few young girls in parks, deserted areas, that sort of thing. He tried to throw himself off Waterloo Bridge and that was when they put him into hospital for the criminally insane after he was found to have pictures of murders and mutilations in his rucksack. He was released in April 1999 as being completely cured and of no danger to the public. He had been a model prisoner in Broadmoor and had reacted well to the medical treatment he was given. He was supposed to be on medication for life but obviously he never took it. He came back to this house, only it had been purchased by a family, a doctor and his wife, they had two little girls. They disappeared in 2001 and of course because the mortgage had not been paid for over six months the bank repossessed the house. In his sick mind he thought the house still belonged to him, it was the property of a developer who sold it to the young couple. He killed the people who owned the house and they have never recovered the bodies; that is what we think had happened anyway, he was still living here until your husband bought the house. Amanda, Paul had become a real obstacle to him he was there every corner he turned, he was like an intruder and the more Paul seemed to be in the way the angrier he got! So, he decided to kill him. So you were right all along and I was wrong! There I was looking for a serial killer, and he was standing right next to me all the time, I would never have guessed it was Evan Wilson never in a million years." He hung his head.

Haldane closed Evan's rich dark eyes. Amanda looked up at Collins and said.

"I'm sorry Sergeant, I'm sorry I blamed you it wasn't your fault, none of us could have known, Evan was so kind, he was so thoughtful, he had been with Madeline for a long time in fact I thought they would get married." She looked at his limp body, her eyes avoiding the spike that protruded from him.

"Still, I should have taken more care, the only thing was you see, his plan backfired, he didn't expect the house to go on the market like it did, he was too stupid to realise, he killed the owners and thought he could just step into the house, but unfortunately Paul bought it from right under his nose, I'll let D.S. Haldane tell you the rest."

"Amanda, I was one of the investigating officer on the assault cases in London, they were vicious nasty cases and I knew it would not take long before this man murdered, but before we caught him on the bridge in Waterloo I was transferred to North Wales, I always wanted to move to a nice little country area away from London, it was for my family really, my wife wanted to live out of London so when this posting came up I jumped at it. I saw Evan in the café, he looked familiar to me but I couldn't remember where I'd seen him, in this job you meet hundreds of people, but I was more interested in the case up here, so it slipped my mind, that was until I went back to Scotland Yard to look up some files, and that's when I saw the picture of the man that had been arrested for the assaults. This time I knew who it was…it was Evan Wilson, the hair was slightly different but it was him alright."

"But how did you know it was him?"

"I'm coming to that, I remembered seeing him before that night I met him here when I popped into the little café in town, the night I came to see Paul, but I couldn't remember where I had seen him it was such a long time ago, It nagged me, I knew it was not in a social capacity I had seen him, and of course being in the Police you deal with so many criminals you forget what they look like after a considerable time, if I hadn't left at the time he was caught on the bridge I would have got him straight away. I had a sudden hunch that's why I went back to London to have a look at Rogues gallery; I also saw him get into his car so I took down the number plate and kept it in my mind on simmer if you like. He drove a dark blue Nissan Sunny 1.6. I then took the photo to the hospital for Mrs Jeffries to identify, she was the only one who actually saw his face without the mask and she positively identified him as the man who attacked her, so my persistence paid off, we went to Evan's house to arrest him but of course he wasn't in, he was here! But we did find the body of a young homeless girl in the boot of his car! And by the way, his name was not Evan Wilson, it was Evan Steed, Wilson was the name his mother used."

For a moment he turned away, the look in Amanda's eyes was unbearable.

"Oh Madeline!" She sobbed. "I knew all along something had happened to her." She looked at Wilson's body again and almost gagged. "Bastard!" she murmured. "Madeline liked him so much; I think she was falling in love with him! He took her out a few times! God it's unbelievable."

"Well, it's over now." Haldane said.

"Maybe." Amanda replied. "For all of you it is, but not for me, I feel the end has no end, nothing is ever going to be the same for me again, I have lost everything, Madeline was the best friend I have ever had in the world…I don't know how I'll cope without her!"

Her tears came in one big gush, her mind anaesthetized by her grief she felt as if she was falling into a ravine of hopelessness into a pit of hell.

"Paul, my husband was the love of my life I hope he and Madeline are together in death now."

Haldane bent down and took her in his arms rocking her gently as he felt her body's heaving sobs.

Amanda's mother stood at the top of the cellar steps with David at her side. "Mum!" she called.

"I know darling, it's going to be alright now."

Tears ran down David's face at the thought of never seeing Madeline again, but also with relief that Amanda and little Bethany were alive. Madeline would leave a gaping wound so open in their lives it was never going to heal, at least not for many years to come.

As Amanda was taken from the house by stretcher with her shoulder badly fractured to the waiting ambulance, she could hear Madeline say,

"I will always be here for you Amanda." And then she turned her head to the wind.

That same evening Forensic scientists moved into the house to discover the remains of the other victims, the decomposed body of a man in his early thirties, a young woman of about the same age and the tiny remains of a three month old baby, and of course the four year old girl Amanda found under the floorboards. They were the original owners of the house. The house was eventually sold to an American couple that were absolutely thrilled to own a house that had been at the centre of a massive murder hunt that had taken over three years to solve.

ABOUT THE AUTHOR

At a very early age Linda realized that she wanted to be a writer, after being top of the class in reading, writing and literature, she left school and started writing small stories in between working and raising a family. Her main interests, when she is not writing books are wildlife, she lives in Islington London with her husband and three adored Persian cats, and a very vivid imagination